200

IF THIS BE TREASON . . .

For Jill Conway and for most of the humans in Primavera, the issue seemed simple. The civilized centauroids in the south needed their help against the invading northern barbarians . . . and the advanced weapons of Earth would secure their victory.

For Captain Yuri Dejerine of Earth's Navy, the matter was also simple. Earth was fighting a far-flung space war, and all of Primavera's resources were now military property. Any use of these weapons in the internal affairs of Ishtar would surely be treason.

But Jill Conway was Ishtar-born—though an Earthwoman by ancestry—and she knew of no greater treason than abandoning a friend!

FIRE TIME

Poul Anderson

A Del Rey Book

BALLANTINE BOOKS • NEW YORK

A Del Rey Book
Published by Ballantine Books

Library of Congress Catalog Card Number: 74-5928

ISBN 0-345-28692-8

This edition published by arrangement with
Doubleday & Company, Inc.

Manufactured in the United States of America

First Ballantine Books Edition: November 1975
Second Printing: March 1980

First Canadian Printing: December 1975

Cover art by Darrell K. Sweet

Maps by Karen Anderson

FOR HAL CLEMENT,
worldsmith

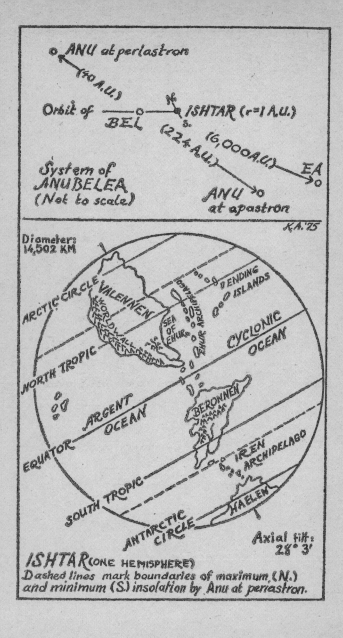

ANU at periastron

(40 A.U.)

Orbit of ——o——— N. ISHTAR (r=1 A.U.)
BEL   S.   (6,000 A.U.)
(22¼ A.U.)   EA
                                        o

System of
ANUBELEA   ANU o
(Not to scale)   at apastron

K.A. '75

Diameter:
14,502 KM

ARCTIC CIRCLE   VALENNEN   D'ENDING
                                        ISLANDS
        WORLD WALL MTS.   SEA OF   CYCLONIC
                          EHUR   OCEAN

NORTH TROPIC

ARGENT   BERONNEN
OCEAN

EQUATOR   IREN
                           ARCHIPELAGO

SOUTH TROPIC   HAELEN

ANTARCTIC
CIRCLE
                           Axial tilt:
                           28° 3'

ISHTAR (ONE HEMISPHERE)
Dashed lines mark boundaries of maximum (N.)
and minimum (S.) insolation by Anu at periastron.

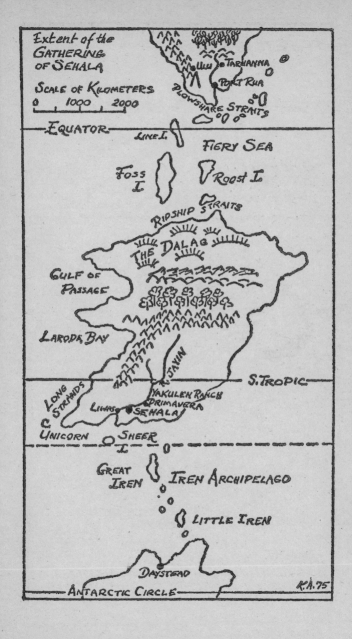

FOREWORD

It is a fearful thing to fall into the hands of a wholly just man.

His image had been chilling enough in court. Now we were summoned to himself. Dusk took us as we stepped from the flyer, blue-gray around, deepening to black where the mountainside toppled into the valley, overhead still a violet touched by the earliest stars. A guardian satellite hastened among them, entered Earth's shadow, and vanished as if the thin cold wind that whittered about us had blown it out. There streamed a smell of glaciers and distances.

The house was built of native stone, enormous, a part of these heights. Few men on man's mother planet can afford solitude. The president of the Tribunal commands it. A light in a bronze frame glowed above an ironbound oaken door. Our pilot gestured us that way. His whole body said we had better not keep Daniel Espina waiting.

Though my heart stammered, we all walked steadily. The door opened to show an attendant, live and nonhuman. *"Buenas tardes,"* the thing said. *"Siganme ustedes, por favor."* We followed down a hallway darkly wainscoted, to a room perhaps intended for meetings such as this.

It was broad and tall, full of antiquities and silence. The carpet muffled footfalls. Chairs and a couch stood rigid-framed, leather-covered, with a teak and ivory table. A grandfather clock from centuries agone ticked opposite an owl carved in marble. Shelves lined the walls, carrying books in the hundreds, more codices than reels. A modern desk and console—communications, data retrieval, computation, recording, projection, printout, disposal—somehow likewise belonged.

The far end of the room was a transparency. Beyond it reached the mountain, forest below and valley nighted below that, remote snowpeaks, more stars every minute. Before it, in his mobile chaise longue, sat Espina.

1

As always, he was loosely black-clad; nothing showed except the skeletal head and hands. A look from him halted us.

And yet, "Good evening," he said, tonelessly but quietly, as if we were guests and not criminals whom he would sentence. "Please be seated."

In our separate ways we bowed and lowered ourselves to the edges of chairs facing him.

"I believe English will be the most convenient language?" he inquired.

The question was rhetorical, I thought. How could he not know the answer? To mask the stillness, I replied, "Yes, your honor—sir—You recall ... on Ishtar it's been the common human language for a long time. Most permanent residents aren't very good even in Spanish, for lack of practice. It happened the original base personnel were mainly Anglo—pretty isolated since then—"

"Until recently," he cut off my foolish noise.

Dk, went the big clock. Dk. Dk.

After a minute Espina stirred the least bit and said, "Well. Who prefers coffee and who tea?" We mumbled. He beckoned his servant to him and gave the order. While the being departed, he took a silver case out of his robe, put a cigarette between yellowed fingers and inhaled it into lighting.

"Smoke if you like," he invited, neither hostile nor cordial, merely informing us that he didn't care. We made no move. His gaze felt like the alpine wind.

"You are wondering why I called you here," he said at last. "Isn't that quite irregular? And if a judge should feel a need to interview prisoners confidentially, why haul their bodies halfway around the globe?"

He drew smoke into lungs and let it out again to veil his Rameses face.

"As for the second point," he proceeded, "hologramy saves me the traveling I no longer wish to do. But it is not the same as the living flesh"—he glanced at his hand—"which you still have so abundantly. For you to be here, in my place and presence, is not the same as us confronting each other's colored shadows. I wish more officials understood the difference."

A cough racked him. I'd seen replays of his historic

2

decisions and speeches. No such attack of mortality marred them. Did he instruct the 3V computers to microdelay and edit their transmissions? That's standard political practice, of course, along with the other glamorizers. But Tribune Espina had always scorned any softening. Hadn't he?

He snapped after air, breathed in fresh poison, and continued:

"As for the first point, in my office there are no regular actions. Every case is a freak.

"Think," he said into our astonishment. "Mine is the final court for matters which fall under no single jurisdiction. Thus complete precedents never exist. Not only can entire legal systems be at odds; philosophies can." Contempt spoke forth. " 'Mankind' is a word about as meaningful as 'phlogiston.' Tell me, if you are able—in this allegedly unified World Federation of ours, just how much in common have a prosperous Japanese engineer, a gang lord in the Welfare district of a North American city, a Russian mystic, and a Dry African peasant? Besides, more and more of our business originates off Earth altogether"—his voice dropped—"in a damnably peculiar universe."

Our looks followed his. He touched a control on the chaise, interior lighting dimmed, the quickly fallen upland night grew clear to see.

Stars crowded blackness, nearly space-bright and space-many. The galactic belt glimmered from horizon to horizon; I remembered that in Haelen they call it the Winterway. Low to the south, Sagittarius stood across it. There I sought, and believed I found, the patch of glow that drowns out from sight of Earth the triple sun called Anubelea. Close by, the trail of light was cloven by dark dust. Elsewhere, invisible to us, fared worlds being born, worlds alive with other flesh and spirit than ours, burnt-out neutron clinkers, those pits of alienness men called black holes, galaxy after galaxy around the curve of reality; and the question is unanswerable, unaskable, what this all came from and what it will return to and why.

Espina's desiccated utterance brought me back. "I've studied the files on you at some length, as well as hearing testimony. My learned colleagues deplore the time

3

I've spent. They remind me of problems they consider more urgent, especially now during a war. The mutiny was a very small affair, they say, and had no obvious important effects. The defendants have not denied the charges against them. Let us punish and be done.

"Regardless, I've persisted." He nodded at his infotrieve. "No doubt I can conjure up every fact about you which the law could possibly call germane, and a good many additional."

He paused before finishing, "Yes, quite a few facts. But how much truth?"

I dared take the word: "Sir, if you mean the moral issues, justification, we requested a chance to explain and were denied."

Exasperation crackled. "Certainly. Did you imagine a court handling intercultural, often interspecies problems, could get anything done if it permitted emotional scenes at preliminary hearings?"

"I understand, sir. But we've not been allowed to make public statements either. We've been held incommunicado, and those hearings were barred to spectators. I doubt the legality of that."

"My ruling, under wartime powers. You may come to see that I've had my reasons."

The crippled body leaned forward, too old for repair, too alive for its captivity. The eyes assailed us. "Here you may orate as you please," Espina said. "I counsel you against it, though. What I hope to get from you is rather more subtle, more difficult than your personal objections to certain Federation policies. I mean to inquire about matters juridically irrelevant, incompetent, and immaterial. I want hearsay and conjecture. You are prepared to sacrifice your futures for those beings yonder. Why?"

His hand chopped air. "Set yourselves aside if you're able. Tell me about them as you know them or, likelier, imagine them. Oh, yes, I've gone over several xenological treatises. I've actually returned to childhood and reread that saccharine *Tales from Far Ishtar*. Words and pictures, nothing else!

"Give me some blood and bone. Make me feel how it feels to know doomsday is coming again in one's own lifespan."

4

The servant entered with a tray. "You may have alcohol, or whatever drug you need to relax, later if you desire," Espina said. "But best not at once. We've a formidable task ahead."

He sipped from his teacup. I caught the tarry odor of Lapsang Soochong. Presently he began to search us out.

I

IN FIRE TIME the north country got no peace from the Demon Sun. Day and night, summer and winter, it blazed aloft until there was no longer any day or any winter. But those were the Starklands, where few mortals had ever gone and none could ever dwell, whether the year be good or evil. Dauri from that realm, bound south on their unknown errands, saw the Red One sink as they fared, until at last it sometimes wheeled under the horizon behind them.

Having crossed the Desolation Hills, such travelers were in among the Tassui, the Frontier Folk, who held the south end of Valennen and hence were the northernmost of mortals. Here land, life, and sky alike were strange to theirs.

When the Stormkindler was far from the world, hardly more than the brightest stars, these parts knew small difference between seasons. In winter some rain might be hoped for, and the days were a little shorter than the nights, but that was nearly all. (Traders and soldiers from the Gathering said that meanwhile in the far north the True Sun never rose, and the cold grew so strong that ice lay in the very valleys.) But Fire Time changed this, as it did everything else. Then at midsummer the Tassui got the Invader by day, two suns at once, while at midwinter they got it by itself, not one moment of blessed darkness.

The same held true of a person traveled South-Over-Sea: except for seasons changing, winter in Beronnen when summer was in Valennen—and the Burner always lower to northward. Finally he reached a place which never saw it during Fire Time, merely afterward when it had retreated too great a distance to wreak harm. Most Tassui thought this must be a country favored by the gods, and disbelieved foreigners who told them that it was, instead, chill and niggardly.

Arnanak knew the story was right. He had visited Haelen himself a hundred years ago as a legionary of

7

the Gathering. But he seldom gainsaid his fellows and followers about matters of that kind. Let them keep wrong ideas if they wanted, especially ideas which fed envy, suspicion, and hatred of the outsiders. For he was at last ready to open his full attack.

A horn blew in the hills above Tarhanna. Echoes toned off crags and scarps. Louder brawled the Esali River, hastening through a canyon toward the plain. Not yet had drought, already setting in elsewhere, shrunken it to the trickle, among stones that scorched the feet of the thirsty, which Arnanak's grandfather had remembered from cubhood. But the air hung still and hot, with a smoky smell out of lia and bushes where they withered.

Alone, the True Sun drew near to the western ridges. Haze turned its shield a dull yellow, ash-dust off a woodland or a range that flame had grazed upon. Otherwise the sky was clear, a blue so hard that it might ring if struck. Deeper blue ran the shadows of wrinkles on slopes; down in clefts and dales they were purple.

Again Arnanak winded his horn. The warriors left their shady spots and loped toward him. They would not don war-harness, those who had any, until just before the battle. Baldric, scabbard, pouch, quiver were the sole clothing of most. Their green pelts, green-and-gold-glinting red-brown manes, black faces and arms, stood vivid against the dun growth and strewn rocks around them. Spearheads gleamed high. Tails switched hindquarters in eagerness. When they crowded together beneath the low bluff on which he stood, their male odor was like a breath off damp iron.

The pride in Arnanak did not keep him from making a rough count, now when he had them in a group. They numbered about two thousand. That was much fewer than he expected soon to need. However, it was a good response for the start of an undertaking as venturesome as this. And they had come from everywhere, too. His own contingent had had the longest journey to rendezvous, he supposed, from Ulu under the Worldwall. But by looks, bearing, gear, ornament, scraps of talk, he recognized others out of all South Valennen, mountaineers, woods runners, plains rangers, sea

8

reapers of coasts and islands. If they proved able to seize the trade town, their kindred would flock after them.

A third time he sounded the horn. Silence spread in its wake till the unseen water had the single voice. Arnanak let him see him, weigh him in their minds, before he spoke.

Since his people admired anyone who had strength to gain and wit to keep wealth, he wore an abundance of costly gauds. Studded with gemstones, a golden coronet rose spiky from the leaves of his mane. Gold coils wound along arms and legs. Rings glittered on all four fingers of either hand. A many-colored Sehalan blanket decked his back and hump. The longsword he raised in sign of command was damascened steel forged South-Over-Sea; but *it* had seen ample use.

Behind him a phoenix tree rose umber and mighty till branches spread out to make a wide blue roof of foliage. Under that shelter a canebrake had lately sprouted, a curtain of tan stalks and rustly shadows. Arnanak had chosen the rendezvous well ahead of time, and taken care that he arrived first, partly in order to claim this spot for his own. He did not forbid it to others because he begrudged them its comfort; rather, he had made a point of staying out in the open, in unbroken sunlight, like the least fortunate newcomer. He needed it for the show he had planned.

Gravely he trod to the bluff edge, met their eyes, filled his lungs and let roll forth:

"You Tassui, hark. I, Arnanak, Overling of Ulu, speak; and you will understand.

"My messengers who carried the war-daggers from household to household could tell of little more than a place to meet when the moons sail thus-and-thus among the stars. You knew that over the years I have made allies and oathgivers of many in the west, and no few elsewhere. You have heard how my wish is to drive the foreigners into the sea and beyond, unbarring our way to the south before Fire Time waxes its fiercest. You have guessed I may strike first at Tarhanna.

"But this the legion also knows, has heard, and can

9

guess. I would not risk spies or traitors telling our enemies more closely what we will do.

"Therefore I am not wroth that most males hung back. Some fear me, some fear my failure; moreover, now is the season when every household must garner what it can, that it may feed itself through a hard year to come and worse years afterward. No, I find the best of omens in seeing this many of you here.

"We move at sunset. I will tell you the plan.

"A reason I had for chosing springtime is just that then the Tassui are toiling. The legion will not await more from us than a few raids—surely not an onslaught against the chief inland stronghold of the Gathering. I know how they think, those from South-Over-Sea. Through double agents I have helped them come to look for any large movement of ours only in summer, when we have something in our larders at home, and have full nights for cover and coolness as we travel.

"Yet we have half a night here before the Red One rises—time to reach Tarhanna, given both moons up to help us fare speedily. I have myself made the trip, twice, and know. Besides, I know the garrison is small. The legion has withdrawn part of it to help fight buccanneering along the Ehur coast . . . buccaneering that I got started this past winter for that same purpose!"

A murmur went through the array. Arnanak overrode:

"Today your leaders and I have hammered out what to do. You have but to cleave to their standards. In two divisions, we will go at the north and south gates. Then when we have the soldiers well busied, a little band will scale the riverside wall—a tricky act, therefore a surprise, but not too tricky for my sailors, who have rehearsed it on a copy of the wall which I had built at Ulu. They will carve a bridgehead for others, who will fall on whichever gate looks more weakly defended, and get it open; and thus we take the town.

"If there is hunger in your home, warrior, remember that you can go to islands in the Fiery Sea which are still fat and still too well held for us to overcome; and you can barter your share of the loot for food. Before all, remember that here we barely begin the overthrow of the Gathering. Your children shall dwell in lands the gods love.

"Of this I give you a sign."

He had been pacing his words to the sun. When it slipped beneath the hills, dusk went like a wave across the world and the first stars leaped forth. From the same western rim lifted Kilivu, its jaggedness aglint as it tumbled. Frosty light shivered among suddenly uneasy darknesses. Somewhere a prowler howled; the noise of the river seemed to louden; though soil and boulders breathed forth heat, the air felt at once less heavy.

Arnanak's tail signaled the dauri. They slipped from the canebrake like seven other shadows, until their weirdness entered the moon-glow. Beneath its petals, their leader bore in its arms the Thing.

Fear whistled and bristled in the murky mass gathered under the bluff. Spearheads slanted forward, blades and axes flew free. Arnanak took the Thing. He held its gleams and blacks on high. "Hold fast!" he shouted. "Stand firm. No curse is here. These beings are with me."

After a while he had the warriors calmed enough that he could say more quietly: "Many of you have heard how I am become a friend of the dauri. You have heard how I fared into the Starklands which they haunt, where never mortal trod before, and brought back from their tomb city a Thing of Power. Behold, it was no lie. We cannot but conquer.

"Tonight we begin. I have spoken; and you will understand."

Before the troop had set off, Narvu rose in the east, smaller, duller, slower, but full, which Kilivu was not. That meant full in the light of the True Sun. The Invader cast its own wan red glow on both; no longer were they always eclipsed when they crossed the top of the sky at this phase. Between moons, stars, and Ghost Bridge, the Tassui saw well.

Nonetheless, descent to the valley was hard. Often Arnanak must grip with all three toes on all four feet, lest he tumble down a slope eroded to treacherousness. His hearts thumped. His throat felt sere as the brush

11

which clawed at his pasterns. He could well-nigh sense the leaves of mane and brows, the blades of his pelt, go likewise dry. The night brooded thick. He knew it must be growing milder, but his overburdened body did not.

He had left his riches and the Thing behind in care of the dauri. No Tassu—belike no legionary—would try to steal them from those creatures. Rather, such a person would run or, if uncommonly bold, make an offering on the spot in the hope of good luck later on. Now Arnanak carried war-gear on his back. Made in Beronnen for him when he served the Gathering, it was heavier than what most of his followers bore.

He heard them behind him, foot-thuds, metal-clink, rattle of stones, muttered oaths and harsh breath. Stiffly, he kept ahead. If he would be obeyed, he must ever be in the van of trek or battle.

Foolishness, he thought. Civilized folk were wiser. His commandant in his soldiering years had been lamed by wounds long before, but stayed in charge because there was no better tactician or day-by-day administrator. Barbarians—yes, barbarians—could win against civilization only by default, when it was breaking down.

He was glad that the legion he meant to throw out of this land was the Zera, not his old Tamburu Strider.

Of course, the latter might chance to come here as reinforcement. But that was beyond likelihood. One by one, the Gathering was abandoning its outer territories, as civilizations did each thousand years when the Stormkindler returned. Let Valennen be lost, and the Gathering would hardly try to regain it . . . even though this would presently mean the fall of the Fiery Sea islands, and thereafter—

Unless the humans— What could a male really know about beings more eldritch than the dauri, beings from so far away that their sun was lost to sight—if that story of theirs, or any other, could be believed—?

Arnanak clutched the hilt of the sword sheathed at his torso. If he had heard, and understood, and guessed aright, the humans would be too busy around Sehala to help in this remote outpost. Foreign as they were, they shouldn't grasp the meaning of the Valenneners' ad-

vance until too late. Then . . . why should they not be
willing to deal with the High Overling? He would have
more power, more to offer, than the shards of the
Gathering.

If Arnanak had caught the truth and planned well.

If not, he would die, and most of his people with
him. But Fire Time would have killed them anyhow, in
worse ways than battle. Arnanak let go the sword and
gave himself to making haste down the stony, scored
flanks of the hills.

Travel was easier in the flatlands. On orders from
their chief, the warriors stayed off a trade trail along
the river, save twice when they slipped thither to
quench thirst and lave their skin-plants. They might
have met a patrol, a few of whom might escape to give
the alarm. Instead they trotted cross-country.

The fields there were free of brush if not of thorn
fences. Taught by the towndwellers, folk hereabouts
had been cultivators for two or three sixty-four-years.
Speargrain, breadroot, and tame animals grew well. But
come Fire Time, farms where food was would draw
more hungry raiders than the legion could handle, until
weather destroyed crops and cattle from the gentler
climes of Beronnen. The cultivators were leaving their
homes while a chance remained to take up different
ways of life. Arnanak's band met no one in the few
steadings it passed. However, pasture was not yet completely ruined; the fighters foraged sparingly as they
went.

The east had lightened when they swung back
toward the stream. Black ahead of them, limned against
western stars and moon-shimmer on water, bulked the
walls and watchtowers of Tarhanna. Leaders uttered
low-voiced commands to halt and arm quickly, before
the Demon Sun rose and betrayed them to yonder sentries.

By now, air and soil were nearly cool. The Invader
would not by itself bring back great heat. Though
somewhat larger in the sky than the True Sun when
passing nearest the world, it gave less brightness and
warmth—about a fifth as much, a philosopher in Sehala had once told Arnanak. Indeed, the worst part of

13

a Fire Time came after the Marauder was again outward bound.

Still, by True noon today, when it set, the plain would be fevered. (And this was only spring, in an early year of the evil!) Arnanak hoped to be inside the town before then. Whether or not he would be out-of his armor depended on the garrison. He believed the legionaries would surrender on promise of being allowed to depart disarmed. Civilized soldiers reckoned it an empty bravery to die in a lost cause. But their captain might decide death was worthwhile for the sake of killing as many barbarians as might be.

Well, then the bone kettles would seethe; and kindred from end to end of South Valennen would join the Overling of Ulu in revengefulness.

He unpacked his kit, fastened helm and mail to his body with the help of his standard-bearer, took shield on arm. The bad dawn broke, crimson across the land. Arnanak lifted his sword to grab that light. "Come!" he roared. "Attack and win!" He trotted into a run. Behind him the ground drummed under the weight and haste of his warriors.

II

THE DOOR CHIMED. *"Entre,"* called Yuri Dejerine. Rising, he waved the phonoplay to silence. Had it been drawing something classical from the data bank—a piece by Mozart, say, or a raga concert—he would have reduced the sound level to a gentle background. But most humans dislike Gean music, all of it, never mind that that planet has as old and wide a variety of traditions as ever did Earth. To understand, one needs the interest from which springs patience, plus a good ear.

The door admitted a young man whose uniform bore air corps pursuit squadron insignia. They shone very new, and his salute was a bit awkward. He handled himself well in Lunar gravity, though; he wouldn't have qualified for his service if he weren't more quickly weight-adaptable than most. His frame was tall and powerful, his face handsome in a blond Caucasoid mode. Dejerine wondered whether he really bore subtle indications of having been born and reared beyond the Solar System. Knowing he was, an observer could too easily read clues into a look, a stance, or a gait.

Accents were more reliable. Dejerine spared his visitor wrestling with Spanish by taking the word in English: "Ensign Conway? At ease. In fact, relax. It was good of you to come."

"The captain sent for me." Yes, Conway did speak an odd brand of the language, markedly different from Dejerine's pan-European version. It was the dialect of a people whose mother tongue this had been for a long time, but carrying a softness and a lilt that were ... partly nonhuman?

"I requested you visit me, only requested." The door having closed, Dejerine astounded the other by extending a hand. After an instant, the clasp took place. "You can do me a large personal favor, and conceivably Earth too. Perhaps I can make a return, but that isn't certain. What is certain is that we both ship out quite shortly, and I am taking time you could spend with the girls or enjoying several unique sports. The least I can do is give you a drink." He took Conway's elbow and guided him to a lounger opposite his own, while he chatted on. "That's why I suggested we meet in my quarters. A dormitory or clubroom is too unprivate, an office too austere. What would you like?"

Donald Conway sat down under the arm-pressure. "I ... whatever the captain wishes, thank you, sir," he gulped.

Dejerine stood over him and smiled. "Do fall free. Forget rank. We're strictly alone, and I'm not a lot older than you. What is your age—?"

"Nineteen—I mean twenty-one, sir."

"Still used to Ishtarian years, are you? Well, last month I had my thirtieth birthday, terrestrial. No yawning gap, true?"

Conway eased a trifle. His nervousness had not taken away candor from a gaze which now grew thoughtful, regarding his host. Dejerine was medium-sized, slender, his hands and feet small, his movements catlike; he had been a championship tumbler in

15

Academy days. His features were regular and fine-boned, complexion olive, nose short, lips full, eyes as brown as the sleek hair and neat mustache. He was in mufti, blouse, sash, flared slacks of iridescent cloth, tabi and zori. His class ring was standard, but the tiny gold circlet in his right earlobe bespoke a measure of brashness.

"Mainly," he continued, "I became a cadet at sixteen and have stayed in the service. You reached Earth two years ago, enlisted when war began, and have barely hatched out of hurry-up training." He shrugged. "What of it? Later you will finish your studies, and go on to become a distinguished professor of fine arts, and be president of a major university when I am beached at half pay. So, what is your pleasure?" He moved to the minibar. "I am for cognac and a timid hint of soda."

"The same, then, thank you, sir," Conway said. "I haven't had much chance to learn, uh, the science of drinking."

"You have no large choice on Ishtar?"

"No, mostly homebrew beer and local wine." Conway forced loquacity on himself. "They taste different enough from Earth's that many lifetimers don't care for what little import we get. We're self-sufficient, our agriculture flourishes, but, well, everywhere else is a whole other ecology to affect the soil, plus weather and radiation and—Anyhow, a few people operate stills, but they admit what they produce is nothing to brag about."

"You see, already you've helped me," Deierine laughed. "I've been warned to stock up before departure."

While he prepared the refreshments, Conway glanced around. Though not an admiral's suite, the chamber was large and well furnished for Tsiolkovsky Base. However commodious in peacetime, facilities here grew overloaded when men were shunted in by the thousands for ready transport to scenes of action. They must be doubled into barracks; power shortages developed till interior Earthweight generators must be shut down; that meant everybody must suffer tedious extra hours of exercises; on liberty they must stand in line for a chance at sightseeing crawlers, climbing out-

16

fits, slide-ski slopes, or catch a train to Apollo and hope not to get very badly rooked. . . . A half-wall transparency, dimmed against glare, showed majestic desolation. A cargo ship crossed the view, backing down on gravs toward an auxiliary field hastily scraped from the basalt.

This room held few personal traces of its occupant. You travel light through space, barebones in wartime. Some printouts lay on a table: a book about Anubelea, a girlie periodical, a mystery novel, the collected poems of García Lorca. Beside them stood a humidor.

"Here you are." Dejerine handed Conway his drink. "And would you care for a cigar? . . . No? I suppose tobacco also turns peculiar on Ishtar? Well, I'll ignite if you don't mind." He settled into the facing seat and lifted his own glass. *"Salud."*

"Uh, cheers," Conway responded.

Dejerine chuckled. "That's right. You are becoming your true self. I expected you would."

"You checked me out, sir?"

"Nothing more than your open file. I don't pry. What I did was ask the bank for data on personnel from Ishtar whom I might contact. Your name appeared. According to the entries, you were born there and never got off the planet until lately. I doubt if a coward or incompetent would have been tolerated that long, assuming he survived. Then in spite of growing up among—what is the figure?—about five thousand scientists, technies, and their children, more than three hundred parsecs from Sol and seldom visited—you showed such promise in visual art that you were offered a scholarship here. And *then,* when the war broke out, you didn't continue safe in your studies, you enlisted, in one of the toughest branches at that. I need no more information to know you fairly well."

Conway flushed, took a considerable sip, and ventured: "Obviously you've been assigned there, sir, and you'd like to hear what I can tell you. Isn't that surprising, for a man with your record? The assignment, that is."

Dejerine frowned a bit. "Such things happen."

"I mean, well, after your message I used the bank too." The brandy had no doubt gone fast to Conway's

17

unpracticed head, for his words came rapid and needless—not flattery, Dejerine judged, but a gauche attempt at responding to the senior's amicable overtures. "You were my age when you got the Diamond Star for a rescue off Caliban. You went on to be exec of a blastship, captain of a ranger, operations chief for constructing a base on Gea. Quite a variety, even if the Navy does like to rotate jobs; and you're quite young for your rank." He checked himself. His cheeks reddened. "I'm sorry, sir. I didn't mean to be forward."

"That's all right." Dejerine waved his cigar in dismissal. Discontent remained on his mouth.

"If I may guess, sir—Gea has natives who're pretty strange by our lights. I found no mention of them registering any complaints against you. Which must mean you treated them right, wisely, cleverly, kindly. Maybe Cincpeace figures you're our best representative to the Ishtarians."

"Then why aren't you posted back there?" Dejerine demanded. He took a savage puff of smoke. "You've lived in their midst. Your community has for a hundred years."

Conway hesitated, glanced aside, finally said low: "Well, it isn't a place for my kind of unit, unlikely as combat is. And . . . whether Staff thought of it or not . . . I'd be none too good on Ishtar. Emotional conflicts—You see, my family, parents, sisters, my old friends . . . they're against the war. Many are really bitter."

Dejerine smoothed his countenance. "How do you feel about it?" he asked.

Conway met his look square on. "I enlisted, didn't I? Oh, sure, rights and wrongs on both sides. But—humans have been attacked. Their presence has been challenged, on real estate they made theirs with blood and sweat. If we don't stop that kind of thing early, we'll be in a bad way later. I recall the Alerion affair."

Dejerine smiled. "You don't, son," he replied. "I myself was busy getting born that year." His humor faded. "But, yes, we try to learn lessons from history. Besides, speaking as an individual, I've seen the Welfare and Backworld misery on Earth—been there in person, felt it, smelled it—and I've seen people who left

18

it for Eleutheria, and what they've done and what they hope for—

"Well, I am not being sent to help them. I'm bound a thousand light-years in the opposite direction!"

He drained his glass, rose in a single motion, and sought the bar. "Are you ready for a refill?" he asked quietly.

"No, thanks." Conway searched for words. "Captain, Cincpeace must have reasons. Suppose the Naqsans did make a long surprise move and occupy Ishtar. It has resources. Or I suppose it has more hostage value, less in those few people of ours than in all the high-powered man-years we've got invested for scientific knowledge that's finally begun to pour in. Come negotiations, Ishtar could be a mighty good bargaining counter for Naqsa."

"Do you truly think so?" Dejerine brightened a trifle. "My orders just are to establish a reconnaissance base against the possibility, remote but still a possibility, that action may move toward that volume of space."

Conway nodded. "And unless it's well done, it's a waste of effort. That's why you're in charge, sir. Once you've got it running, I'll bet my Y chromosome you'll be reassigned—to the front—if we haven't finished the war before then."

Dejerine laughed anew. *"Tiens,* you do know how to make a chap feel better, don't you? Thanks." He returned to his lounger. "Those Naqsans are tough and smart. I expect fighting will go on for years."

"I hope not."

"Well, naturally. If anybody likes the idea of war, any war, past, present, or future, let him speak forth so we may shoot the son of a bitch and get on with a rational discussion. The lesser of two evils doesn't stop being evil on that account. And I . . . have had friends on the opposite side, in happier days."

Dejerine paused before he added, "It is that, you understand, I want to have a part in ending this thing. I happen to take seriously the theory that our service is the space police arm of the Peace Control Authority of the World Federation." He stirred. "Tell me, since you say they generally oppose the war on Ishtar, why?

19

Most Earthside intellectuals support it with crusading fervor."

Conway drank. "I'm afraid at that distance, the issues look kind of unreal," he said, and leaned forward. "Mainly, though—from what I heard and read before leaving home, when the conflict was only potential but the news kept getting uglier—and from letters and tapes I've gotten since, and talking with visitors here— mainly, they see it as a disaster to their special cause, to the whole planet. If nothing else, the supplies they need are being pinched off. Let the affair go on awhile, and they won't be able to get any stuff for their projects. At the worst possible time, too."

"Ah." Dejerine blew a smoke ring and followed its progress through squinted eyes till it had dissipated. "We come to what I want from you. Information. Background. Advice. The care and feeding of Ishtarians and of the small but venerable scientific-altruistic colony which the Exploratory Consortium maintains among them. Anything you can tell. You see, my orders were cut last week. Nearly all my waking hours and half my sleeping ones have gone to getting my command organized, and will until we leave, which is soon. I suppose it would be indiscreet to tell a junior officer how much high-level sperm I receive—"

Seeing Conway's bemusement, he stopped. "Uh, sperm, sir?" the younger man asked.

"What, you haven't heard? You are an innocent. Standard Procedure, Entropy Reaching Maximum. The point is, you are my single chance to learn about my objective. Ignorant as I am, I could do every kind of harm, perhaps actually compromise my mission."

"But—you're educated, you've been around in space—"

"Oh, yes, yes, yes," Dejerine said impatiently. "I understand the celestial mechanics of the Anubelean System. I know a little something about the natives of Ishtar, including their unique biological situation." He drew breath. "Planets where men can walk around in shirt sleeves are few enough that everybody alive between the ears can at least name you those we know. By the same token, however, they're thinly scattered. Our main involvements are with races and bases closer

20

to home. Also, never forget, any planet is a whole world, too big and complicated to comprehend. *Bon Dieu*, man, I live on Earth and I can't describe its littoral ecology or the dynastic history of China or what the current squabble in the Kenyan Empire is about!"

He dropped cigar in ashtaker, slammed his drink down next to it, and from the table snatched the book on Ishtar. "I have been studying this, for instance." His words came quick and harsh. "The latest published, ten years old. Neatly assembled information." He flopped it open, more or less at random, and thrust it under Conway's nose. "Observe."

The left page:

ANUBELEA B (Bel)

Type: G2, main sequence
Mass: 0.95 Sol
Mean diameter: 1.06 Sol
Mean rotation period: 0.91 Sol
Luminosity: 0.98 Sol
Effective temperature: 5800° K.

PLANETS
Elementary parameters (Earth = 1.0)

		Mean orbital radius	Sidereal period	Mean equatorial diameter	Mass	Mean surface gravity
I	(Nabu)	0.29	0.163	0.41	0.061	0.363
II	(Adad)	0.54	0.402	0.78	0.45	0.738
III	(Ishtar)	1.03	1.072	1.14	1.53	1.18
IV	(Shamash)	2.67	2.735	0.95	0.83	0.928
V	(Marduk)	4.40	9.56	5.1	5.1	1.96

Note: Asteroids are distributed semi-randomly, due to the companion stars. For complete orbital data, see Appendix D. For fuller description of planets of B other than Ishtar, see Chapter XI.

The right page:

ANUBELEA B III (Bel III)
ISHTAR
Elementary parameters
Earth (E) = 1.0

Mass: 1.53 E.

Mean equatorial diameter: 1.14 E = 14,502 km.

Mean density: 1.03 E = 5.73 H_2O.

Mean surface gravity: 1.18 E = 1155 cm/sec².

Sidereal year: 1.072 E = 392 Terrestrial days = 510 Ishtarian days.

Rotation period: 0.775 E = 18 h 36 m 10.3 s.

Axial inclination: 1.14 E = 28° 3'.2.

Mean irradiation (from Bel only): 0.89 Sol/Earth.

Mean angular diameter of Bel: 1.03 Sol/Earth = 33°.

Mean sea-level atmospheric pressure: 1.12 E = 810 mm Hg.

Normal % atmospheric composition by volume: N_2 76.90, O_2 21.02, H_2O 0.35, A 1.01, CO_2 0.03, + misc.

Water/land surface ratio: 1.20 E = 2.94:1.

Satellites

		Mean orbital radius, km.	Sidereal period, hours	Mean equivalent diameter, km.	Mean angular diameter
I	(Caelestia)	2.40 × 10⁴	8.34	188	38'
II	(Urania)	7.35 × 10⁴	44.61	265	13'.5

Note: Both moons being of irregular shape, especially I, diameters and angular diameters as seen from Ishtar are calculated for equivalent spheres. For fuller information and discussion, see Chapter III.

"What's there that I couldn't get better and quicker from the navigator's bible?" Dejerine said. "Oh, yes, *sí, oui, da, ja,* also text, pictures, anecdotes. Not bad material for a tourist to study in advance, if anybody could afford to play tourist over such a distance. And I've gone through other stuff too, projected hours of 3V records, I know the shape of an Ishtarian—" He had been riffling pages as he talked, and for no logical reason halted at such an illustration.

A male and female were shown, plus a human who gave scale. The male was the larger of the pair, about the size of a small horse. "Centauroid" was a very loose description. The burly two-armed torso merged smoothly with the four-legged barrel, taurine hump above the forequarters leading from the horizontal to the almost vertical sections of the back. The body looked leonine rather than equine, with its robust build, long tail, padded feet whose three toes (more prehensile in front than behind) bore purplish nails. The arms resembled, somewhat, those of a Terrestrial weight lifter; but the hands each had four digits, the first three not unlike man's thumb and two of his fingers though spreading more widely, the last like a less-developed extra thumb with one more joint, all possessing nails too. The head was big and round, ears large and pointed (slightly movable), jaw showing a chin and near-anthropomorphous delicacy, teeth white and small except for a pair of upper fangs which barely protruded from the mouth. Instead of a nose, a short muzzle opened in a single broad nostril which curved downward and flared at the ends. Beneath, feline whiskers surrounded the upper lip. The eyes also suggested a cat's, whiteless, his blue, hers golden.

Face and arms were glabrous, the skin (in the race depicted, native to Beronnen) light brown. Most of the body bore a tawny-green mosslike pelt. The lion impression was heightened by a rufous mane which covered head, throat, and spine down to the hump: composed not of hair but of thickly leaved vines. A familiar growth formed a shelf of eyebrow.

Sexual dimorphism was considerable. The female stood fifteen centimeters shorter. She had a mere stub of tail. Her hump was large and softly rounded, unlike

23

his blocky cluster of muscles; her rump was broad and her belly deep; two nipples on an udder which wasn't large, and the external genitalia, were brilliant red. Accompanying text noted that her odor was sweet and his acrid, and that she commanded a wider range of frequencies in both speech and hearing.

They were unclad aside from ornaments and a belt to support pouch and knife. He carried a spear and a stringed instrument slung across his shoulders; she, a longbow, quiver, and what might be a wooden flute.

"—I know the biochemistry is basically like ours, we can eat a good deal of each other's food though some essentials are lacking in either case—why, they get drunk on ethanol too." Dejerine snapped the volume shut. "Homelike, no? Except that men have spent a century on Ishtar, working hard to understand, and you can better tell than I how far off they are from their goal!" He sent the book spinning over to his bed.

"A long ways," his visitor admitted.

"And those humans. True, true, more than half the population of Primavera is floating: researchers who come for a while to carry out specific projects, technies on time contract, archeologists basing themselves there till they can go on to ... Tammuz, is that the dead planet's name? Nevertheless, they must all have a special devotion to Ishtar. And the core of them are the long-term residents, the careerists, a fair percentage second- or third-generation Ishtarians who have scarcely an atom from Earth in their cells." Dejerine spread his palms. "Do you see how badly I need a, a briefing? I need more than that, of course, but can't possibly get it. So ... my friend, will you kindly finish your drink and take another? Loosen your tongue. Free-associate. Tell me about your past life, your family, your comrades. In return, I can at least bring them your greetings, and whatever presents you wish to send.

"But help me." Dejerine knocked back his second glass. "Give me ideas. What shall I say to them, how reconcile them and get them to co-operate, I who come in as the agent of a policy that dashes their fondest hopes to the deck?"

Conway sat for a space, his vision lost in the overlook across Luna, before he said carefully: "You know, you might start by showing them that documentary of Olaya's which made the big splash last month."

"On the background of the war?" Dejerine was startled. "But it was generally critical."

"No, not quite. It tried hard to be objective. Oh, everybody knows Olaya is no enthusiast for this thing. Too aristocratic by temperament, I suppose. But he's a damn fine journalist, and he did a remarkable job of getting a variety of viewpoints."

Dejerine frowned. "He skimped the fundamental issue: the Eleutherians."

Emboldened, Conway answered, "Frankly, I, and I'm not alone, I don't agree they are the fundamental issue. I admire them, of course, and sympathize, but mainly I think we, humankind, we have to stay on top of events for our survivial as a species. On Ishtar I've seen such chaos rising—" Earnestly: "But that's what I'm getting at. Somebody like, oh, my sister Jill, her whole life spent there ... she, her kind of people, they only see the horrors Anu is bringing to *their* planet. If they could realize that sacrifices have to be made for a higher good— But they're intelligent, you know, trained in scientific skepticism; they've spent their lives coping with the wildest jumble of cultures and conflicts. No slick propaganda pitch is going to win them over.

"That Olaya show, it was honest. It touched reality. I felt that, and ... I can tell you my people on Ishtar would. If nothing else, they'd understand we still have free speech here, Earth isn't a monolithic monster. It ought to help."

Now Dejerine was quiet for a time which grew.

At the end, he jumped to his feet. "All right!" he exclaimed. "I asked for your advice, and—Donald, Don, may I call you? I'm Yuri—immediately you begin. Come, do have some more. Let us settle down to the serious business of getting drunk."

III

SOUTHBOUND, LARREKA AND his attendants neared Primavera about noon of the day after he had left his wife at Yakulen Ranch. The human settlement lay three marches upriver from the city of Sehala. No longer was that site a precaution against possible trouble. Surely everyone in Beronnen, and most dwellers elsewhere throughout the Gathering, had come to understand that the Earthfolk were their friends, the last best hope of saving their entire civilization. But the aliens still needed space to raise crops and cattle which could nourish them in ways that raingrain or breadroot, the flesh of els or owas, could not. And those who studied nature, like Jill Conway, preferred readier access to wildlife than the plowlands around Sehala afforded. And those who studied people declared that their own constant presence in the city would be too upsetting.

Not that any such effect could amount to a dustpuff—Larreka had often thought—alongside the upsettingness built into this world.

He swung briskly down a road which paralleled the wide, sheening flow of the Jayin. An important highway, it was brick-paved; he felt heat as well as gritty hardness. But that was enough for a tough-padded old soldier to show himself by putting on buskins. Bad though the time was becoming, South Beronnen always escaped the worst of what the Rover passed out ... except indirectly, of course, when starveling hordes invaded this favored land. Furthermore, right now was mid-autumn in the southern hemisphere, the airs easing off toward rainy winter, no matter how hard the Rover tried to screw things up.

Its red glower, low above northern hills which it turned amethyst, was near setting. The Sun stood high and brilliant. Double shadows and blended hues made the landscape strange. It rolled gently away from either bank of the river. This shore was given over to human cultivation. Wheat, corn, and the rest had been harvested, leaving stubblefields; but apples flushed in an orchard, horned fourlegged animals chewed grass behind fences—how green everything was! The opposite side remained native: turf of golden-hued lia studded with scarlet firebloom, trees in coppices tawny (swordleaf) or ocherous (swirlwood and leatherbark). Wingseed bushes were propagating yonder, and many pods flapped across the stream before they ran out of stored energy and fell to the ground. Nature's carelessness: they could no longer take root over here; the soil had been changed too much.

The breeze into which they beat was pleasant after the morning's sultriness. Larreka heard his mane rustle. He drank the sweet weird odors of Earthside growth with an appreciation learned through a hundred years. The grimness of his present mission didn't lessen that. A soldier shouldn't let worry spoil whatever bonuses life tossed his way.

"How much further, sir?" asked one of the half-dozen males at his back. They weren't needed in these closely settled, food-rich parts. But it had expedited the trek across North Beronnen and over the Thunderhead Mountains, to have some who could be detached to hunt and forage while the rest kept going, and extra hands for camp chores. Larreka figured he might as well let them come the whole way to Sehala and its fleshpots. Poor bastards, they wouldn't get a lot of fun during their youth. He who had spoken was a native of Foss Island in the Fiery Sea, recruited there and posted directly to Valennen because that was where the Zera was stationed these years. He had never before visited the mother continent.

"*Chu,* maybe an hour." Larreka used a unit denoting the sixteenth part of a noon-to-noon, coincidentally quite near to the Earth measurement. "Keep moving. I told you we'll overnight there."

"Well, at least Skeela'll soon be down."

"Huh?—Oh. Oh, yes." With as many names as he had heard for the red orb, Larreka could generally spot another.

He himself thought of it as the Rover, since he belonged to the Triadic cult. There it was central, together with the Sun and that Darkness on whose brow

27

smolders the Ember Star. As a youth in Haelen, he had called it Abbada, and had been told it was an outlaw god who returned every thousand years; later he became skeptical, and considered the pagan rites of propitiation a waste of good meat. The barbarians of Valennen were in such awe of the thing that they gave it no name whatsoever, just a lot of epithets, none of which should be used twice in a row lest its attention be drawn to the speaker. And so the business went, different everywhere, including among the humans. They called the red one Anu, and denied a soul of any kind was in it; and likewise for the Sun, which they called Bel, and the Ember Star, which they called Ea.

In many ways, their concept was the creepiest of the lot. Larreka had had to nerve himself to master their teachings. He couldn't yet believe that there was nothing to the Triad but fire. And whether or not that was the case, he'd carry out the rites and commandments of his religion. It was a good faith for a soldier, popular in the legions, excellent for morale and discipline.

From the outside, Larreka didn't look like a person who would study philosophy. He might have been a veteran sergeant, slightly undersized but heavily muscled, less graceful than most though exceedingly fast when needful. Wounds deep enough to leave permanent scars had seamed his body in places; a gouge crossed the bone of his brow, and his left ear was missing. Haeleners being of South Beronnen origin, he had skin formerly pale brown, turned dark and leathery by many weathers, wherein his eyes stood ice-blue. His speech kept traces of a rough homeland accent, and his most conspicuous weapon—practically his trademark—was the heavy knuckleduster-handled curve-bladed shortsword favored in that antarctic country. Otherwise he wore only a purse-belt for small articles, and the arms and travel kit strapped in a bundle on his back or loaded in two wicker panniers. This included a hunting spear and a hatchet which could double as a weapon. Nothing was ornamented; it was well-worn cloth, hide, wood, steel. His sole jewelry was a gold chain around the thick left wrist.

The soldiers behind him were gaudier, sporting

28

plumes, beadwork, jingling links. They were also very respectful of their shabby leader. Larreka Zabat's son of Clan Kerazzi was perhaps the most demanding of the thirty-three legionary commandants. After two centuries in the Zera, he was far into middle age, three hundred and ninety on his last birthday. But he could expect another hundred years of health, and might well hope for more—if a barbarian didn't get him first, or any of the natural catastrophes the Rover was brewing for the world.

It slipped under the horizon. For a brief while, clouds to the north were sullen from its rays. Then the sane light of the Sun shone free. Cumulus loomed tall and white above a blue shadowiness hinting at storm.

"Think it'll rain, sir?" asked the male from Foss Island. "I sure wouldn't mind." Though near the equator, his home was refreshed by winds off the sea. Here he felt hot and dusty.

"Save your thirst for Primavera," Larreka advised. "The beer there is good." He squinted. "N-n-no, I wouldn't look for rain today. Tomorrow, maybe. Don't be in a fume about it, son. You'll soon get more water hereabouts than you can handle, enough to drown a galleyfish. Maybe then you'll appreciate Valennen better."

"I doubt that," a companion said. "Valennen's supposed to go even drier than it futtering well already is."

"Futtering ain't the word, Saleh," a third put in with a crow of laughter. "Female pelts'll get baked so stiff you could sand a hole in your belly."

His exaggeration was moderate. Loss of moisture did coarsen the mat of fine green plant growth covering most of a body. "Why, as for that," Larreka said, "heed the voice of experience," and described alternate techniques in blunt language.

"But, sir," Saleh persisted, "I don't get it. Sure, Valennen sees a lot more of the Wicked Star, a lot higher in the sky, than Beronnen does. I understand how it gets hotter than here. Only why'll the country dry out that bad? I thought, ng-ng, I thought heat draws water out of the sea and dumps it as rain. Isn't that how come the tropical islands are mostly wet?"

"True," Larreka answered. "That's what's going to

29

spill rain all over Beronnen for the next sixty-four years or more, till we're in mud up to our tail-roots when we aren't flooded out—not to speak of snowpack melting in the highlands and whooping down, to add to the fun and games. But Valennen's saddled with those enormous mountains along the whole west coast, where the main winds come from. What little water the interior's got will blow away eastward over the Sea of Ehur, while clouds off the Argent Ocean crash on the Worldwall. Now shut your meat hatch and let's tramp."

They sensed that he meant it and obeyed. For some reason he recalled a remark which Goddard Hanshaw had once made to him:

"You Ishtarians seem to have such a natural-born discipline that you don't need any spit-and-polish—hell, your organized units like in the army hardly seem to need any drill. Only, is 'discipline' the right word? I think it's more a, well, a sensitivity to nuances, an ability to grasp what a whole group is doing and be an intelligent part of it. . . . Okay, I reckon we humans catch on faster to certain ideas than you do, concepts involving three-dimensional space, for instance. But you've got more, uh, a higher social IQ." He had grinned. "A theory unpopular on Earth. Intellectuals hate to admit that beings who have wars and taboos and the rest can be further evolved than their own noble selves, who obviously have none."

Larreka remembered the words in the English which had been used. Fascinated by humans since their first arrival, he had seen as much of them as he could manage and learned everything about them and from them that he was able. This was rather more than he let on to his followers or his brother officers; it wouldn't have fitted his character as a rough, tough old mudfoot. Language had been no problem to a fellow who'd knocked around half the globe and always quickly found how to ask local people for directions, help, food, beer, housing, sex, whatever he wanted. Besides, English was very narrow in range and choice of sounds. Humans could never match the voice or hearing of even a male Ishtarian. He admired them for plowing their way through Sehalan anyhow.

When they were so pitifully short-lived, too. A single

sixty-four or less, and they needed special medicines to keep their strength. Before the end of the second sixty-four, that was no help either. . . . Larreka unconsciously quickened his pace a bit. He wanted to enjoy his friends while he had them.

More urgent was his errand among them. He carried evil news.

Primavera was houses and other buildings along asphalt streets shaded by the red and yellow foliage of big old native trees which had been left in place when the area was originally cleared, their soil tended to keep them alive amidst alien growth. It rose in gentle slopes from a landing on the Jayin where boats docked and vessels of Ishtarian river traffic paid calls; the inhabitants manufactured a few articles like rotproof fabrics to trade for many of their needs. They built largely in native materials, wood, stone, brick—though the glass they made was superior to anything of Beronnen—and added light bright paint. A road ran east, vanishing over a ridge, eventually to reach the spacefield. A kilometer outside of town it passed by the airport, where flyers were kept for long-range transportation. Around home people used groundcars, cycles and feet.

Ishtarians were too common in Primavera to draw special attention unless they were individually well-known. Larreka only was to long-term residents. And not many persons were outdoors at this hour, when adults were at work and children in school. He had reached Stubbs Park, was about to short-cut through it and grab a drink of water at the fountain in the middle, before he was hailed.

First, he heard the purr of a large flywheeler at high speed, followed by a squeal of braking. To drive like that in town would have been unforgivably reckless in most, but not quite all. He wasn't surprised to recognize Jill Conway's throaty shout.

"Larreka! Old Sugar Uncle himself! *Hi* there!" She unsnapped her safety harness, sprang from the saddle and out between the roll bars, left the vehicle balanced while she hurled herself into his arms.

At length, "M-m-m," she murmured, stood back,

31

cocked her head, and surveyed him centimeter by centimeter. "You're looking good. Worked some fat off, have you? But why the deuce didn't you let me know you were coming? I'd've baked a cake."

"Maybe that was why," he teased in her English.

"Aw, switch it off, will you? The trouble with a lifespan like yours is you develop no sense of time. My culinary disasters didn't happen yesterday, they were twenty years ago. I'm a grown lady now, people keep wistfully telling me, and you'll be surprised how well I cook. I must admit, you never did anything more heroic than eat those things a little girl made for her Sugar Uncle."

They smiled at each other, a gesture common to both species though human lips curved rather than quirked upward. Larreka returned her searching gaze. They'd swapped radiograms and sometimes talked directly by phone, but hadn't met in the flesh for seven years, since the Zera Victrix went to Valennen. He'd been kept too busy by worsening natural conditions and the rise of banditry to take leave, while she'd first been studying hard, then embarking on her own career. When little was yet known about the ecology of Beronnen and the Iren Archipelago to the south, he couldn't blame her for choosing to do research in their congenial environments. In fact, he would have been distressed had she decided to investigate the greater mysteries of Valennen. That continent wasn't safe any longer, and Jill was among his loves.

She'd changed. In a hundred years of close acquaintance with humans, close friendships with several, Larreka had learned to tell them apart as well as they could themselves, person by person or year by year. He had left her a lanky, late-maturing adolescent who had scarcely outgrown a tomboyishness which, no doubt, he had helped foster. Today she was indeed adult.

Clad in the usual blouse and slacks of townsfolk, she stood tall, long-legged, barely on the feminine side of leanness. Her head was long too, the face rather narrow though bearing a wide full mouth, nose classically straight, eyes cobalt blue and heavy-lashed under level brows. Sunlight had browned and slightly freckled a fair skin. Dark-blond and straight, her hair fell to her

32

shoulders, controlled by a silver-and-leather filigree band he had given her. She had stuck a bronzy saru feather in the back of it.

"You're ready to be bred, all right," Larreka agreed. "When and who to?"

He hadn't expected she would flush and mumble, "Not yet," then immediately ask: "How's the family? Did Meroa come along?"

"Yes. I left her at the ranch."

"Shucks, why?" she challenged. "You've got a far nicer wife than you deserve, for your information."

"Don't tell her." His pleasure faded. "This is no furlough for me. I'm bound on to Sehala for an assembly, afterward back to Valennen as soon as may be; and Meroa will stay behind."

Jill stood quite still for a space before she responded low: "Are things getting that bad there?"

"Worse."

"Oh." Another pause. "Why didn't you tell us?"

"The trouble blew up damn near overnight. I wasn't sure at first. We could just have been having a run of foul luck. When I knew better, I called to demand an assembly, then took ship."

"Why didn't you call us for air transport?"

"What use? You can't bring in everybody. Even if you had enough aircraft, which I doubt, a lot of speakers wouldn't ride in them. So we couldn't get a quorum together sooner than I could arrive by sea and land." Larreka gusted a sigh. "Meroa and I needed a vacation anyway—it's been spiky, this past year—and the trip gave us that."

Jill nodded. He had no cause to explain the reasons for his route to her. Under better conditions, the fastest way would have been entirely waterborne, from Port Rua in the South of Valennen to Liwas at the mouth of the Jayin and upriver to Sehala. But at present there were too many equinoctial gales, swelled by the red sun. Besides risk of shipwreck, sailors faced the likelihood of a voyage that contrary storms lengthened by weeks. Safest was to island-hop through the Fiery Sea, make harbor on the North Beronnen coast, then hike across the Dalag, the Badlands, the Red Hills, the Middle Forest, and the Thunderhead Range to the Jayin

33

Valley: mostly wilderness and a lot of it pretty barren, but nothing that an old campaigner couldn't get through at a goodly clip.

"Well, I've been out in the field awhile," she said. "Fossicking around in the Stony Mountains till day before yesterday. Probably I've not gotten what news God or Ian Sparling now have." Her reference wasn't theological; Goddard Hanshaw was the mayor.

"They don't, aside from doubtless having heard the speakers will assemble soon. How could I've called them on the march? That's why I've stopped off here, to see your leaders and try for a word from them that I can bring along to Sehala."

Again Jill nodded. "I forgot. Silly of me. I'm too used to instant communications, simply add hot air and stir."

She was in a different boat from him, Larreka reflected indulgently. A standard-size portable transceiver would reach to one of the relays the humans had planted throughout the southern half of this continent, and it would buck the voice on. But greater distances required a big transmitter and those relays the newcomers had put on the moons. Thus far they hadn't built more than four such stations—being, after all, at the end of a mighty long and thin supply line from Earth—Primavera, in Sehala, in Light Place on the Haelen coast, and, barely ten years ago, in Port Rua. It was ironic that, posted away off to Darkness-and-gone in the northern hemisphere, he'd been able to talk from end to end of the Gathering, a meridian arc ten thousand kilometers in length; and then, as he approached the center of civilization, his walkie-talkie had gone deaf and dumb.

Jill took his arm. "They don't expect you, hey?" she said. "C'mon, let me make the arrangements. I want to listen in."

"Why not?" he answered. "Though you won't like what you hear."

An hour passed. Jill whirled off to collect the men she had mentioned, who were carrying out jobs in the neighborhood. Meanwhile Larreka led his troopers to the single inn Primavera boasted. Mainly it dealt in beer, wine, pool games, darts, the occasional dinner

34

out; but it had accommodations for humans, whether these be transients or new chums who'd soon get permanent digs, and for visiting Ishtarians. Larreka saw his squad settled in and told the proprietor to bill the city for them as per long-standing agreement. He didn't warn them not to run it riotously high. They were good lads who'd keep the honor of the legion in mind.

Nor did he make arrangements for himself. Jill had written two years ago that she'd moved from her parents' home to a rented cottage which had an Ishtarian-outfitted chamber—it dated back several of her generations, to when scholars of both races were working constantly and intimately in an effort at mutual understanding—and if he didn't stay with her anytime he was in town, she'd be cut to the squick. ("That's 'squick.' It bleeds more.")

He proceeded to the mayor's home-cum-office. A community like Primavera needed little steering. Most of Hanshaw's duties involved Earth: shipping companies, individual scientists and technies considering a job here, bureaucrats of the World Federation when they got the urge to meddle, national politicians who could be a bigger nuisance.

The house was typical, built for a climate the humans called "Mediterranean." Thick walls, pastel-painted, gave insulation as well as strength; to the rear, a patio opened on a flower garden. Sturdy construction, steel shutters for the windows, an aerodynamically designed heraklite roof, was needful against tornados. Larreka had been told that Ishtar's rotation made storms more frequent and violent than on Earth.

Hanshaw's wife admitted him but didn't join the conference in their living room. Besides the mayor and Jill, Ian Sparling was present. Those were ample. Get more than a few Terrestrials together, and it was incredible what time they'd dribble away in laborious jabber. Sparling was chief engineer of the rescue project, therefore a key man. Moreover, he too was a good friend of Larreka's.

"Howdy, stranger," boomed Hanshaw. He'd changed almost shockingly, the commandant saw, turned gray and portly. He still seemed vigorous, however, and still insisted on shaking hands rather than clasping shoul-

35

ders. "Flop yourself." He gestured at a mattress spread on the floor to face three armchairs. Nearby, a wheeled table held an executive-desk console. "What'll you have? Beer, if I know you."

"Beer indeed," Larreka replied. "In many large mugs." He meant brew of breadroot flavored with domebud; to him, the stuff gotten from Earth grains tasted vile. That wasn't true of all such plants. After a hearty shoulderclasp with Sparling, he drew a pipe from his pouch and drawled, "Furthermore, I haven't blown tobacco for seven years."

The engineer grinned, ordered his supply, and on getting it back stuffed a briar of his own. He was a tall man—two full meters, which put him brow to brow with Larreka—in his mid-forties, wide-shouldered but otherwise gaunt and rawboned, hands and feet large and knobbly, movements looking awkward though they did everything he wanted them to. High cheekbones, curved nose, deep creases around thin lips, weatherbeaten skin, unruly black hair tinged with gray, tuneless voice, eyes big and brilliantly gray-green, had little changed since last time. Unlike Hanshaw, Sparling was as careless a dresser as Jill, but lacked her flair.

"How're the wife and youngster?" Larreka asked him.

"Oh, Rhoda's about as usual," he replied. "Becky's a student on Earth—you didn't know? Sorry. I always was a rotten correspondent. Yes, she's back there. I saw her last year on a trip. She's doing fine." Larreka recalled that humans were entitled to home leaves every four of their native years. Some, like Jill, had never taken any; this was home to them, and they were in no hurry to make an expensive tour. But Sparling returned oftener than that, to present his latest plans and argue for support of them.

"I've kept better track of your work than of your family." Larreka meant no offense. Whatever would ease the disasters ahead was top-rank in every civilized mind. "Your flood control dams—" Seeing the engineer scowl, he stopped.

"That's become part of our whole problem," Sparling said stiffly. "Let's settle down and get at it."

Olga Hanshaw brought the refreshments her husband

36

had ordered by intercom, and announced lunch in an hour. "I'm afraid it'll be nothing fancy," she apologized to Larreka. "The storms this past summer hurt the crops, your people's as well as ours."

"Well, we realize in your position, you've got to set an example of austerity," Jill said to her. "I know a hog from a Hanshaw."

Sparling alone chuckled. Maybe, Larreka thought, her English-language remark referred to something on Earth, where the engineer had been born and spent his earlier youth. Did she notice how his gaze, having gone to her, kept drifting back?

"Let's save the jokes for later," the mayor urged. "Maybe this evening we can have a poker game." Larreka hoped so. Over the octads he'd become ferociously good at it, and kept in practice by introducing it to his officers. Then he saw Jill gleefully rub her hands and remembered how she'd played slapdash chess but precocious poker. How tough had she become since?

They sobered when Hanshaw continued, "Commandant, you're here on unpleasant business. And I'm afraid we've got worse news for you."

Larreka tensed on the mattress where he couched, took a long gulp of beer, and said: "Unleash."

"Port Rua sent word the other day. Tarhanna has fallen."

Larreka had kept too much Haelener in him to yelp or swear. He sought what comfort he could find in the smoke-bite of tobacco before saying flatly, "Details?"

"Not a hell of a lot. Apparently the natives—the barbarians, I mean, not the few civilized Valenneners you've got—apparently they made a surprise attack, took the town, threw everybody out, and told the legionary chief as he was leaving that they weren't there for loot, they intended to garrison it."

"Bad," Larreka said after a while. "Bad, bad, and bad."

Jill leaned forward to touch his mane. Disturbed, a few of the seleks therein leaped out from among the leaves, then scurried back down to the proper business of such small entomoids, keeping it free of vermin and dead matter. "A shock, huh?" she asked softly.

"Yes."

37

"Why? I mean, as I understand the case, Tarhanna is . . . was the Gathering's main outpost in the interior of Valennen, 'way upriver from Port Rua.' Right? But what purpose had it except trade? And you always knew trade'll go to pot as conditions deteriorate."

"It was a military base too," Larreka reminded her. "Thence we could strike at robbers, uppity households, whatever. Now—" He smoked for a second before he proceeded. "Maybe this hits me hardest as a sign. You see, the Zera's still in good shape. Tarhanna should've been able to throw back every landlouper the whole inhabited end of the continent could raise against it. Or, anyhow, hang on till Port Rua sent a relief expedition. Only it didn't. Also, the enemy feels he can keep it. Therefore he's got himself an outfit. Not a bunch of raiders: an organized outfit. Maybe even a confederation."

He appealed: "Do you see what that means? Final proof of what I'd decided had to be the case. The bandits and pirates were growing too bloody bold, too successful, to be the kind we'd routinely coped with. And of course we were getting a little military intelligence from the outback—and now this—

"Somebody's been uniting the barbarians at last. Probably he's finished, and ready to put the crunch on us. To cast the Gathering out of Valennen altogether.

"Except that's a bare start for him. It has to be. In the past, the Rover drove desperate people south. They fell on civilization and helped tear it apart. This time around, it looked like civilization had a chance to pull through. Only somebody has organized the Valenneners to match us. He can't have but one long-range purpose—to invade the south, kill, enslave, kick us out of our lands, and take over the ruins.

"That's what I've traveled for. To tell the assembly we can't withdraw 'temporarily' from Valennen, we've got to hold fast at every cost; to get reinforcements, a second legion at a minimum, up there. But first I want to ask what help you in Primavera can give. It may not be exactly your war. But you're here to learn about Ishtar. If civilization falls, you'll have a thin time carrying on."

That was as long a speech as he had ever made, even

38

addressing the Zera on a high occasion. He turned half wildly to his pipe and beer.

Sparling's voice yanked him back: "Larreka, this hurts like a third-degree burn to say, but I'm not sure what help we can give you. You see, we've been stuck with a war of our own."

IV

SEEN FROM SPACE, all planets are beautiful; but those where humans can breathe have for them a special poignancy. As his flagship maneuvered toward parking orbit, Yuri Dejerine watched Ishtar through the least haze of tears.

Its globe was radiant blue swirled with white and marked with darker hues of continents. The unlikenesses to Earth gave it the kind of glamour that a foreign woman may bear. There were no polar caps and fewer clouds, despite a somewhat larger ocean cover. The browns of soil had no greens blent in, but shades tawny and ruddy. No great scarred Luna swung widely around, only two close-in midget moons; he glimpsed one, flickering as it tumbled, like a firefly against starful blackness.

And the light was eldritch. Most came from Ishtar's own Bel, slightly less intense than Sol on Earth but the familiar yellow-white. Anu, however, was now so close that it evoked roses and blood in the clouds and tinged the seas purple.

Stopped down to preserve his eyesight, a vision of both suns stood in the viewscreen before him. They appeared nearly the same size, a trick played by their distances. Bel was haloed in a glory of corona. Anu had no clear disc. At the middle was a furnace red where seethed monstrous spots; this dimmed and thinned outward until at last it writhed in a hazy intricacy of flame, tendrils which made Dejerine think of the Kraken.

He turned his look away. As if for companionship, he tried to find sister planets, and believed he could

39

pick out two. And, yes, that really brilliant star, ruby-colored, that must be Ea, six thousand times as remote from here as Bel and outward bound. It wasn't a reminder of mortality like Anu; as a dwarf, Ea would have a tremendously long though quiet life.

Nevertheless it touched Dejerine with a sense of its loneliness, and his, and everybody's, ineluctable. And the splendor of Ishtar held an oncoming agony. His thought went on to Eleanor, how fair she had been and how miserable, on the day she told him that after two years she could try no longer and wanted a divorce. *I was trying too,* he told her again. *I really was.*

He shook himself. No notions for the commander of a flotilla, these. A voice out of a speaker rescued him from silence: "Orbit assumed, sir. All satisfactory."

"Very good," he replied automatically. "Men not on regular watch may go off duty."

"Shall I have a call put through to ground, sir?" asked his exec.

"Not yet. It's night in that hemisphere—as far as the proper sun is concerned, anyway. They've adapted to an eighteen-and-a-half-hour day there and must be mostly asleep at present, whether or not Anu is aloft. We'd be discourteous to rouse their leaders. Let us wait—um-m-m—" Dejerine balanced Ishtarian rotation against Earthspin Navy clocks. "Say till 0700. That'll give us a few hours to relax, too. If any messages are received before, switch them to me in my cabin. Otherwise beam Primavera at 0700."

"Aye, sir. Have you further orders?"

"No, I'll simply rest. I advise you to do the same, Heinrichs. We've a busy time ahead."

"Thank you, sir. Good night." The thick accent cut off. Dejerine had required talk to be in English, practice for a community where that was well-nigh the exclusive language. (No, native speech also. Don Conway had used a number of words which he explained, on inquiry, were of nonhuman origin.) The captain suspected a lot of Spanish, Chinese, or what-have-you went on in his absence.

He himself had no linguistic problem. His upbringing had made him fluent in several major tongues, and his wife had been from the United States.

He brushed aside the returning memory. He had loved her, and he still wished her well, but after three years it would be ridiculous to pine. There were plenty of other women—had been since his middle teens. He wondered if any on Ishtar would prove available.

Again he considered the planet. Orbit had brought the cruiser into view of its civilized parts. The opposite half held a single continent and countless islands, where no significant number of Ishtarians lived and about which humans had to date learned little. They had more enigmas where they were than they could handle, in spite of indigenous help.

Anu light lay sinister across a slice which ought to have been dark. By that dull glow he picked out the continents he had read about. Conway had tried to teach him how to utter their names.

Australia-sized Haelen decked the south pole, extending an arm past the Antarctic Circle. Thence a series of archipelagos, visible from here only as changes in the pattern of clouds and currents, led north to Beronnen, roughly India-shaped, dry land from a bit south of the southern tropic to a bit south of the equator. Beyond were more islands, many volcanic—could he identify murkiness in some of the clouds?—until his eye reached Valennen, not far north of the equator. Like a Siberia stood on end, it stretched nearly to the north pole. The curve of the planet hid its further three quarters from Dejerine, that unknown territory whose life had not been born on Ishtar.

He searched for the rest of his command, parked in advance of him, but failed to see any vessel. No surprise; they were widely spaced for safety and radio relay. Their names made a litany in his head: *Sierra Nevada,* where he was; ranger *Moshe Peretz,* first vessel he had skippered; scout mother *Isabella,* who bore in her womb ten wasps; workshop *Imhotep,* which the fighting craft were here to serve and protect. Yes, he thought, he'd come a long way, spectacularly fast, in two senses. That he had been dispatched here, remote from action, was in truth an honor, a mark of trust.

Nevertheless, since his duties were off him for a while, the control bridge felt like a cell. He rose and left it, in search of what home existed in his cabin. His

41

shoes clacked loudly on empty decks. During the voyage he had had the field generators set for 1.18 g. His men and he must arrive at Ishtar with bodies adapted to its heavier pull. Tired, he felt the fourteen kilos added to his weight as if it were lead hung at shoulders and ankles.

Well, he'd be okay after a nap.

But when he had exchanged high-collared blue tunic and white trousers for pajamas, his hermit's bed held no attraction. He decided to allow himself a small cognac, and lit a cigarette. For a few minutes he prowled about looking at personal things.

His father's picture . . . Why didn't he keep his mother's? Their marriage had broken when he was six, their sole child, and she had reared him. She had been conscientious about it, too, as much as a growingly important administrative job in the Peace Control Authority permitted. Their life hadn't lacked excitement, either—frequent moves to different European cities, vacation trips to the rest of Earth and to Luna, parties where eminent guests discussed matters big in the news. . . . Yet somehow, maybe because they rarely saw each other, maybe because he was always cheerful, ambitious for little more than the enjoyment of life, Pierre Dejerine came through to the son in a way that Marina Borisovna never could . . . though surely a part of her in that boy had seen him through the Naval Academy, even if it was a part of his father that had sparked him to apply. . . .

The captain shook his head and grinned at the contents. If he must be stuffy-serious, why not put the mood to use and read over what he had on Ishtar? If nothing else, the boredom of this latest repetition might make him sleepy.

He took the best of the books, relaxed in the lounger, sipped brandy and smoke, and began leafing through.

—Babylonian nomenclature. Other Terrestrial mythologies were spent on planetary systems nearer home. But by chance, the Anubelean was among the first visited, so soon after Mach's Principle led to the cracking of

42

the light-speed barrier that Diego Primavera's voyage was an epic of daring.

His main goal was the globular cluster NGC 6656 (M 22) in Sagittarius. At three kiloparsecs' remove, this is comparatively close, and additionally of special interest to astrophysicists for being small and dense: thus a good place to begin research on groups of its kind. Spaceborne instruments had picked out an isolated stellar system much nearer, which happens in this epoch to be on a direct line between Sol and the cluster heart. That background had camouflaged it from Earthside astronomers, and confused the results of observation from orbit. Accordingly, Primavera's ship was scheduled to visit it en route.

What he found there was vastly more exciting than what he was bound for—from a biological and psychological, hence human viewpoint. Bear in mind how new in galactic space man was. He had not hitherto come upon worlds at once so like his home and so remarkably unlike.

Primavera led a second expedition for the specific purpose of exploring those planets. His report caused a sensation. A scholarly dilettante, Winston P. Sanders, proposed the Babylonian names as being appropriate on numerous counts, and the suggestion was soon adopted. . . .

However, by that time travelers who had gone elsewhere were bringing a flood of exotic tales. . . . Anubelean studies languished until a global association of scientific and humanistic institutions had been founded and funded. . . . Not only the fascination of Ishtar and Tammuz spoke for establishing a permanent base on the former. A wish did, to help the living natives through the next of those crises which had dogged their entire history, indeed their evolution. . . .

Rhetoric. Dejerine wanted dullness. He skipped to a chapter self-proclaimed as dryly factual.

Per se, the system is nothing extraordinary. Companion stars often have widely differing masses, therefore developmental histories, and eccentric orbits are more a rule than an exception.

The three members of Anubelea seem to be approximately as old as Sol. Hence Bel, the G2 star, can expect four or five billion years of steady shining in the future. Ea, the red dwarf, will endure far longer than that. But Anu, the most massive, has inevitably aged faster.

It is not enormously bigger than Bel, 1.3 times, which is to say the mass is 1.22 Sol. In its heyday it did not shine too fiercely for at least one of its planets to spawn protein-in-water life and oxygen-releasing photosynthesis. But perhaps—we continue pathetically ignorant—the greater irradiation hastened evolution. Whatever the causes, we do know that about a billion years ago, Tammuz (Anu III) had brought forth intelligent beings who had in turn brought forth a technological civilization.

By then, their sun had burned sufficient hydrogen that it could no longer stay on the main sequence. It had begun to swell, to become a red giant. At present its total luminosity equals 280 Sols; and this is slowly, inexorably rising.

To understand the situation on Ishtar, let us imagine its sun, Bel, as stationary, Anu and Ea revolving around it. Needless to say, in actuality the three stars move around a common center of mass. But given their changing configurations, only mathematics can well describe this. (See Appendix A.) A Bel-centered diagram is valid geometrically, to a first approximation, though false dynamically.

In this picture, Anu moves around Bel in a huge ellipse. At its maximum distance, it is some 224 astronomical units off, scarcely more than the chief star in the skies of Ishtar. At closest approach, it comes within 40 astronomical units of Bel, i.e. between about 39 and 41 of Ishtar, depending on the planetary position. The orbital period is 1,041 Terrestrial years. That is, each millennium the red giant sweeps near. . . .

The path of Ea is still more majestic and eccentric. It is always too remote to have a measurable direct effect, although it looms large in every known Ishtarian mythology. And it is interesting in its own right for the single planet it possesses, a superjovian. . . .

In the present epoch—which for all practical purposes covers millions of past and future years—Anu at

44

periastron to Bel adds approximately 20 per cent to the irradiation which Ishtar normally receives. This corresponds to a rise in black body temperature of 11° C.

Theoretical calculations must be used carefully. A planet, especially if it has atmosphere and hydrosphere, is *not* a black body. For example, heat will cause the formation of clouds from evaporated water, which will reflect back more radiation than formerly; but meanwhile greenhouse effect will operate the more strongly as more water vapor enters the air. And then there are the differing, though always large, thermal inertias of various regions. . . .

Since periastron passage is necessarily rapid, the time during which Anu is important to Ishtar is arbitrarily estimated at a century. As it approaches, at first there is small result except its increasing apparent size and brightness. Time is needed to heat an entire planet. Storms, droughts, and similar disasters do not become major until about the period when Anu is closest. Thereafter, while the red giant recedes, they grow progressively worse—just as the hottest time of an ordinary year comes after the summer solstice and may last beyond the autumnal equinox.

All in all, it is thus for about one century out of ten that nature on Ishtar is in turmoil. . . .

Having no large moon, the planet precesses slowly. Through this past geological era, the inclinations of orbits and spin axes have made Ishtar's northern hemisphere bear the brunt. If periastron occurs at midwinter, Anu will be ca. 26° from the north celestial pole; if at midsummer, ca. 28°. This means that these colatitudes get the maximum exposure. Their temperatures rise well above the "theoretical," with everything that that implies. At their antipodes, a third of the globe never sees Anu during this time, not until it is swiftly moving away. Although the passing star is probably responsible for the lack of ice caps at either pole, the antarctic continent remains bleak. We could wish for a more reasonable energy distribution; but the universe has never shown much interest in being reasonable. . . .

The book fell on Dejerine's lap. He woke merely to enter his bed.

V.

Its Tassu garrison would not yield Tarhanna to seige before they had plucked the leaves of their manes and shaved the turf of their pelts to eat—and then not until they had burned what strength that last starvation ration gave them. Belike many would still try to lift ax or pike when the legionaries broke down undefended gates. Knowing this, a regiment of the Zera Victrix moved north with engines trundling among them for the demolition of walls: ballistas, trebuchets, testudo-roofed ram.

Larreka wouldn't have ordered that, Arnanak thought in glee. *He's too wise.* But Larreka had gone South-Over-Sea. His vice commandant, Wolua, was less patient, less able to foresee possible countermoves. Arnanak had hoped his enemies would seek to regain the town quickly, and laid plans for this. When he was sure, his couriers went out; drums cast word across canyons; and where they would not be seen by outland forelopers, smoke signals puffed by day and beacon fires flashed by night.

Wolua was no fool. It was merely that two or three hundred years in service seemed to have made his thinking run in deep channels, not become free-ranging like Larreka's. As he led his force up the road, he kept a web of scouts far-flung on either side of the Esali. The Tassui had nothing to match that corps—chosen and trained for fleetness, schooled to read maps and use compasses, equipped with telescopes, portable heliographs, bottles of tiny bluesmoke bugs which were not found in Valennen, even magical voicecasters from Humanworld in the hands of a few key officers. The scouts did not simply prevent an adversary from surprising their main body; they found and killed hostile counterparts, to keep foes in the dark about their own side.

Or thus it had been until lately. Arnanak had a new response.

Small, swiftly scuttering, his dauri were not likely to be seen; if seen, they would likely be taken for animals; if a legionary who saw one chanced to know a little Tassu folklore, the most he would likely think was: "Holy Sun, those stories may be true! Maybe there *are* spooks in the Starklands, that get down here sometimes ... yes, doesn't the legend say they come in numbers as harbingers of the thousand-yearly destruction—?"

Arnanak's grasp of their whistling, trilling speech was not firm. Nor could they move as fast as the legionary outrunners. But they told him what he needed to learn. He knew the size and composition of the force from Port Rua, he knew day by day where it was, and on this basis he could direct his plan of battle.

He stood waiting to call the charge. Beside him was Kusarat, the Overling of Sekrusu. News of the capture of Tarhanna had decided that powerful but hitherto unsure chief, and he had lately arrived at the head of three hundred armed oathgivers. They were very welcome, as much for their example as their strength. Arnanak was willing to show their leader every sign of honor, pretend that he and he were equals. The Overling of Ulu understood it would take years to bind all households to him in such wise that they agreed he had in truth become the master of South Valennen.

"What did you do?" Kusarat asked.

"I brought half my males down out of the hills as if we were blundering blind in search of fight or plunder," Arnanak told him. "As I'd awaited, the legionaries struck cross-country with the idea of their larger force surprising and slaughtering us. We, ready for them, retreated in better order than they saw, drawing them upland. Meanwhile the second half of us, scattered hidden, have gathered here."

"How could they stay hidden from yon foul-be-their-name scouts? Many of those must have gone ahead."

"Aye. But the dauri aided our folk to know where most scouts were and whither bound. Hence they could shift about as needed."

"Dauri—" Kusarat grimaced and made a sign.

"Word reached me a short while ago," Arnanak

went on to hearten him. "The enemy left a few soldiers to watch his war engines on the road. They had no idea that through the dauri I had means to tell the warriors in Tarhanna of this. Our males have sallied thence and slain that guard. They are pulling the engines back to town."

Kusarat forgot his unease. He smote sword on shield and roared for joy.

"Softly, if you will, my friend," Arnanak said. "They have no need to know in the Zera that we are not a desperate rabble brought to bay."

From the clump of cane lia that screened them, he peered down into a dry gorge. There tramped the enemy troops, two thousand strong. Barren, the defile was more easily used, in spite of strewn boulders, than the ground above, where claw grew. The Valenneners whom they pursued had taken this way themselves. Wolua kept detachments out across the canyon sides and along the rim: plain common sense. But in these cramped quarters, his scouts were of scant use. He had no way of telling what gathered against him forward and behind. Skirmishing on the slopes, fighting a dogged rearguard action along the bottom, the Tassui blocked him off from any frontward signs and kept him too busy to think about those parts he had already passed.

A wind boomed cruelly hot. The canes where Arnanak stood rattled in its blast. It smelled of seared brush. Red and white light together cast double shadows of different lengths and colors, weirdened the whole landscape, sparse yellow shrubs, cracked gray soil above and raw-shaped ocherous crags and bluffs tumbling into the cleft beneath. A carrion ptenoid hovered far, far aloft in a heaven which seemed less blue than brazen.

There stood the True and the Demon Suns; and it was as if the first had learned wrath from the second. As summer drew nigh in Valennen, so did crimson glow to gold-white blaze. They smote the land with hammers.

Plenty bad here in his patch of shade, Arnanak thought. Soon he would have to sound the charge and lead it down into an oven.

Well, he was better outfitted than his followers, in

his old legionary gear. No Tassu smith had skill to copy that, though some made clumsy tries. Most barbarians must be content with a shield for protection, or nothing. The best a wealthy male could get might be chain mail for torso and body. The underpadding it required wouldn't let his pelt breathe or drink sunlight. Thus he weakened and began to pant; heat entered his blood; after a time he must withdraw and rest or else swoon. Therefore many who could have afforded it chose, instead, to wear little more than a cuirass and helmet. But the North-made helmet was merely a visor riveted to a conical top. Strapped on, it crushed leaves of the mane.

Arnanak's was a round steel cage supported on his shoulder harness, which in turn attached to a breastplate of metal and leather. Hoops from this arched across his back from neck to hump, warding that part of his mane while giving it freedom to work for him. The breastplate did not fit snugly; yielding pads here and there were points of contact to let his whole torso absorb the force of a blow. The plates which protected his barrel were fitted likewise, curved outward to clear most of the pelt, the cinches doing small harm. Iron-studded gauntlets and steel greaves also gave air space to his limbs, while reinforced leather straps dangled across the upper portions. Everything was painted white.

The oblong shield on his left arm was not. Its steel cover had been polished to cast light into an enemy's eyes. The boss was a beak for stabbing, the upper and lower edges were ground sharp to cut at chin or foreleg. Handy to his right arm hung sword, hatchet, and dagger.

More was needed for a rig like this than the means to buy it. A male must get legionary training in its use. Arnanak had served for an octad in the Tamburu Strider; and the years since then had often found him at practice.

The troop had pushed to within a half kilometer of him. He deemed his moment had come. Raising horn to lips, he winded the battle call, burst from the canebrake, and sped down the slope.

Stones clicked, bounced, slashed at his buskins. Heat

49

billowed, sunshine dazzled, metal below flung star-gleams at him. He felt how muscles throbbed and beat, air whistled through his nostril, hearts slugged, mane and pelt poured stress-juices into his blood till he tasted sweetness. On his left bounded Kusarat, and left of him a standard-bearer whose green flag the Sekrusu males followed. On his right sprang Tornak, a son of his, holding on high the Ulu emblem—pole-mounted, the great-horned skull of an azar from North Beronnen. Behind them came their folk.

And elsewhere, Arnanak saw in eye-flashes, elsewhere were the other bands, a wave of warriors pouring down upon the soldiers of the Gathering. They overwhelmed the outer legionary squads without stopping, hewed them into the ground and plunged onward.

Trumpets and drums called the soldiers below into close formation. Arrows, javelins, slingstones flew. Arnanak saw a male of his smitten, stumble and fall, roll flopping downward while he screamed and his veins threw gobbets over the thirsty ground. "Forth, forth!" Arnanak bawled. "Get in among them! Swordwork, axwork! For your lives and your households'—when Fire Time comes!"

After the battle, all were weary and most had suffered wounds. Fain were they to lie down and strive at naught but willing the pain out of their minds. But toil remained. Those hurts must be dressed, stitched if need be; one could not long spend heedfulness on forcing them not to bleed, at the cost of urgent tasks. The throats of hopelessly maimed legionaries must be cut, and of comrades unable to do it for themselves. What foes had not died or escaped must be hobbled and hand-bound, to be led off for enslavement unless the Gathering paid a goodly ransom. And then, although a water hole was nearby, Arnanak said they would camp at the next, an hour's march hence.

To angry shouts he replied: "These whom we fought today, who now lie slain, fought well. If we stay here, the carrion eaters will not dare come, and thus their spirits will be trapped that much longer. We can let them have quick release, can we not? Luck follows an honorable deed."

He himself closed the eyes of Wolua.

So the host loaded themselves and their prisoners with what they had stripped from their adversaries, and with their own dead. The latter would not be brought home; that was too big a trek. But they wouldn't greatly mind waiting a day or two in the anguish and bewilderment of flesh, if it would be boiled off them and eaten in Tarhanna. The final service to war-friends was as noble a liberation into the afterworld as when one gave that feast to one's family. And of course their bones would travel back, to be used for conjuring oracular dreams before getting final rest in the dolmens.

Arnanak did not, in truth, share this belief. While a soldier of the Gathering, he had been initiated into the mysteries of the Triad. They made more sense to him than the raunchy gods of his people. But he held his peace about that, led the sacrifices as became an Overling, and today did what he did because it would add to his name.

The Sun had almost followed the Rover below the hills—or the True Sun had almost followed the Invader—when they reached the spring they sought. Already it lay shrunken in a ring of dried and cracked mud. But low-growing buff-colored lia and scrubby red-leaved yan trees hung on, a meager oasis. Arnanak noticed blue shoots here and there, the early encroachments of Starkland life. Lore, handed down from ancestors who had outlived former Fire Times, said that plants of this kind could better get along then than plants of mortal sort; they became common, and drew beasts that could feed on them, which drew dauri. In this wise the parched, burnt, storm-lashed country also became haunted.

Afterward, when the Marauder had retreated, the blue plants did too, and their animals—save for kinds like the phoenix, which always throve in South Valennen; and folk could again beget children with hope that these would grow up.

Arnanak ordered the prisoners tethered in the best grazing the oasis offered. There was no other food. Any dried meat or fruit that anybody had brought was long since eaten; and who had strength to search for game?

51

Free to range, he and his warriors could get something into their guts from the sparser parts of the vale.

Night fell as they plucked and cropped. The years around Fire Time were doubly strange in that each night of advancing spring was (hereabouts) longer than the last—for the Red One so moved through heaven as to share it with the True Sun about midsummer.

Stars glittered forth, Ghost Bridge, doubly lit small rock of Narvu, above shadowed steeps and pinnacles. The air stayed hot, but a breath of breeze came like a well-wisher's hand. At last the victors could take their ease. Arnanak heard sighs go through the dimly seen mass of them as body after body dropped and chins sank down onto arms laid across forelegs. He settled himself by a low fire. Tornak lay at his side, and three more sons. Kusarat of Sekrusu asked if he might join them. "Unless you would sleep," he added politely.

"No, I would liefer rest awake for a little," Arnanak said.

"And I. My thoughts are still a jumble. Did I drowse off straight-away, I'd have no hope of making a good dream for myself."

"*Vu?* Do you have skill in the dream art? I knew that not."

"No, I can't bring any forth that are worth telling," Kusarat admitted. "But I can make them pleasant ... or useful."

Arnanak nodded. "Thus is it for me."

"And me," said Tornak. He laughed. "Tonight I want dreams of beer and females—not in Tarhanna nor my father's hall, but Port Rua when we take it—that should be something!—or even Sehala."

"Be not over-eager," Arnanak warned him. "Those conquests lie afar in time; and we may not live to make them."

"The more reason to dream them," said Tornak's half brother Igini. Their father signed them both to silence. They were young, their manners not yet honed. The other two were older, sober married males, though since neither had passed his sixty-fourth year, Arnanak's power continued over them too.

His desire was that Kusarat be shown respect. Seemingly the latter was just as anxious to please, for he asked, "Are these lads yours, Arnanak?" and upon getting a yea: "Then you must have the rest out widely, those who've gotten their growth. I hear you've sired very many, by more different females than most of us ever get at."

Arnanak didn't deny it. Besides several advantageous marriages and a row of concubines, no doubt he had made fruitful a fair number of wives he borrowed on his travels. Husbands were pleased to give him that hospitality, in the hope of strong children born into their houses. Above the fame and power he had won, there was himself, huge, soft-footed, eyes as vividly green in the black face as teeth were white, the worst of the wounds he had gotten in a gale-driven life all healed without a scar.

What he did say, gravely, was: "Aye, some are raiding at sea, some bear my messages across land. But most are at home doing their work, by my orders. I never forget how thin an edge we must live on till we've won new homes in better countries. Even a victory like today's means less than the garnering of what food and goods we can."

"Ng-ng-ng . . . you speak like a Gathering dweller," Kusarat murmured.

"Which I have been. Since then I've dealt with them here in Valennen, watched them, listened to them, always trying to learn. Why do you suppose they wield power across the whole known world? Aye, they've more skills than us, their heartland is more wealthy and populous than ours, true, true. But mainly, I do believe, mainly they have this habit of thinking ahead."

"You'd make us into their image?" Kusarat asked warily.

"As far as we can gain thereby, and are able," Arnanak said.

Kusarat regarded him for a silent while, by the flicker of spitting, shadow-weaving flames, before he replied: "And yet you deal with the dauri . . . who knows with what witchcraft?"

"That question is often shot at me," Arnanak said. "The best answer I can give is the truth."

Kusarat erected his ears and switched tail against flank. "I listen."

"I first met them, *kyai-ai,* maybe two hundred years ago when I was a youth, hardly out of cubhood, and the world not troubled by the Torchbearer. Already then its brightness cast shadows by night, and we knew it was on the way back to us. But the young do not fear a distant tomorrow and the old have no reason to. We lived well in those days—do you remember?

"My parents dwelt in Evisakuk, where Mekusak was Overling. My father was a full freeholder and had given no oath. Their house lay in the woods on Mount Fang, without close neighbors. Nevertheless my parents thought Mekusak must have sired me, an eventide when he chanced by and got shelter from them. For I grew to be like him in size and short temper and hating to scratch the soil. We kept a niggard plot where we raised a few herbs. Mainly my father and we lads were hunters. When sent out alone, I often stayed away for days on end, and afterward lied about having had a long chase. They doubted me, since they had seen what I could do when we fared together. Thus year by year I grew more estranged, and chafed more.

"Then once by myself, on the western side of the mountain and high enough that I could see a gleam where the ocean was, I found a daur. I had glimpsed a few dauri before, though barely. They came to our parts less seldom than to most of South Valennen. Maybe it was because here was wilderness, thinly peopled by mortals; maybe because here were more of the plants they live on though we cannot; maybe they had a land-magic to work here. Who knows? I don't, not to this day.

"But there the small uncanny thing was, trapped beneath a tree which had blown over in a storm the night before. Its arms and legs moved feebly, in ripples under a skin which, at hot noontide, had gone from purple to white. The petals on the branch—the branch where a head should have grown—the petals clenched and unclenched, as if they gasped, and the tendrils below them writhed. From the belly three eyes stared, dark as holes. But the hole itself had been punched by a sharp-ended bough; thin ichor trickled out.

"For a two-pulse beat I wanted to flee, and for another I wanted to slay. However, I held fast. And

54

a thought came to me: We fear them, and sometimes set out offerings, because they are unknown to us. Not because they are evil; there are few stories about their doing harm, which may all be false, and there are some about their having done things jointly with mortals, which may all be true. Would it not be wonderful to have the friendship of a daur?

"I lifted the tree off him, not too heavy for me. I bore him to a cave nearby, treated his wound as best I was able, made him a bed of lia. For days thereafter I brought him water, and food of his kind. I say 'him' but know not if 'her' would be right, or 'it,' or what. Nor do I know if we became friends as mortals do. Who can tell what a daur thinks, deep in his belly or petals or wherever his soul abides, if he has a soul? I do know we lost shyness of each other and began to swap a few words. I could not utter his trills and squeals well, though I did better than he did at my speech. Yet we learned the meaning of certain signs and noises.

"When he was healed, he gave me no treasure or magical power as I had hoped. He only made me understand that he wished me to come back whenever I could. I went home mightily thoughtful. Of course I said naught to anybody of what had happened.

"I did return often. Most times nobody met me, but now and then I would go off with a whole little band of those beings. They used no metal, and gave me tools of stone, useless to my size and shape of hand but finely chipped and perhaps lucky to carry. For my part, I guided them around—remember, they did not live here, they just came south over the Desolation Hills and along the Worldwall on brief trips—and I helped them catch the small game which could not nourish me, and gave them bones from my larger kills to make into tools. I think that must be one thing they sought. Animals in the Starklands are all dwarf, as I would learn long afterward.

"Meanwhile I began courting a female. In rashness I boasted to her at last of my comradeship with the dauri. Less bold than I'd supposed, she fled from me in terror. Soon two of her brothers sought me out and accused me of trying to cast a spell on her. Anger kindled

55

anger till they were stretched dead. Parents on both sides were quick to compose the quarrel, before a feud could start. I've since wondered if that's not the real reason fathers have absolute power over sons and grandsons, mothers over daughters and granddaughters, till the age of sixty-four—not 'upbringing,' not 'rightness,' not the word of a god, whatever we believe today—but simply that before this law, too many young were getting slain.

"Regardless, my father saw he had best give me leave to depart. I went right blithely. For the next hundred years or such, there were more exciting things to do than run on Mount Fang with the dauri. I was a hunter, and brought skins to Tarhanna for trade. When I heard that the outlanders paid better for phoenix wood, I became a lumberjack. We would raft our logs down to Port Rua, and thus I got to know that town. What its soldiers, sailors, and merchants told me about South-Over-Sea fired me and I took to the water myself.

"At first I was a buccaneer. But that was a poor trade in those days. We dared raid no island that held a legionary post, and most did. Soon I shipped as a deckhand on a Sehalan freighter.

"Long I wandered the lands of the Gathering, taking what work I found, until I joined a legion. I liked that, but when my octad was over I didn't re-enlist; for I had grown thoughtful. No, I went to Sehala itself and lived on my savings while I read books—I had learned to read; it's not a wizard's art, whatever you've heard—and hearkened to wise folk.

"You will understand. Year by year the Burner was brightening.

"They grew troubled in Sehala. Always civilization had gone under, in flood, storm, famine, breakdown, and the onset of wild people driven out of countries still more ruined. Nevertheless, they had hope. In the last two cycles, legionary organizations had saved something, more the second time than the first. Aye, several of the legions are that old, the Zera among them. They have outlived nations, and brought new ones to speedier birth and growth. Moreover, this time the humans had come, those aliens of whom you surely know rumors—

"Yes, I have met humans, though not to talk with at any length. But another evening, Kusarat. You have asked about the dauri and me.

"Legionary records showed that the Cruel Star would stand straight above Valennen. In the past, said those records, most Valenneners—belike our forebears didn't call themselves Tassui—most had perished. Dim and broken word-things bespoke northerners who in still earlier ages, before any legions were founded, overran the Fiery Sea and parts of Beronnen. Their names are lost; their descendants are part of today's civilization; but they themselves lived through Fire Time. They lived!

"I thought: If the Gathering keeps its might, there can be no such invasion of it now; and most of my people will die. I cared for them still. What quarrels I had among them I saw as lovers' quarrels.

"I thought: But the Gathering will at best be much weakened. If Valennen meanwhile is strengthened, united, knowingly led— Do you see? And before you say it, I will. Yes, of course I want to be he who shapes the whole next cycle. I want the humans to come to *me* while I live, not to Sehala, and deal with me in wonders. And when I am dead, I want my memory to stand, my skull enshrined for an oracle, till the next Fire Time after this, and beyond. That is no more than soldier's pay for saving a folk.

"Therefore I came home.

"You have heard the rest: how I cleared new land at Ulu; how I built wealth and power through trade with the Gathering, and reaving of those places from which the Gathering withdrew; how lesser families who saw worsening years ahead came to me, gave oath in return for land and leadership, learned from me how to fight with the head as well as the hands. They are the bone of my strength.

"But the spirit in it—"

"Kusarat, I will say frankly, I have hunted out word about you, because you are an Overling of weight. Thus I know I can speak to you more openly than to some. You are no back-country huddler who gulps

57

down every cackle of old wives' gossip about the gods. When I say that our shortsighted, wrangling Tassui cannot be brought together by force alone, not to save their very lives—that only an Otherness can melt them to an ingot from which I may forge a sword—you will understand.

"I sought my dauri again.

"Long and long was that search. Yet they do make ever more treks to mortal realms, in ever greater numbers, as the Stormkindler draws nigh. Their Starklands dry out worse than our grounds do; and meanwhile, as the waxing heat kills off our kind of life, their kind— which can better take it—moves in, to nourish them. Thus in the end, it matters not how, I found me a daur. We spoke what little we could. Later I met more dauri and we spoke further.

"I do not know if he I saved was among them, nor even if they had heard that tale. I tried to find out, and failed. What I did have was a slight command of their speech and knowledge of their ways, to show I had formerly been friendly with their sort. I worked hard to add to this.

"For . . . in Fire Time, it is not only mortals who seek what allies they can get.

"They are leery of us. And, frankly again, too much closeness might make my followers not leery enough of them. I needed a sigil, a Thing, which I could bear for a mark of their favor while they mainly kept away from the Tassui. But I could not make this clear; they are so utterly sundered from us. Or if they understood me, perhaps they did not know what would serve. After all, I myself was blind as to what there might be. A token of stone or bone was no use; I could have fashioned that myself.

"The upshot was that they took me into their homeland.

"You have heard that I went. You may have heard that I came back in mummy skin and bones a-rattle, and took a year to regain my health. But you have not heard of the quest.

"I spent three years merely readying. First the dauri took food of mine and made caches for me along the way. In the Starklands it would not rot, nor would

58

beasts eat it. Regardless, I almost starved. They had laid down too little; the load a daur can carry is small, and I had not foreseen how grim that country is. Still nearer did I come to death by thirst. It is not a desert northward, or was not before the Red One returned. But it is dry, its life needs less water than ours does, and this too we had not allowed for.

"Yet in the end we won to certain ruins. I groped half mad among them, until a daur showed me the Thing that is full of unknown stars. I clutched it to me and sent my feet back across that land which scorned and scorched them. Somehow they bore me.

"Since, the dauri and I have grown closer. We have secrets I am not free to share. But their will toward me is good; and my will toward you is good. My friends they will help, my foes they will harm. This is enough to say. I have spoken; and you will understand."

Later, as he drifted toward sleep, Arnanak thought: *Enough to say to him. Humans would surely pay well to hear more. What I can tell them about the dauri might buy me their abandonment of the Gathering.*

VI

ANU WAS A few hours under the horizon and Bel quite low above. Light streamed yellow under the trees along Campbell Street. Where it passed through the translucent leaves of jackfruit, it flecked the shade beneath with spots of coral. The air lay quietly cooling, full of spicy autumn fragrances from across the river. Several children played hopscotch on the pavement. Their shouts flew thin and sweet to Ian Sparling's ears. A bicyclist dodged around them. Otherwise nobody was in sight. The laboratories and industries whose low, garden-surrounded buildings lined this thoroughfare were closed for the evening, their workers at home or—a few score—outside the mayor's house to see the Earthlings come forth and hope for a scrap of news.

Actually, that first conference was finished. The

Hanshaws had invited participants to stay for dinner. Sociability might ease a little of the stress between them. Sparling had excused himself on the ground that his wife would be disappointed if he didn't return for a special dish she'd prepared. He suspected Hanshaw knew it was a lie, but he didn't care. By taking the rear exit to an alley, and thence a roundabout way home, he avoided questions from the crowd.

Pipe cold between teeth, fists jammed into pockets, he scissored space with his legs, scarcely aware of the world. Fingers must close on his arm and shake before he noticed. But then he saw Jill Conway. He stopped. The blood quickened and sang in him.

"Wow," she said. "What's the hurry? You're traveling like the devil to a tax collector's wake." Scant mirth was in her tone, and after a second she added, "Bad, huh?"

"I shouldn't—" He nearly lost his pipe, crammed it away, and swallowed before he demanded, "What're you doing here?"

"Waiting for you."

He stared at her slenderness. Light ran down the street and struck gold from her hair. "Huh? But why—?" *No, obviously she didn't wait for me. Just for a chance to talk to me.* Sparling collected himself. "How did you know when or where?"

"I asked Olga Hanshaw to phone me as soon as the official discussion ended. She wasn't forbidden to, and she feels she owes me a favor." Jill had rescued the couple's youngest child from drowning a couple of years before. This was the first time Sparling had heard of her claiming any reward. "Don't mention it, please, Ian."

"No," he promised at once; then: *But God did request we keep things confidential till he's planned how to tell Primavera and ... the whole Gathering.* Then: *Well, I won't go back on my word to Jill. I can't. It's harmless. If anybody on this planet can be trusted, she can. She should've been invited to sit in on the conference. Though that would've roused jealousies, and distracted me—or inspired me— Throttle that nonsense!* he ordered himself. *You old fool!*

"As for how I knew where to wait," Jill told him,

"why, I know you. Campbell to Riverside and on home. Right?"

He attempted a smile. "Am I that transparent?"

"No." She regarded his gaunt features carefully. "No, you're a mighty private person. However, chances were you'd leave early; you're never much for polite banalities. You'd choose a route which avoided people. At this hour, it has to be this way. Primavera isn't exactly a labyrinth." Her voice snapped: "You know my methods, Watson. Apply them!"

He couldn't but chuckle and shake his head. "Why not loosen your collar?" Jill suggested. "You don't have to choke any more to impress the Navy with our earnestness. Besides, that cowlick of yours spoils the effect."

"Well—okay." When he had done, she took his arm again, tucked hers beneath, and started them off in the free-swinging stride they both favored.

"What happened?" she asked after a while.

"I'm not supposed to—"

"Yeh, yeh, yeh. You're not under oath of secrecy, are you? I'll give you my promise if you like, not to let anything go any further." She was silent for a space, during which he heard their boots thud and felt her touch. When she spoke anew, it was most softly. "Yes, Ian, I am presuming, I am begging for a privilege. But I've got a brother in the Navy. And Larreka's always been like a second father to me. The night he stayed at my house ... hardest to take was the way he kept working to crack jokes, tell anecdotes, whatever he hoped might amuse me. I wanted to cry. Except naturally he'd've known what that meant, and soldiers' daughters don't show grief."

"The legionary tradition," he said for lack of better words. "It'd be dangerous to morale if allowed. We're different, we humans."

"Not that different. And if I knew what— The sooner I know, the sooner I can start thinking about something real to do, not sit inside myself and gnaw my guts."

He must look at her then, less far downward than a man of his height need do with the run of women. Her

61

blue gaze was steady, yet she smiled no more and the level sunbeams caught sparks in her lashes.

"You win," he rasped. "Though you won't like the news."

"I didn't expect to. Oh, Ian, you're such a laren!" The word meant, approximately, "good trooper," overtones of kindliness as well as strength and fidelity. She let go his arm and took his hand. He checked a wish to squeeze back. No use, worse than useless, to let her guess how she had altogether gripped him. But he could keep a very gentle hold, couldn't he?

They reached the landing and turned north onto Riverside, a road cut from the left bank of the Jayin. On their right, trees screened them from view of town, a long row of deep-rooted swordleaf, preserved amidst this terrestrialized ecology to be a windbreak when tornados whirled out of the west. Opposite, the stream flowed broad, murmurous, evening ablaze upon it. Snags and shoals made ripples; an ichthy would leap in a gleam of silver and a clear splash; rocket flies darted brilliant. On the farther shore, native pastureland rolled into blue remoteness—tawny turf of lia, scarlet firebloom, scattered trees crowned with copper or brass. In the middle distance a flock of owas grazed, and the larger els individually, six-legged kine in a peacefulness that Sparling wished Constable could have painted.

Here the air was cooler still, damp, breezy, many-scented. Westward under sinking Bel, a few clouds glowed orange. Elsewhere the sky stood unutterably clear. A ghostly, waning Caelestia drew eastward. Beneath, so high as to be only a pair of wings, hovered a saru. It did not stoop on any of the iburu which flapped along lower down; maybe it waited for easier prey than those big bronzy-green ptenoids. A cantor sat on a bough, small, gray-feathered, fearless, and sang its autumn song.

Sparling remembered how Jill had continued the work of her mentor, old Jim Hashimoto, on the many functions of song in the cantor and related species, for her first serious research project, and how she'd run whooping across his sight in the joy of a breakthrough idea. Had that been when he first— No, probably not. She was a long-legged youngster then, six or seven

62

years older than his, merely one of three kids born to the Conways. Since, Alice had married Bill Phillips, and Donald had followed Becky to college on Earth till the Navy pulled him in. . . .

"We'll soon be at your place, Ian," Jill warned. "Unless you want to stop and talk."

"No, let's get it over with," he said, called back. "Not much to tell, anyhow."

"I don't suppose the ships brought mail?"

"No. At least, nobody mentioned any. Captain Dejerine, their top man, did promise regular communications will be maintained. If nothing else, his courier boats will carry civilian messages too."

"What're they here for?"

"That was announced yesterday, right after they first established contact. To protect us from possible Naqsan attack."

"Ridiculous, I'd say. Wouldn't you? Ridiculous as the whole war."

"Maybe not."

"Well, if their presence would guarantee the supplies we need—for your kind of work in particular—I'd be duly grateful. But no, the word is that the war effort will take nearly all shipping, and doubtless assorted key items as well. Captain Whosie confirmed it today. Didn't he? You wouldn't look so fierce otherwise."

Sparling jerked a nod.

Jill studied his countenance again before she said, "The news was worse yet. Right?"

"Right," came from him. "They're supposed to build a base here. For reconnaissance operations. Which means depots, backup facilities, and a local war industry to save on interstellar transportation. Dejerine has orders to mobilize everything we've got that isn't required for our survival. Effective immediately, we must justify whatever of our production we consume rather than stockpile for the Navy."

Jill halted. And he did. "Oh, no," she whispered.

He let the stiffness slump out of his shoulders.

She caught both his hands. "Your cement plant?" she asked raggedly. "You can't keep on making concrete for your dams?"

"That's right." He heard how flat his voice fell. "It's requisitioned for the base."

"Couldn't you *explain?*"

"We tried, for our different projects. Me, I pointed out how flooding of valleys by melted snowpack has always been a major factor in wrecking civilization in South Beronnen, and if we could prevent it this periastron, then we could hope— Hell, why am I telling you? Dejerine asked when the floods'll start. I gave him our estimate—he'll surely have my files checked out—and he said that in five years the war should be over and we can carry on the same as before."

"You mean he's never heard of lead time? He thinks you can build a set of dams in high country, with native labor and a miser's consignment of machinery, by rubbing a lamp?"

Sparling grimaced. "He and his fellows weren't unsympathetic. They're not evil men, nor stupid. We're free to protest and petition to Earth, they said, and they won't necessarily argue against us. That'll depend on what they decide after reviewing matters for themselves. Meanwhile, they have their orders." He drew breath. "God asked them, what about military assistance to the Gathering? Dejerine said no. He's been strictly and specifically instructed to stay out of local disputes. That includes us, he said. We must not risk equipment which may be valuable to the war effort, or risk getting his force embroiled, diverted from its task. Besides, a Parliamentary commission has declared that our past 'interference' should be investigated, since it looks very much like 'cultural imperialism.' "

Jill stared. "Judas . . . hopping . . . priest," she said.

"I'm not too surprised," Sparling admitted. "When I was on Earth last year, that seemed to be the newest intellectual fashion, that nonhumans should be left to develop naturally."

"Unless they're Naqsans on Mundomar, of course."

"Of course. At the time, I wasn't worried about Ishtar, because the rebuttal was too strong: if we don't step in to help civilization survive, millions of sentient beings will die. But now—" Sparling shrugged.

Jill finished for him: "Now they'll have to rationalize the fact that they let it happen, the better to prosecute their own pet war. A 'noninterference' doctrine ought to make excellent conscience grease." She spat. "Do you wonder why I've never bothered to visit Earth?"

"Hey, don't judge entire nations by recent politics. I thought your reason was you didn't feel in any hurry to see a lot of buildings and crowds when you've got a worldful of marvels right here. Even that isn't true. There are still beautiful areas on Earth."

"You've told me." Jill beat fist in palm. "Ian, what can we do?"

"Try to get those orders countermanded," he sighed.

"Or find loopholes in them?"

"If possible. Mainly, though, I'd say we should start by getting the Navy men on our side. Make them agree the Gathering of Sehala is more important than a minor base way outside the theater of war. Their word should bear more weight in Mexico City than any amount of impassioned pleas from us. I repeat, Dejerine and his staff strike me as basically decent, reasonable persons. They support the war, but that doesn't mean they're fanatics."

"Do you plan a grand tour for them?"

"Not yet. I'm bound for Sehala tomorrow, to tell the assembly that . . . whatever help they were counting on from us, they'll have to wait for." Sparling winced. "It won't be easy."

"No," Jill said low. "I wish it didn't have to be you, Ian. It does. You must empathize with them better than anybody else, and Lord knows they think the cosmos of you. But I wish you didnt have to take on the pain of it."

He looked at her through thunder. *She cares this much about me?*

Turned thoughtful, she went on: "Suppose meanwhile I have a go at persuading those Earthsiders. Well, not persuade, that can't be done overnight, but putting our case to them, laying out the facts. I've no professional ax to grind; a naturalist can continue research unaffected. And I do have a brother in uniform. So they should listen. I'll be polite, yes, downright cordial. Do you think that might help, Ian?"

"Would it!" he blurted. At once: *I don't believe the idea's crossed her mind, what a charming young woman*

65

can accomplish. She has no conscious notion of how to flirt. It moved him, though at the same time he was wrenched to understand that her concern for him was that of a friend, only a friend.

She tossed her head. "Okay. We ain't licked yet. Which may mean we're dry behind the ears. Not between them, let's hope." Seriously: "When you see Larreka in Sehala, tell him from me, *'Yaago baraol'* "

"What?"

"You don't know? . . . Well, it's not Sehalan. From a dialect in the Iren islands, where the Zera was stationed, oh, decades ago." She hesitated. "A rough equivalent of 'I have not begun to fight.' If Larreka hears it from me, he'll feel better."

Sparling squinted at her. For both of them, the banter which had long been a shared pleasure could become a refuge. "Rough, did you say?" he murmured. "How rough? What's the literal translation?"

"I'm a lady," she retorted. "I won't tell you till I've decided I need practice in blushing—or you do."

They stood silent for a little, hand in hand.

"Too lovely a sunset for anything but itself," she said, looking across the river. Light from clouds and water poured hot gold across her. "Does Earth really have places left like this?"

"A few." He was chiefly conscious of her clasp.

"Your stamping grounds?"

"No, they're different. Woods, mountains, sea, wet climate—"

"Silly! I know you're from British Columbia. You've now confirmed what I also knew, that you're as literal-minded as a computer. If I said 'frog,' you wouldn't simply jump, you'd do your best to turn green."

He smiled across an inward flinching. "Come to Earth and meet a frog. Kiss him and change him back into a handsome prince. Then you'll be sorry. You see, the conservation of mass will require you become a frog."

Did she see that she had called him old and stodgy? For she spoke with renewed seriousness. "Sure, they've kept enclaves of nature on Earth, and you had the luck to grow up in one. But didn't you first truly luck out when you came here? Aren't you happier where *we* are

66

the enclave? Freedom—" Abruptly she pointed. "Look! Look! A bipen!"

Sparling's gaze followed her gesture. The animal which flew lumberingly from above the row of trees was less birdlike than the other ptenoids in view. Instead of four legs and two wings, it had four wings and two legs—and endless further differences, from bone to feather-plant. He was familiar with the dipter, which dived after ichthyoids off the South Beronnen coast. But the majority of fourwingers, less successful than two-wingers, were confined to Haelen. He'd never seen a bipen before. It was a large and comely creature, plumage violet in the sunset rays.

"They're beginning to move north," Jill breathed. He glanced at her, saw how her eyes shone, and lost interest in the bipen. "I thought they would. Remains from the last cycle—shifts of storm belts—Ian, am I awful for being fascinated by what Anu passage does to the ecology?"

No, he wanted to say; you can do no wrong.

He couldn't have voiced it thus, but he groped after a word more meaningful than "Certainly not." Her cry interrupted him. He cast his attention back skyward.

The saru which had been at hover descended. Its wings drove clawed feet and hooked beak; Sparling heard air whistle behind. He heard the impact which broke the bipen's neck, and saw blood spray. The blood of ortho-Ishtarian life is purple, and wildly fluorescent. The saru labored off with the heavy catch it had made.

Jill choked. Again he glimpsed tears. She mastered them. "Bound to happen, I suppose," she mumbled. "Every thousand years. Maybe the species has even gotten dependent on this kind of thing." She turned to him. "But we don't need to. Do we?"

He shook his head.

"By God, and I mean the original," she went on between her teeth, "we will not quit." Gulping: " 'Scuse me. I'll try to be brave and all, but—that poor birdling coming this far to die— Let's give 'em hell, Ian. Thanks for everything. Good night." As she let him go and walked swiftly back, Bel went under the world-rim.

Sparling stayed where he was, loading his pipe, till

she had gone from his view and for minutes after. Clouds darkened in a blue dusk, save where the moon tinged them. The early stars trod forth, and mellowly shining Marduk. He thought how tormented that planet was by the storms Anu raised in its immense atmosphere. But across a few hundred million kilometers, nothing is visible except peace. The air around him grew cooler still, water clucked, smoke gave his mouth an acrid kiss.

Indeed, he thought, this moment and place were more serene than his birthland. No matter that Earth was blessed above Ishtar, except maybe in having brought forth man; the West Canadian coast and the Inland Passage were never like the Jayin Valley, they were clouded, wave-beaten, storm-swept, and upon a sunny day what you saw was a stern majesty.

Jill's right. I have been lucky. His daughter had said the same last year, when he took her on a cruise through the remembered country. Her college was in megalopolitan Rio de Janeiro.

Boyhood among trees and clean currents, because his father happened to be a space architect who commuted to Vancouver when he didn't leave Earth entirely, his mother a programmer who could work right out of her house, and they between them able to afford Ocean Falls—*I've seen Welfare and the Backworld too,* he told Yuri Dejerine as he had not during the day's discussions. *Don't get me wrong, I sympathize, I agree those people deserve a better break. And as far as pride in being human goes, I was at the formative age of fifteen when Gunnar Heim brought us to our victory over Alerion. I don't merely know, I feel what that meant.*

But working outsystem as a young engineer, I met Naqsans, and Satan take it, they're our kind. Then for the last twenty years I've been on Ishtar, this has become my world, here's where my duty lies—

He shook himself. Past time to report in. His boots racketed.

Twilight was deepening toward night, more and more stars out, when he finished the short climb up Humboldt Street from Riverside and opened his gate. Window-gleams caught wilted roses and bald patches in grass. Terrestrial plants didn't give way to weeds if neglected. For that, some years would first have to pass, killing off imported earthworms and soil bacteria, restoring the original balance of acidity, nitrogen, and trace elements, letting native microbes rebuild humus. Untended exotics simply sickened and died. *I've got to fertilize, drain, whatever's needful,* he thought. *When I get the chance. If I do.* No groundsmen were for hire in labor-short Primavera. Becky had handled the work.

Be honest. I could find the necessary hours if I wanted, Sparling knew. *Truth is, I enjoy gardens but not their maintenance. Rather do carpentry for my fun, or whittle toys to give to kids human or Ishtarian. And Rhoda has what Jill (Jill) calls a sere and withered thumb.*

He walked in the front door. His wife laid down her book. He recognized a novel which had caused considerable excitement on Earth when he was there. The library had ordered a reel for making printouts. Curious about what went on in the novel nowadays, after its long eclipse, he kept intending to read this specimen. However, he always seemed too busy, or he was tired and preferred to relax with an old familiar like Kipling, or he was intrigued by a piece of Ishtarian literature, or—

"Hello," she said. "What happened?" Her English kept a trace of Brazilian accent. Once he had learned Portugese and they spoke it at home; but they'd drifted out of the habit and he lost his vocabulary.

"I'm afraid I can't tell you for a while," he grunted. Guilt reminded him weakly that she was no blabbermouth and Olga Hanshaw had been free to listen in. He replied that he was too worn out to discuss the miserable business any further—the more so when Rhoda, isolated in a minor supply-department position, would need everything explained at length which Jill saw on the instant.

"It is not good," she said after watching his face.

"No, not good." His lankiness flopped into a chair. A minimum he must reveal: "I'm leaving for Sehala tomorrow. Got to, uh, make liaison with the assembly while it stands. I expect I'll be gone a few days."

"I see." She rose. "Do you care for a drink before dinner?"

"Absolutely. Rum and a dash of lemon. About two fingers." He held them upright in a row.

When she smiled, a trace returned of that which had drawn him to a shy, studious girl he met on a job. She'd never been an unusual sight; he'd originally rated her at a millihelen, the amount of beauty needed to launch a single ship. But he'd always been awkward with women; he saw he could have Rhoda Vargas if he wished, and she'd be a good partner; he proceeded systematically to fall in love. "I have been looking forward," she said.

Younger than he, she nonetheless showed more gray in her hair. The snub-nosed countenance had gone pudgy, as had the short body. Yet passing by on her way to the kitchen, she stroked a palm across his head, and he recalled their first years.

Alone, he puffed his pipe and wondered if Becky's difficult birth had brought on the slow change. The doctor had said there was no point in cloning her a new uterus; she'd lose it afresh, and the baby too, next time. But they hadn't been required to try for more children, had they? Did the loss inside carry some consequence too subtle for meditechnics to see? The blunt fact was, she remained gentle, popular in the community, an excellent cook, et cetera, et cetera, but drop by drop they came together less often, in spirit and in flesh.

Or, he thought, not for the first occasion or the hundredth, *was the change mainly in me?* For his work had sent him adventuring across half the planet, while hers and the child kept her behind. He got the Earthside business trips, while she—who missed her kinfolk more than he did his, though she never complained—must settle for a few weeks every four years. On the other hand, she kept her human associations in Primavera, her interest in human creations, while his involvement steadily increased with Ishtarians and their minds.

Be the cause what it might, these days he felt little for her beyond a certain liking and compassion: a truth which he only had the heart—or the nerve—to tell himself. When his projects began to demand he spend most of his time here, planning and directing, instead

70

of in the field, his main emotion was resignation to dullness.

Until he grew fully aware of Jill Conway.

He tamped his pipe with his thumb, almost savoring the slight burn.

Rhoda brought in their drinks. "I'm glad you got away this early, dear," she said. "You have been straining too hard. I thought tonight, if you didn't come in late, for dinner I would make something special."

VII

CAPTAIN DEJERINE ACCEPTED happily an invitation to a day's guided outing with a person who could explain what he saw. Besides a chance to start making friends in a community whose co-operation he needed and which he knew was hostile to his purposes, he welcomed the sheer recreation, after a wearying space journey. When the person whom Goddard Hanshaw mentioned turned out to be Jill Conway, his pleasure boosted to delight.

She called for him before Belrise, in the eerie red light of Anu low in the north. He and a few associates were temporarily lodged at the inn; most of the men must remain in orbit till their prefab shelters could be erected. He had been supplied a flywheeler. ("Might as well do you the courtesy before you requisition it," Hanshaw had growled half amiably.) Jill's was a great deal larger and livelier. He was appalled at the prospect of matching her driving style, but clenched his jaws and presently found himself enjoying the speed. By then they had crossed the river—on a small automatic ferry, since his machine lacked a skimmer—and were well into untouched Ishtarian countryside.

Bel arrived in heaven, shadows doubled and the ember illumination became rosy. Jill halted at a grove where a spring flowed. "How 'bout breakfast?" she proposed. "Afterward we'll go more leisurely."

"*Magnifique.*" Dejerine opened the carrier box on his vehicle. "I regret being unable to make a real con-

71

tribution, but here is an Italian salami, if you will accept—"

"Will I!" She clapped her hands in glee. "I've had that exactly once before in my life. Believe me, a first love is nothing compared to a first Italian dry salami." *Liar*, she thought, remembering Senzo. And yet . . . the hurt of that was well healed over. *In you also, darling, I trust.*

Dejerine helped her spread a cloth on the ground and unpack the food she had brought, bread, butter, cheese, jam. *He is pleasant*, she thought. *Damn good-looking, too.* As she was plugging the coffee maker into her wheeler's capacitor, he startled her: "I have not had a minute to say this before, Miss Conway, given your whirlwind procedure. But I know your brother Donald. He asked me to send his best greetings."

"Huh?" She sprang from her hunkering position. "You do? How is he? Where's he bound for? Why hasn't he written?"

"He was in excellent shape the last time I saw him," Dejerine replied. "We had spent quite a few hours talking, in the course of days. You see, when I was assigned here, I—you say?—I looked up whoever I could get from Ishtar, in hopes of a briefing. That happened to be Don." His smile was quite captivating, easy, warming the whole face, accompanied by a regard which was not a stare but an appreciation. "He told me considerable about you." He turned serious as quickly as she herself might. "Where is he posted? I know only that it is to the front. Please don't worry too much about him. In every way, equipment, training, organization, we are far superior to the enemy. And as for the rest, he was busy and preoccupied; he admitted he hates to write letters, and so he entrusted me with his word. I did make him promise he would write soon."

Jill sighed. "Thanks a billion. That's Don, for sure." She returned to the coffeepot. "Let's save the details for later. Like this evening, if you don't mind, we can land on my parents. My sister and her husband would want to hear too."

"As you wish," he said with a slight bow. He had the sense not to try to help when he would obviously get in her way. Instead he admired their surroundings.

72

The grove stood on a rolling plain. It was chiefly tall red-topped swordleaf, though domebud added splashes of bright yellow. The turf shaded by the trees was that low-growing, tough lia which humans called dromia. The spring issued from beneath a boulder spotted orange with clingwort, ran down in a rivulet, and soon vanished into the soil. Nevertheless it nourished a wide area, for many kinds of shrubs grew around the coppice. Further out, sward gave place to waist-high fallowblade and head-high plume, waves of dull gold across kilometers. The wind blew warm and dry, bearing scorchy odors, awakening a thousand rustlings above the faint gurgle of the water.

"Do you know the names of all these plants?" Dejerine asked.

"The common breeds," Jill said. "I'm no botanist. However"—she pointed around—"most of what you see is assorted kinds of lia. It's as varied and important as grass is on Earth. Bushes— That little fellow yonder is bitterheart; the Ishtarians use it for seasoning and a tonic, and it seems to have medicinal properties for humans as well. But watch out for the scraggly thing, night thief. It'll make an Ishtarian sick, and kill you or me if we eat it. There's no firebloom around here— needs more moisture—but the thunderweed gets really spectacular in the rainy season, which we're heading into; and then in spring, the pandarus."

"The what?"

Jill giggled. "I forgot you wouldn't know. That'n. It draws entomoids to pollinate it by duplicating their sex attractants, both sexes. Quite a spectacle."

For an instant she regretted her remark. Dejerine might take it as an invitation. He simply inquired, "Do you use translations of the native names?"

"Seldom," she answered, relieved. She could fend off a pass, but— *Well, if there are going to be any, I prefer to initiate them.* Wryly: *Not that I'd win trophies, of whatever shape, in a contest for femme fatale of the year.* "Most aren't translatable—how would you say 'rose' in Sehalan?—and we aren't geared to pronounce the originals properly. So we invent our own. Including 'lia,' by the way. The first scientific work on the family was done by Li Chang-Shi."

73

"M-hm. I understand the photosynthesizing molecule here isn't identical with chlorophyl, only similar. But why are both red and yellow this frequent?"

"The theory is, the yellow color is basic, but red pigment orignated in Haelen as an energy absorber. A heath of sundrinker is a wild thing to see. The phylum proved sturdy enough to spread across the globe and differentiate every which way. Just a theory, you realize. Lord, a whole world! In a century we've barely begun to get the outlines of how little we know. . . . Let's eat, shall we?"

As they did, the sky was darkened by a flock of pilgrim, made thunderous by their wings and clangorous with their cries. Startled, several azar broke from a swale where they had been grazing and bounded off, their six legs undulatingly graceful. Through binoculars, the humans saw details which Jill explained.

"No true horns on Ishtarian theroids. These stubby things you see are more like what grows on a rhinoceros. A few kinds of azar—it's a whole clutch of genera—a few big types in North Beronnen do develop an impressive spread, but mainly for display. Look . . . can you make out how the front legs have a special shape? And their hoofs are sharp striking weapons. Seems to be a general tendency on Ishtar, for the forward pair of limbs to do something besides help locomotion. The extreme case, of course, is the sophonts and their relatives; forelegs become arms and forefeet become hands."

When the splendid parade had ended and quiet dwelt again beneath the wind, Dejerine looked gravely at her as he said, "I get a glimpse of how you who were born here must love this planet."

"It's ours." Jill replied. "Though in a peculiar way. Our race will never take it over, will never be more than a few. It belongs to the Ishtarians."

He dropped his gaze to the cup he held. "Please understand, I appreciate how dismayed you must be that your humanitarian plans are set aside. Always in war, many hopes are interrupted or destroyed. I pray for an early end of the fighting. Meanwhile, perhaps we can work something out for you."

Maybe, Jill thought. *Don't push too hard, girl.* She

smiled and, very lightly and briefly, patted his hand. "Thanks, Captain. We'll talk about that. But today we're enjoying a peek-around. I'm supposed to be your docent, not your nag."

"By all means," he said. "Ah . . . you mentioned relatives of the natives. My sources describe equivalents of the apes——"

"Kind of," Jill nodded. "Like the tartar, which really corresponds more to a baboon. The closest kin is the fellow we call a goblin."

"The semi-intelligent species? Ah, yes, I was coming to those. How much do you know about them?"

"Very little. It's rare and shy in Beronnen. Fairly numerous—is our impression—in the opposite hemisphere; but fully developed Ishtarians have hardly penetrated there yet. I can't tell you a lot more than that goblins make crude tools and appear to have a language of sorts. As if Australopithecus survived on Earth."

"Hm." Dejerine stroked his mustache. "How strange that they have been allowed to."

"No, not really. Remember what an enormous amount of ocean, stormier than any on Earth, lies between."

"I meant that where ranges overlap, the higher species hasn't exterminated the lower."

"Ishtarians wouldn't. Not even the most warlike barbarians have our casual human bloodthirstiness. For instance, nobody here has ever tortured prisoners for fun or massacred them for convenience. You probably think of the Gathering of Sehala as a sort of empire. It isn't. Civilization has developed without any need for the state. After all, the Ishtarians are a more advanced form of life than us."

His surprise took her aback, until she reflected that an idea with which she had always lived must be new to him. After a moment he said slowly, "My readings did mention post-mammalian evolution. They never made too clear to me what was meant. I assumed—*Tiens*, you are not claiming they are more intelligent than us? This was not in my books." He drew breath. "True, they seem better at some things than we are, but less quick and original in others. That's usual among

75

contrasted sophont species. The totals always seem to even approximately out. I think the explanation is reasonable, that beyond a certain point there is no selection pressure to increase brain power further, and indeed this would grotesquely unbalance the organism."

She studied him with rising respect. Had he, the military man, taken that much trouble, that much thought? *Okay, I'll pay him the compliment of answering in kind, not talking down any more than necessary.*

"Can you stand a lecture?" she asked.

He smiled, leaned back against a bole, offered her a cigarette from a silver case, and, after she declined, helped himself. "When such a lecturer gives it?" he murmured. "Mademoiselle, I try to be a gentleman, but my glands are in good working order."

Jill grinned. "We will have a twenty-minute quiz at the end," she said. "Ay-hem.

"You know life here—ortho-life, that is, not T-life—developed quite similarly to Earth's, the original environments being so similar. Mainly the same chemicals, two sexes, vertebrates descended from something like an annelid worm, and so forth. We can eat most of each other's food, though we'd come down with deficiency diseases if we tried to exclusively, and certain things that one breed likes are poisonous to the other. The fact of hexapodality versus quadrupedality appears to be fairly trivial, a biological accident. Ishtar has its equivalents of fish, reptile, bird, mammal, et cetera. The differences are important enough that we lay on names ending in -oid. For instance, the theroids are warm-blooded, give live birth, and suckle their young; but they don't grow either hair or placentas—they've got astonishing alternatives—and in general, the variations are endless.

"Maybe they'd be more like us yet, except for Anu's going off on a red giant kick about a billion years ago. It's spent the whole while since growing bigger, and nastier each time it passes close. This means poikilothermic land animals—whoops! Cold-blooded, if you prefer—they've been at a still worse disadvantage than on Earth, and never got far. No trace among the fossils

76

of anything analogous to dinosaurs. The theroids grabbed an early lead and kept it.

"Okay. On this basis, which you're doubtless familiar with already but I wanted to spell out—on this basis, we think—we think, mind you; the actual evidence to date is pitifully slight—we think the theroids have had more time to evolve than mammals on Earth. (Yes, I realize mammals are very old, but they didn't really take off till the Oligocene.) The trick they invented here that we haven't, is symbiosis. Oh, sure, you're symbiotic with a few organisms yourself, like your intestinal flora. One definition would even include your mitochondria. But the well-developed Ishtarian theroid is a whole zoo and botanical garden of co-operating species.

"Let's take a sophont, for instance—a few of his most conspicuous partners. His pelt, or hers, is a mossy plant, shallowly rooted in the skin but connected to the bloodstream ... because his skin is a lot more complicated than ours. His mane and brows resemble ivy. Their branches make a tough armor for the upper backbone and a fairly thin skull. The plants take out carbon dioxide, water, and other by-products of animal metabolism for their own use. They give back oxygen directly, plus a whole string of vitamin-like materials we've barely started to identify. True, the plants don't furnish a complete respiratory-eliminative system. They supplement lungs, double heart, intestines, every organ—all of these with their special symbionts—but the upshot is an individual who functions better than we do. He can live on a far wider variety of food. He's less extravagant of water, through sweat or wastes or simply breathing. Thanks to Anu, water is in short supply over large areas of Ishtar. And, ah, our native also carries a built-in emergency food supply, those same plants. He can eat them and still survive, however handicapped by the lack. They'll soon grow back from their roots or from spores in air and soil, same as they do on the newly born."

Jill paused for air. "Whew!"

"I can see the advantages," Dejerine said slowly.

"Did you know this already?"

"I have read, yes. However, I'm glad to hear it repeated in a larger context."

"I'm coming to one, I hope." Caught in an excitement which for her never faded, Jill said: "Those advantages go beyond the obvious. Look, symbiosis like this isn't merely helpful directly. It frees genes." Observing his puzzlement: "Well, think. Genes, which Ishtarian life also has, genes store information. Their storage capacity is bodacious, but it isn't infinite. Imagine a set of 'em which governs some metabolic function. Now imagine that function being taken over by your friendly neighborhood symbiont. The genes aren't needed for it any more. They can go into new lines of work. Mutation and selection see to it that they do. The mutation rate's probably higher among Ishtarian theroids than Terrestrial mammals anyway, because body temperature is. The problem on Ishtar is much oftener keeping cool than keeping warm; and the theroids solve it partly through their plants—assorted endothermic chemistry more than transportation—and partly by being naturally warm themselves. . . . I'm digressing all over the place, hm? Well, nature does. The point I'm trying to make is that the Ishtarians have advantages over us, including a longer evolutionary history as homeothermic animals. They may not have reached their present level of intelligence as early as humans—though Lord knows when that was—but they phased into it more gradually. This is one reason those goblins are still around. And the history shows. It shows."

Dejerine frowned. "In their brains, do you mean?" he asked.

Jill nodded. The ends of her hair tickled the bare angles between neck and shoulders. "Nervous systems as a whole," she said. "Man is rather hastily built, you realize. Jerry-built, even. It's been said we have three brains, one cobbled on top of the next. The stem first, the reptilian brain; then the mammalian cerebellum; finally the overdeveloped cerebral cortex. They don't work together in awfully good harmony—hence ax murders, mobs, and socialism. The Ishtarian has more unity in his head. You can see it if you do a dissection. Insanity seems to be unknown—literally doesn't exist,

78

unless you count amentia due to massive physical damage. Not to disease. Ishtarians have precious little disease, with all those specialized helpers living in them. As for neurosis—" Jill shrugged. "That's a matter of definition, isn't it? I'll just say I've never known an Ishtarian whom *I* would call a twitch. And I might point out that alien and powerful as we happen to be, we humans have never produced any culture shock here. They respect us, they accept from us what things and ideas they find useful, but it all integrates easily with their old ways."

Hoarse and a trifle dizzy from rapid-fire talking, she leaned back against the trunk which supported Dejerine, sipped coffee grown cold in the cup, a bite from her piece of bread and jam. She'd made the preserve at home, half strawberry, half native newton fig, and been pleased when the Earthling wanted seconds.

"M-m-m," he mused, "no doubt the general life-physiological superiority accounts for the long Ishtarian life-span. Three to five hundred years, correct?"

Jill nodded. "I think, though, another factor's been at work as well," she said. "On Earth, fairly short generations mean fast genetic turnover, fast evolution. That should be an advantage for the species. I'm inclined to agree with the theory that we're programmed to start seriously aging as early as about forty, for this exact reason. But Ishtar suffers these Anu passages every thousand years. The effects are powerful for only a century or so. Longevity probably helps conserve adaptations to the cycle, and thereby helps species survival."

He gave her a considering look. "What a bleak philosophy."

"Oh? Doesn't bother me." Jill thought for a moment. *Okay, let's be frank with him. We need his ... empathy ... more than his intellectual understanding.* "Well, no use denying, everybody'd like to have that number of healthy years," she said. "But since we can't, no use crying, either. The Ishtarians get their share of woe. Every second lifetime, Ragnarok. And they don't whine."

He was silent awhile, in the blowing morning warmth, before he murmured, with his eyes aimed away from her, across the curve of the planet: "It must

79

have curious effects on you in Primavera. The same unchanged centaur who was your grandfather's friend is yours, and will be your children's—but before you were grown, he was your teacher for many things, was he not, your protector, conceivably your idol? Forgive me; I do not wish to be impertinent; but I am interested to know if my guess is right, that for some of your lifelong residents, some autochthons are father figures."

By Darwin, he is a surprising bastard!

His gaze back upon her, he must have seen he had touched a nerve. Why deny what he could learn by leading any gossipy townsperson into talk? "Yes, I s'pose," Jill said. "Maybe I'm an example. Larreka, the commandant of the Zera Victrix . . . we've always been close. I daresay I absorbed a lot of attitudes from him." Impulsively: "He saw me through a bad experience in a way nobody else in the universe could've."

"Oh." Dejerine paused. "Do you wish to discuss it?"

Jill shook her head. *Why should I trust him this much, this fast? He's the enemy, isn't he?* "No, I'd rather not; for now, anyway."

"Of course," he said gently.

She remembered—

Big land animals are rare on Ishtar. Each thousand years, food becomes too scarce in most regions. Central and southern Beronnen can support a few, like the tree lion and the almost elephantine valwas. But in its farther north, the continent turns into a reach of dry savannahs known as the Dalag. There lesser game abounds, in between Anu passages: at least fifty kinds of azar, for instance, serveral quite large. The beasts which kill them for food are dog-size or less, running in packs, though with massive jaws capable of frantically fast devouring; and no scavengers are visible to the naked eye other than certain swift small invertebrates. The sophont population is thin, mostly herders who do not do much hunting. Yet here and there cyclopean ruins rise out of the burnt-yellow sea of lia; and it is thought that civilization was invented in this country.

The thing which binds together these paradoxes is the sarcophage.

For her eleventh birthday, which on Earth would have been a few months short of her twelfth, Jill got leave to join Larreka's party on a trip to the Dalag. Aside from sport, the commandant planned to look over sites of possible strong points against barbarian incursions when the red sun came. An adult human went along too, Ellen Evaldsen, Jill's well-beloved young aunt, a planetologist who wanted to study rock formations besides adventuring around inside new horizons.

They marched merrily overland. Often the girl rode on Larreka or a friend of his. Ellen said they spoiled her rotten, but didn't interfere. And in camps firelit, starlit, moons-lit, ominously Anu-lit, the woman traded stories from Earth for native tales until Jill could not decide which were more wonderful. Then they reached the Dalag, and it was grander than anything that could be said.

Whispering, billowing golden reaches, broken only by darker shrubs and single flamelike trees; mysterious shadowy coolness of a water hole beneath a mineral-painted bluff; hard blue glare overhead and unmerciful heat, before night brought chill and a diamond swarm of stars; encounters with herder folk, a few words and a cup of herb tea under a felt canopy, the noble sight of a wo bounding skillfully to round up its master's els and owas; then onward to seek an immensity of wild grazers, whose hoofbeats boomed from the bottom of the world— Oh, yes, cruel sights as well, less her comrades chasing down an animal and cleanly killing it with bow or spear, than a pack of tartars driving an azar into a stand of the bush called claw, then ripping flesh from it while it hung there hooked and screaming—

"But they've got to," Larreka told Jill. "We can save meat by quick-like soaking it in gut juice. Animals can't. Or, those that make gut juice inside themselves, they can, by eating fast. Tartars aren't able to. If they couldn't eat most of a prey alive, they'd have to kill eight times as many to get a square meal. And . . . if there were no beasts of prey, the rest 'ud chew the range bare and starve."

"But why do things have to be awful right here?"

81

she protested. "Meat doesn't rot away this fast anywhere else, does it?"

Larreka appealed to Ellen, who repeated in different words what Jill had been warned of beforehand. The airborne mold named arcophage by humans is harmless to living tissue. But it settles instantly on dead flesh, multiplies explosively, and in two or three hours reduces the hugest animal to bones. It seems to require a particular climate, for it exists only in the Dalag and the nearer Fiery Sea islands. Or is climate what limits it? And what strange adaptations to it has evolution brought forth? "It's not a horror, Jill, dear, it's a mystery for us to solve."

"I've heard as how it caused the first civilizations," Larreka added.

Jill gave him a wide-eyed look through the furious sunlight.

"Well, a notion," Larreka said. "An old mudfoot like me can't judge. However, some of our philosophers and your scientists think it might've happened like this. When people first tried living in these parts, they had to be vegetarians; couldn't keep any meat to speak of. But then they found, certain beasts of prey make juices in their guts that kill the, uh, sarcophage. 'Course, all those people knew was, the juice'd make the meat last. They needed apparatus, like kettles for boiling down the animal guts and bowls for soaking slaughtered critters in. Those had to be herd critters; treatment isn't very practical for hunters. You've seen that, watching us. The apparatus is pretty heavy, being made out of stone or pottery. So those early people settled down in sod huts—which helped 'em stay cool, anyway—and kept flocks, and started raising feed. . . . Later on, these ideas about houses and ranches moved south, where life is easier, and South Beronnen's been the heartland of civilization ever since. But here's where it began, maybe."

"Including a great many myths, religions, rituals, concepts of life and death alike, from Valennen to Haelen," added Ellen Evaldsen. "The transience of the flesh may be as basic, as widespread on Ishtar, as the dying god is on Earth."

"Huh?" grunted Larreka. "Well, if you say so, lady."

And thus wonder had kindled in Jill too. She had already known that ruin visited the world, again and again and again. As far back as she could remember, Larreka had been matter-of-factly preparing for the next time, and humans planned ways to make it less dreadful than before. She was quick to accept the Dalag for what it was.

Until the day when Ellen died.

It happened brutally fast. The woman had climbed a high black rock thrust out of the savannah which, she laughed, had no business being here. It appeared safe. But it held an invisible weakness (from the heat and storms of a million years of Anu passage?). In the camp beneath, they saw the stone break, they saw her fall.

She lay with her head at a grisly angle. By the time Larreka reached her, dissolution had begun. Flesh bloated, stank, shone iridescent blue-green, collapsed into foul liquid, and puffed away. The Ishtarians couldn't dig a grave speedily with their limited tools. What they buried was white bones and hair which remained Anu-red.

Larreka sought Jill. He gathered her curled-together body in his arms and trotted off, beyond sight of the camp. Bel set in fire, the stars bloomed forth, Ea burned like a candle. He settled down in sweet-smelling mildness of air and lia, drew her close against his breast, and stroked her for a long time.

"I'm sorry, sweetheart," he said. "I didn't think. We shouldn't've let you see."

Jill wept.

"But you belong to the legion," he said. "Don't you, soldier?" He laid fingers below her chin and raised her face toward his and the stars.

She nodded violently, for there was nothing else.

"Then listen," Larreka said, almost too low to hear. "You may have heard, when we four-leggers lose a person we care about, it hits us harder than it does you humans. If you've known somebody for a few hundred years . . . Well, we've had to learn how to take it. Let me tell you what we do in the legions."

And first he told her of banners, rewoven century after century, which bear the names of the fallen; and then he told her of much else; and when dawn broke, she danced the dance of farewell with them, as best she could, at the grave: the earliest step away from grief.

Jill rose. "Come on," she said. "Let's get packed and be on our way. I want to show you a typical ranch, but if we stall too long, the most intersting members will be off to hell and gone on the range."

"I hearken and obey," Dejerine responded. While they stowed their material, he added seriously: "Miss Conway, you are kind to show me around like this. I am grateful. However, is your main hope not to enlist my feelings on behalf of the natives?"

"Sure. What else?"

"Well ... will you give my side a similar attention? I know you see us as destructive intruders. Will you believe that we may have reasons—over and above our orders—for being here?"

She let him stand a second before she said, "I'll listen to you, yes."

"Good." He smiled. "As a matter of fact, I would like to start by collecting an audience, everybody in Primavera if possible, and showing a tape I have along. It is not official propaganda—it's rather critical—but that's important too." He paused. "You see, I wish for you to believe that I am not a fanatic."

Jill snapped laughter. "I've got to watch your show to prove I'm not?" His mobile features registered hurt, and she felt more contrite than was entirely reasonable. "No offense," she said. "We'll be glad to watch."

VIII

Excerpts from 3V; simultaneous English.

OLAYA

GOOD EVENING. THIS is Luis Enrique Olaya Gonzales, welcoming you again to "Universe of Discourse." Our program tonight is special in both length and, we trust, importance.

Exactly six months ago, the Parliament of the World Federation passed a measure requiring the Peace Control Authority to take "appropriate forceful counteraction" against "agencies, vessels, installations, personnel, and instrumentalities" of the Naqsan League in order to "terminate the emergency and ensure a just settlement of matters in dispute." In plain language, Earth declared war on Naqsa. Officialdom carefully avoids any such phrase—and has better reasons than hypocrisy; some words bring on irrevocable commitments with unforeseeable consequences. Nevertheless, that resolution of Parliament turned a series of accidental clashes into systematic military operations. The powers no longer confine themselves to protest, propaganda, pressures political and economic, increasingly desperate diplomacy; the decision is now to be made through force. War it is, war the people call it, and likewise will we tonight.

We are going to examine this war, its background causes, its past and present and possible future course, its tangled issues. We shall try to be fair. . . .

* * *

View of a planet in space, terrestroid though heavily clouded. Pan in.)

About a hundred and fifty light-years from Sol, a globe where men can live unaided spins close around its dull orange sun. They cannot live there very well—or could not. For them, most of it is hot, wet, tormented by violent weather, vast wildernesses of rain forest, swamp, eroded mountains. The native life can nourish a man for a short while at best; and much is deadly poisonous. . . .

It is a planet better suited to Naqsans. Early in the course of their spaceflight, they founded a few settlements upon it, which grew and had offspring. They called the world Tsheyakka [a set of hawks and gargles, dubbed from a recording]. Humans bestowed the name Mundomar, after they got interested.

For they *could* survive here, if they were prepared to make herculean efforts. Less torrid and humid than elsewhere, the arctic zone was not altogether unsuitable. Water-loving Naqsans had shunned those parts. They saw no reason not to admit colonists from Earth, for a substantial price on the real estate.

[View penetrates clouds, sweeps across jungles, boggy plains, rank growth afloat in oceans. At times it closes up on a particular spot, e.g., one of the modest Naqsan communities. There great seal-like bodies slop and wallow about in the manner natural for them, which many humans find disgusting. The view proceeds northward, finally settling on a brushy plateau. A Terrestrial spaceship lands, a model six decades outmoded: for this is a section from the archives, proud capture of a historic moment.]

Who would come? True, Earth is overloaded with man. True, planets where he can live are rare, and most of those have autochthons. True, what unclaimed globes he had found and settled were, even then, ultracautious about what further immigrants they accepted. But who would be so desperate as to seek out Mundomar . . . or so hopeful?

Those who had no other choice except endless despair.

A long human lifetime has passed since the prophetic voice of Charles Barton—

(Sequence of views; dialogue and BG commentary summarized.

(Drab, sleazy, crowded, the Welfare districts of typical megalopolitan regions, where they huddle for whom technological civilization can find no use. Idleness; boredom; frustration; sense of personal worthlessness; drugs in bottles, in pills, in shots, in sprays; 3V screens for everybody, joyhouses or brain stimulators for those who can scrabble together the money; gang fights among the young, criminal empires among the adult, and the honest majority walking in dread— but the police are the enemy, aren't they? Citizen's allowance, social workers, educational channels, sorry, you don't qualify, sorry, you do qualify but we have no opening; yet sometimes at night an opening appears, on the roof of a housing unit tall enough to block off part of the city glare and let a few stars shine through.

(The Backworld, whose folk can stay alive after a fashion if they get steady outside help, but no more than alive. Technology is not magic; it cannot operate on resources which no longer exist. Peasants in Dry Africa seek shelter beneath an elevated aqueduct insufficient to keep their farms from blowing away, red upon the wind. At night the streets of Indian cities are paved with sleeping people. A pelagic community off the Greenland coast supports itself by sending boys out to nearly exhausted fisheries at the age of twelve. Nobody starves in the Backworld, as nobody does in Welfare. But aid is a mere stopgap, and still taxpayers feel drained.

(All the old panaceas have failed. Education? You can't educate a person—a person of perfectly normal intelligence—into special abilities he wasn't born with; and the demand for routineers is low and falling. Birth control? You can't ask entire peoples to make themselves extinct. Redistribution of wealth? The conservation laws hold as true in economics as in physics. Return to a simple and natural existence? A precondition is the death of 90 per cent of the human race.

(But the stars remain. And given an ideal, the capital

necessary to make a new beginning will somehow come forth. If a man has no other capital, there are his two hands.)

* * *

(Archive sequences of the pioneers on Mundomar, toil, pain, grief, but always that hope which refuses to surrender, that vision which makes sullen Welfare loafers and worn-out Backworld beasts of burden into men and women. Their children grow up afraid of nothing in this cosmos.

(Their children, their children, their children. And as the colony waxes, as it puts seedlings across the whole north of the planet, material wealth burgeons; and likewise do the contributions from Earth, for clearly this mad dream is going to work; and immigrants pour down out of the skies.

(Upon tamed lands, the cities rise clangorous. Nature is harnessed and transformed.)

OLAYA

Friction with the Naqsans began when human enterprises crossed ill-defined borders. Disputes were usually settled by negotiation. But the social structure of the Naqsan colonies was such that individuals among them bore any losses, uncompensated. It also permitted aggrieved parties to combine privately and seek satisfaction. This is quite legal and proper in that culture, that species. However, humans have different, incompatible institutions—or, may I say, instincts? They retaliated against what to them was banditry. . . .

Tension heightened. . . . Incidents multiplied. . . . The Governor General appealed for Peace Authority help. . . . The Naqsan League made clear that it would not abandon its habitants on Tsheyakka. . . .

Meanwhile industrial, ecological, and climatological projects in the human sectors increasingly affected the environment further south, adversely from a Naqsan viewpoint. The nonhuman dwellers moved slowly toward a decision to act in unison. . . .

The nonaggression pact between the two mother

planets satisfied nobody on the colonial world. Both groups felt endangered. Both had widespread popular support at home; but Earth especially was at that time in a pacifistic mood. . . .

Fighting erupted, and soon spread far and wide over Mundomar. The humans showed totally unexpected strength. In numbers they were inferior, in equipment equal to their enemies; in leadership, discipline, élan, devotion, they were incomparably more powerful.

(Scenes of combat. It is limited to the planet, and to chemical weapons plus occasional tactical nukes.

(A flag rises above Government House in Barton; and from a balcony thereon a man in battle dress reads aloud a document to a cheering throng and to the universe.]

PROVISIONAL PRESIDENT SIGURDSSON

—These events have made it tragically sure that we can look to none but ourselves for our rights, our security, our very survival. . . .

We therefore solemnly found and proclaim the sovereign Republic of Eleutheria. . . .

* * *

OLAYA

—Promptly after the cease-fire, Earth recognized the new state, but did not invite it to join the Federation. That may have been from fear of a rebuff by the colonists, who felt forsaken in their hour of need. Or it may have been the result of a secret negotiations with Naqsa. The League diplomats may well have said that a *fait accompli* could be accepted, if not given legal sanction. After all, Naqsa never had claimed the entirety of Mundomar: an oversight, though an easy one for Naqsans to make. What they could not tolerate would be the direct presence of Terrestrial authority in a region they considered stolen.

We do not know if this was the bargain. The record has never been shown us. We only know that the northern fourth of Mundomar was now the independent Republic of Eleutheria, eager for more immigration and more investment from Earth; that Earth recognized it as a legitimate country but Naqsa did not; that the Naqsans in the tropics of that planet felt more embittered and menaced than ever before.

Soon afterward, Earth's attention was diverted by a fresh crisis elsewhere. The Final Society of Alerion occupied the colony world New Europe. This appeared to be a far more determined and formidable opponent than Naqsa. Sentiment in favor of compromise or thinly disguised surrender ran high in the Federation, leading to a series of domestic conflicts with those who advocated firmness. In the end, as we all know, the resistance party prevailed. A short, sharp space war made Alerion yield every important point at issue.

Since then, Earth's temper has changed. The fact that during the war New Europe followed Eleutheria's example and broke away, doesn't seem to have affected the confidence in human destiny which most people today assert. We disavow imperialism, we admit its absurdity on an interstellar scale—but every poll taken for the past generation has found a majority saying that our species must never again allow itself to be domineered by an alien.

Our *species?* Or our Federation? There is a difference.

* * *

(Scenes: The vigorous growth of Eleutheria, in population, industry, and territory; the ill effects on the Naqsan communities and their hinterlands; the next confrontation exploding into the next undeclared war, when the humans overrun the continent of G'yaaru, expel nonhumans, and fortify it.)

—Our children shall not live in fear. The land mass of Sigurdssonia is vital to our security, therefore to the preservation of peace throughout this globe. We will settle it with our citizens. . . .

(Joy tumultuous in Shanghai Welfare. Gigantic on a wallscreen, the image of a politician pledges solidarity with the gallant Eleutherians. He is himself wealthy, but he needs these votes.)

* * *

OLAYA

—replay my interview of last year with Admiral Alessandro Vitelli, Chief of Staff of the Peace Control Authority. . . .

VITELLI

—no doubt about it. None whatsoever. The Naqsan League is behind these latest moves. And I don't mean they're supplying arms and training to the Tsheyakkans. That's no secret, same as we're frankly assisting the Eleutherians. No, I mean that behind the scenes the League is encouraging revanchism. You wouldn't get the sort of talk you hear on Mundomar otherwise. Naqsans don't go in for reckless demagoguery the way many humans do. They tend to keep quiet until they're ready to state facts and take action. Let's not hide behind wishfulness. The Tsheyakkans—through them, all the Naqsans—want more than to regain Sigurdssonia. They want to drive humans completely off that planet.

Do you think Earth should allow this to happen, Admiral?

VITELLI

Please. My service doesn't make or advocate policy, it executes the will of Parliament. . . . Speaking as an individual, I do feel a human presence in that part of space is essential to the balance of power. . . .

* * *

OLAYA

—speech by His Excellency Tollog-a-Ektrush, Ambassador General of the League of Naqsa to the World Federation, just before he was recalled. . . .
[A blubbery-looking mass, bilious yellow spotted green and wetly shining in its nudity, short fluke-footed legs, membranes up to the knobbly elbows, head suggestive of a catfish, fills the screen. The hologram does not convey the odor, but audio brings the mushy voice, irritatingly hard for human ears to follow, into millions of rooms.]

TOLLOG

—historic w'riendshiw wetween ouw two weowles. True, we hawe owwen ween commercial riwals, wut is that not healt'hy, not stimulating? Ewerywody gains wy trade: more inwortantly, wy the inswiration uw ideas, arts, wilosowwies, t'houghts, dreams. I wish wery much to make you know, humans, how we uw Naqsa admire you, how gratewul we are wor all we hawe learned w'rom you and the many owwortunities your enter'rises hawe created wor ewery sentient race, how we wish wor a w'rotherhood uw the swirit. And yet, hawe you not learned somet'hing w'rom us, hawe we not made you some return? What can either weowle gain w'rom war, and what can they not lose?

Yes, we do suwwort our kin on Tsheyakka against naked conquest. I cannot weliewe that Eart'h, Eart'h that we lowe, will really condone, let alone assist, the deswoliation and wereawement uw harmless weings in their homes. . . .

Eart'h has an owligation to those it has imwower-ished? Eart'h is morally wound to see they win to a decent liwe and a land uw their own where they can grow as they will? No doubt. No doubt. They hawe ween long denied. Wut why at our exwense? It was newwer *us* who denied them! . . .

* * *

OLAYA

The third outbreak of large-scale hostilities on Mundomar precipitated a crisis which did not seem to be resolvable. After their initial success, the Eleutherians could make little further progress, and the Tsheyakkans showed no disposition to accept defeat once more. Peacemaking commissions from outside were in effect ignored, not very politely, by both factions. The fear became great that one or the other would acquire major weapons, or might already have them, and would introduce them into the stalemated struggle which was bleeding everyone empty. . . .

* * *

(Scenes: Parades, demonstrations, chanting crowds around all Earth, crying for the rescue of Eleutheria.

(Terrestrial and Naqsan naval units ordered to that

sector. Reports of lethal incidents. Views of broken ships, dead crews, hospitalized live casualties in their agony: many of them prisoners, treated as well as alien physicians are able while they await exchange.

(Summary of diplomatic efforts that failed.

(The Parliamentary session that commits Earth to the survival of Eleutheria.

(More incidents. The ambassador of the League delivers his crucial note.

(The Parliamentary session that tells the Navy to fight.)

* * *

CHAIRMAN AL-GHAZI

—No, of course we don't plan an attack on Naqsa itself, unless Earth is attacked, which I hardly expect. That *would* be an act of war. Worse, it would be morally monstrous and, may I add, militarily idiotic, in view of planetary defense capabilities. No, to the extent that we remain in control of events, this will be an operation on Mundomar and in space, for the sole purpose of inducing our opponents to agree to a fair peace. . . .

* * *

OLAYA

The vote was by no means unanimous. Spokesmen for several countries argued against our involvement, and continue to argue for our withdrawal. A minority of private individuals and organizations urges the same.

(Rain in an almost empty street. A few sad pickets before an Admiralty office. Their signs carry slogans like BRING BACK BROTHERHOOD and HAVE

NAQSANS NO RIGHTS? Occasional passersby in vehicles pause to heckle.)

* * *

OLAYA

—special guest, Gunnar Heim, former Minister of Space and Naval Affairs for New Europe. Three decades ago on Earth, as everyone will remember, Captain Heim took a lonely lead in calling for resistance to Aleriona aggression, and eventually intiated action on behalf of France which caused the entire Federation to move. Later he was in the forefront of declaring and consolidating the status of New Europe as a sovereign planet, and was a major figure in its government for years before he returned to private life, though never to obscurity. Here on a visit, Captain Heim has graciously consented to appear . . .

[The man, white-haired but still erect and bulky, wearing an old service tunic open at the neck, sprawls in an armchair opposite the moderator and leisurely puffs his pipe.]

OLAYA

—you don't think the present situation is like the one you had to meet?

HEIM

Absolutely not. Alerion wanted mankind—and the Naqsans, for that matter, every other starfaring race, but we were the most prominent and therefore first on the list—Alerion wanted us out of space. In fact, I believe Alerion wanted us dead.

95

Why?

HEIM

Call it ideology. We don't seem to be the only species cursed with that. The point is, Alerion's objections were unlimited, therefore Alerion was a mortal threat. We had to apply force to bring its rulers to their senses.

OLAYA

And you don't feel this is true of Naqsa?

HEIM

I know it isn't. When have those beings ever menaced Earth in any way? Unless you count sharp commercial competition, which certain Terrestrial interests would like to see removed.

OLAYA

Well, passing over the space flights, which I suppose could be ascribed to tension—passing over those, there was the business of Earth's mission to the Naqsan part of Mundomar getting bombed, two years back. Zealots, perhaps—

HEIM

Hell, no. Naqsans don't produce zealots.

Then covert official action, it was alleged.

HEIM

Sr. Olaya, that bombing was carried out by Eleutherian agents to provoke fury on Earth. Which it did.
The immediate result was that the Federation broke off
discussions with the League on a joint expedition to
the galactic core; but no doubt the effect on the next
Terrestrial by-elections was more significant.

OLAYA

Pardon me. Can you prove that statement?

HEIM

I have it from friends in New European Intelligence.
Naturally, your government isn't about to tell you.

OLAYA

Let's return to the main subject. Do you feel we
should abandon the Eleutherians to their fate?

HEIM

I'm surprised to hear a loaded question like that
from you.

It isn't really mine. I was quoting innumerable speeches and editorials.

HEIM (after the briefest of smiles)

Well, please bear in mind, I speak as a private citizen of a foreign state. Thank whatever God there be, my government has had the wit to stay strictly neutral! Though I'd like to remind you, New Europe has offered to both sides its good offices—

OLAYA

Understood, Captain. I simply wondered what your personal opinion is. In view of the analogies between what you did and what Eleutheria is doing.

HEIM

I deny they are analogies. I told you before, Alerion threatened our existence and Naqsa does not. New Europe declared independence but has never grabbed off anybody else's property.

OLAYA

Just the same—

HEIM

Okay, if you can stand listening to an old rule-of-thumb engineer who's probably long since obsolete. Let me re-emphasize, this is me speaking and nobody else.

First, yes, I admire the Eleutherians tremendously. What they've done is incredible. It's more than reclaiming land, it's reclaiming their own souls.

But second, the Naqsans on Tsheyakka—Mundomar—they've had their quieter heroisms. Haven't they? And they are sentient creatures too. And they were there first, for whatever that counts.

I don't think they can drive the Eleutherians off the planet. I don't think the League actually wants them to. The original idea was sound. That globe has plenty of different environments. Two species can perfectly well colonize separate parts of it. Their peaceful interaction could benefit all concerned. Cultural hybrid vigor, you know.

Details can be bargained out. You may recall Talleyrand's formula, "an equality of dissatisfaction." The trouble is, the Eleutherians won't settle for it. For instance, by now they and various unpublicized Terrestrial backers of theirs have such investments in G'yaaru—Sigurdssonia, if you prefer—it'd be pretty damn inconvenient for them to disgorge. So they talk about it being vital to their security. Crap. Even though most of them sincerely believe this, crap. The only security between peoples is a common interest.

OLAYA

Then you blame the whole conflict on Eleutheria?

HEIM

Lord, no. Naqsans in their style are every bit as unreasonable as humans.

But, mainly, here is a dispute which could be worked out in some left-handed fashion, the way "Fifty-four Forty or Fight" once was, except that the great powers have let themselves get sucked in and—

Well, you tell me, Sr. Olaya. Why the hell is the

Peace Authority, directed by the Parliament of the World Federation—what possible gain for the ordinary Earthman—why the hell are you underwriting Eleutherian imperialism? If the Eleutherians must conquer more territory, let them do it at their own risk.

* * *

(Embarkation of human marines on a transport shuttle. A band plays and amplified voices are singing.)

Glory, glory, hallelujah,
Glory, glory, hallelujah,
Glory, glory, hallelujah,
His day is marching on!

IX

SPARLING DROVE TO Sehala in a groundcar. A flyer would have been too fast—he wanted a while to think—and a horse was no use on a world where only a few square kilometers grew plants which could properly feed it. The els was an occasional beast of burden or draught animal, though not very satisfactory, a sophont being bigger and stronger; but it reacted explosively to being ridden. The great valwas, sometimes domesticated, was never kept in times when fodder became scarce.

Usually Ishtarians were their own bearers. Traffic went brisk on the river highway, huge-muscled specialist porters, fleet specialist couriers, ranchers self-harnessed to wagons, load-free travelers. These were of many more races and nations than the one which dwelt in South Beronnen from dour Haeleners to wandering semi-savages off the Ehur Islands near Valennen. Most went essentially unclothed, but the variety of plumes, jewelry, cloaks, blankets, harness, every sort of ornament and utility article, was bewildering. Boats, barges, oared galleys plied the water. The Gathering

100

was in trouble, its hold had slipped on territory after territory, but its heartland was still a magnet for trade.

Yet Sparling saw a number of legionary patrols. For a long period, whatever legion had been rotated to Sehala—currently the Tamburu Strider—had not had much to do. Its functions had been civil, police and rescue work, arbitration of minor disputes, the public services it traditionally sponsored such as maintaining certain records or lighthouses. And the obvious duties of a police officer were few in a culture which, created in the first place by a species seldom violent, defined only a single criminal act: failure to obey the judgment of the jury that tried a lawsuit. Nor were firemen often needed, most construction being stone or adobe.

Now the Tamburu seemed as busy as when last it was stationed on a march where brigandage or outright war on civilization was rife. Sparling knew why. More and more people were moving here from northerly parts, in the hope of getting established before the change of weather devastated their homes. With no true government, Beronnen lacked means to bar them. But, itself beginning to feel the scorch and the storms, it also lacked means to provide for them. A lucky few might find steady work, even start new enterprises or marry into landholding families. The rest—

These passerby were not the wholly cheerful, energetic beings whom Sparling had watched in years agone. Many, especially among the outlanders, looked shabby, hungry . . . desperate.

And yet the countryside still lay peaceful, rich, golden beneath blue heaven and towering clouds. He glimpsed large herds and clustered buildings on the ranches which were the foundation of this economy, this society. Further south, the cultivated region around Sehala had been harvested; orchards, stubblefields, reseeded plowlands did not show how scanty that harvest had been when Anu smoldered in the north.

He parked at an inn on the outskirts which had accommodations for humans. "If you don't mind, guest-friend, I'd prefer coin to your paper," the landlord told him. "We've been getting enough clever counterfeits

101

lately that I could have trouble buying anything with a bill. See, here's a sample."

To Sparling the imitation of Terrestrial money seemed crude. But the real thing had never been common outside Primavera. Besides, Ishtarians were frequently insensitive to nuances plain to an Earthling—and vice versa, of course.

"All that foreign riffraff," the landlord grumbled. "Swindling, stealing, robbing; and if you catch them, what's the use? Waste of time taking them to court. They don't own aught to make restitution with. Their labor would be worthless. Excommunication wouldn't hurt them, when no decent person wants their company in the first place. Beating's not likely to teach a lesson, and juries don't kill people who haven't been in contempt at least thrice. Yon homeless rascals need only disappear."

He had listed the sanctions available. Imprisonment, except temporarily for detention, struck his folk as senseless spite, when humans described it; and Sparling thought no Ishtarian would ever grasp the idea of rehabilitation, being too appalled at what seemed a kind of psychic gelding. Maybe the Ishtarians were right.

He felt in his pocket and produced native coins, gold, silver, and bronze, ample for a short stay. The landlord didn't bother to examine those. He could see at a glance they were the genuine article sold by reputable manufacturers. Nobody made a mint off his mint, but demand for new specie was always sufficient to support a few. Or, rather, there had been such a demand while the economy of the Gathering was expanding.

"I'll go into town and look about," the man remarked. "Quite a spell since I was here last." The reason was his work, which among other things required him to seek out native leaders for conference. Virtually none stayed in Sehala, except when an assembly met. This was not a capital city; in many human senses, it was not a city at all. It was merely the largest, most prosperous of the areas where certain activities and institutions concentrated, therefore usually the most convenient rendezvous. Sparling maintained that the South

Beronnen phrase for those territories where civilization was represented in force had been mistranslated and should go into English as "the Gathering *at* Sehala."

Both suns were still aloft, but an overcast had removed glare and a wind with a hint of rain to come blew cool off the river. He didn't mind that, in the absence of streets, he must now walk a few kilometers. Indeed, he wanted to see for himself how matters stood these days. Humans who came here oftener were apt to be blind to many things beyond their special concerns. That was understandable. The concerns required close attention: for instance, working with scholars to understand an old chronicle, or talking with skippers to find out what they could tell of widely strewn countries. However—

The inn stood near the docks. It was typical of buildings where a fair number of people might stay, rising square and sheer around a central court which included a garden and a pond. The first four stories were mortared stone; the remaining eight, adobe with perdurable phoenix half-timbering, a surface varied enough to be pleasing despite the severe outline. That variation was increased by a cookhouse and storage shed; by covered ramps going up from the court; by balconies jutting forth on the outside from every room.

Good architecture, Sparling thought. The heavy walls gave insulation as well as strength. The patio was always cool and the central well gave, through the main gate, a stack effect which louvers on inside windows used to help keep rooms comfortable on a hot day. Balconies, and the battlemented flat roof, gave residents the sunshine their symbiotic plants required, while not exposing them to danger. For the building was more than a thousand years old; it had withstood attack in the last disaster time, and might have to do so again.

Its front entrance looked down a slope to the broad brown river, docks and warehouses, workers, ships which had not unloaded at Liwas on the delta but continued here, lesser craft of the inland waterways. Noise, shouts, thuds, creak of wheels and derrick cables, boom of barrels rolled over gangways, drifted to Sparling. The scene was small and leisured when he recalled, say, Havana. But here was the center of a civilization, the best hope of a race he believed might someday mean more to the galaxy than his. If the red curse could be lifted . . .

He started walking south. At first he was on a trail among fields. Unlike any case he knew of on Earth, towns in Beronnen fed themselves off agricultural hinterlands, actually traded their produce for meat and much else from the ranches. The latter held economic and social primacy. Several in these parts, between them, effectively owned Sehala.

Through Sparling's mind passed a theory he had once heard Goddard Hanshaw advance. In younger days, the mayor had been a cultural xenologist. "I think we've got a twofold reason why the rural sectors lord it over the urban. And no, I don't mean the fact that most of the chieftains who make up an assembly of the Gathering are from cityless places. The Gathering is a historical newcomer. I mean the development of the mother civilization itself.

"First, pastoralism seems to be more efficient on Ishtar than on Earth. Post-mammalian livestock gets more out of a hectare than cows or pigs can. And agriculture is less efficient. If nothing else, herders survive an Anu passage better than farmers; but also, those storms and floods and droughts every millennium have spoiled a lot of land for crops. Then too, I think probably herding is more congenial to the average Ishtarian temperament. (Though that's a plain guess of mine—and maybe at heart most humans would rather be cowboys than nesters.)

"But second is the matter of commute time. That's what made it possible for a fairly high culture to develop among scattered ranches.

"Look. Throughout Earth's history, the range of everyday activity has been limited by how long it takes to go between home and work. It's always been just about the same time, roughly an hour. That's true whether a Babylonian peasant was walking to his most distant field or a bureaucrat in Mexico City catches an airbus from his villa outside Guaymas. You can find exceptional individuals and exceptional circumstances, yes. But by and large, it doesn't *pay* us to spend more than about one twelfth of an Earth rotation going to and fro.

104

Whenever we had to do that as a regular thing, we'd soon move closer to the worksite, maybe founding a new settlement, or we'd get work closer to home. Even primitive hunters camped near where the game was. Even electronic communications haven't abolished the principle, merely changed its application to certain classes of society.

"Things are different on Ishtar. The Ishtarian afoot can travel faster than a man, including a man on a horse, and for much longer at a stretch without tiring. He can see quite well by night, so the shorter day is no inconvenience. He rarely needs shelter, and if need be he can live indefinitely off whatever herbage grows along his path. It's no particular bother to camp out on the job. In short, he's a better traveler than we are, with more speed and scope.

"Therefore ranchers could carry out many different kinds of operation over very wide areas. When they got to the point of wanting fixed marts, at spots where it was desirable to locate other sedentary industries, why, they went ahead and started 'em. The town, the city can send its farmers out far enough to keep itself fed and produce a surplus. Certain kinds of specialists live there. But mainly the population is floating, because for most Beronnen families the ranches are a better, actually a more interesting environment.

"It's a misnomer to speak of 'civilization' on this planet. Shucks, the word doesn't have fewer syllables than 'literate culture.' But I guess we're stuck with the habit."

Sparling continued. Presently he was in among buildings. There was no city wall, such as defended the communities like Port Rua (or lost Tarhanna) that doubled as military strongpoints. War had been absent from this territory for a very long while. Today it was still not considered worthwhile providing more defense than a legion. Should that be defeated, Sehalans would have a better chance in scattering to live off the countryside, than letting themselves be boxed in by an enemy who could do likewise and whose camp would not suffer providential epidemics. Most of the wealth was out on the ranches anyway.

In fact, there was no city plan. Builders chose their

sites at will. Regularly used routes between became trampled, rutted lanes, except where it had been convenient to pave a few sections. Mostly, structures stood well apart, amidst lia, bushes, trees. No type of dwellers or industries occupied any particular area. Many quarters were simple booths or tents, brought in by visitors who didn't care to pay for lodgings. Permanent buildings were large by ancient human standards—to accommodate a larger species—and, while a majority more or less resembled the inn, some were startlingly artistic, whether monumental or exquisite.

Sehala sprawled.

It did not stink, nor was it littered. Sanitation was less of a problem for Ishtarians, whose water-hoarding systems discharged no urine and comparatively little of a dry fecal matter, than had been the case for man. Nevertheless, whoever was in charge of an establishment disposed of wastes and rubbish, if only because otherwise his neighbors would have sued him for making their environs offensive. Odors were of smoke, vegetation, sharp male and sweet female scents.

Folk who saw Sparling saluted him courteously, whether they had met him before or not, but didn't stop to talk. Thrusting chitchat upon a person who might be in a hurry was considered bad manners. Fewer were in sight than usual.

He found out why as he was passing the Tower of the Books. "Ian!" bawled a voice. Larreka, commandant of Zera Victrix, overtook him. They clasped shoulders, and each read signs of trouble upon the other.

"What's wrong?" Sparling opened.

Larreka's tail lashed his ankles. Whiskers bristled above fangs. "Plenty," he growled, "both here and in Valennen, and I don't know which is worse. Word last night, a call from Port Rua. A regiment sent to regain Tarhanna, bushwhacked and wiped out. Wolua himself—you remember Wolua, my first officer?—he got killed. The barbarians' ransom demand for their prisoners isn't gold, it's weapons; and whoever drew up that list knows exactly what he needs to damage us the most."

Sparling whistled.

"So Owazzi called the assembly together again this morning," Larreka continued. "Soon I couldn't take any more speeches and walked out."

That's where the missing townspeople are, Sparling realized. *In the audience.* Assemblies came years apart; and then the group seldom collected. The usual practice was to try for a consensus before casting a formal vote. This was best done by leisured meetings of individuals in private. *Christ! Do I have to go there cold, right now? I'd counted on time to lay groundwork, break my news gently—*

He heard himself say: "Doubtless you told them this strengthens the case you came here to make, for sending reinforcements to Valennen. I take it many are opposed?"

"Right," Larreka answered. "A lot of them want outright evacuation. Give up the whole damn continent, just like that. Well, Ian, what are your ill tidings?"

Sparling told him. He stood silent for a space, save that the wind rustled his mane. The scar on his brow was livid.

Finally: "Let's hit them with that. Hard. Right away. We may shock a little sense into them."

"Or out of them," Sparling muttered. He saw no escape, though, and stalked along beside his comrade.

The assembly met in an auditorium whose marble colonnades always reminded him of the Parthenon. That was in spite of differences being endless, from circular plan to abstract mosaic frieze. Glazed windows above tiers packed with spectators let light down onto a floor where the members stood. At its middle was a dais for the Lawspeaker and whoever happened to be addressing the body.

It was as colorfully mixed a band as any he had seen on the highway. Every society which remained in the Gathering was represented; and Ishtarians were more wildly inventive than men where it came to social institutions. Tribes, clans, monarchies, aristocracies, theocracies, republics, communisms, anarchisms found approximate analogues in this chamber. But what was one to make of a people who alternated the franchise annually between males and females, or who controlled

107

the population of an oasis by staging periodic combats to the death between adolescents of both sexes who might well be close friends, or who changed spouses on a fixed schedule intended to get all possible couples together, or who settled contested public issues by a method of tossing bones which they *knew* gave random results, or— For that matter, had Earth ever seen the like of the Gathering itself?

The assembly was dwindled from its last meeting, a decade ago. Already then, discussion had turned on how much territory civilization might reasonably hope to hang onto, given human help whose exact form had yet to be determined. Since, the legions had pulled back from numerous important islands. Growing storminess, declining economy, pressure from barbarians on the move, had forced them—were forcing them. But to surrender Valennen entirely, at this stage, would be in a new order of magnitude.

As he entered with Larreka, Sparling saw the speaker was Jerassa. He knew him well: a local male, chosen by the masters of Sehala city because he was intelligent, articulate, and in his fashion sophisticated. He had spent a great deal of time in Primavera, made many human friends, and learned much of what they had to teach. In daily life he was among the scholars and chroniclers at the Tower of the Books whom the Afella Indomitable legion subsidized for its own honor. But there was nothing dusty about him; he was rather a dandy. Besides the selek entomoids which lived in his mane as part of the symbiosis, he cultivated rainbow-winged orekas. They made a flittering glory about his head as he talked.

"—in former cycles, I agree we would have been wise to keep a foothold in Valennen, perhaps actually increase our troops there if Commandant Larreka is right about a leader who has been uniting the wild folk for purposes that go beyond pillage. Yes, as long as we possibly could, we should have held the gates against a migration such as we believe helped bring down earlier high cultures.

"But our lifetimes are blessed. To our aid have come powerful allies. Formerly we hoped that, thanks to the legions and to provisions like well-guarded stocks of food, civilization might survive, might keep its continuity, in some countries. But then the humans arrived. We now have hope, yes, expectation that the Gathering will survive substantially unharmed and over a broad range.

"Granted, what the humans can do for us is limited. They have explained that they cannot get large support from their home world. Perhaps more important, they are few; and only they can operate certain devices, or plan the best use of these. Still, a single armed aircraft of theirs is mightier than a legion, let alone a barbarian horde.

"Therefore I submit that Valennen is not worth keeping. We can return at our convenience. Meanwhile, what have we lost? Luxury items like skipfoot leather; fisheries, which the Rover will make unprofitable anyway; and, to be sure, minerals and materials like phoenix, for which we have use. But we can get along without those if need be. Besides, after the Valenneners have broken themselves on the defense line which, with human help, we can hold—I predict they will become desperately anxious to trade with us.

"I submit that we have better work for our people to do, closer to home. The role of the legions in this latest chaos time is likely to be more civil than military, more engineering than fighting. Let us not merely refrain from asking any second legion to join the Zera Victrix in Port Rua; let us request the Zera itself to come back. We need it here, not there."

Jerassa had seen Sparling and Larreka, who did not go into the tiers but stayed at the entrance. He must have adapted his speech immediately, for he ended: "You have heard an abundance from me. Here is a spokesman for the humans. Is it your will that he address you next?"

"Aye," sang from the hundred on the floor, while a murmur went through the watchers above. Jerassa bounded off the dais. Owazzi the Lawspeaker said formally, "Welcome, Ian Sparling. Is it your wish to address us?"

Like hell, the man thought. *And a big reason is you, old girl. You're among the half dozen in this universe*

109

I'd least want to hurt. "Yes," he said, advanced, and mounted.

Owazzi and he clasped shoulders. Hers felt saddeningly fragile. Ancient even on Ishtar, she must have been aging doubly fast under the news of the last few years. That meant she had not long to be, and knew it. For as if a hypothetical deity wanted to make amends for Anu, her race was spared the slow decay which can take half a human's lifetime, and the final horror of senility. She regarded him through clear eyes in a face gaunted but unwrinkled. Her pelt remained bright greenish-tawny, her mane golden-tinged red—young.

"Do you know what has gone on here?" she asked.

"A little," Sparling said; then, to buy time: "Best would be if you told me."

She launched into a crisp summation of proceedings since the assembly convened. This was part of her duty. Though the original function of the Lawspeaker—to know all the codes in the Gathering—had diminished after literacy became widespread, an excellent memory and a gift for seeing the total picture remained essential in the person who presided over these meetings. She had for three hundred years, and nobody had yet suggested retiring her.

Sparling half listened, half struggled to arrange the words he must soon voice. His problem was not really to put a hard truth into soft language; it was to move his hearers toward decision and actions that might ease the span ahead. But what decisions? He couldn't be sure. What actions? This was not a parliament. Almost its sole power was moral.

I've been twenty years on Ishtar, and made myself into a xenologist in order to know better what I could best do as an engineer. But a lot of my studies were done in countries far from here. And in any case, I've never had to play local politics. My politicking has been back on Earth, to get okays and funds for my work. Therefore I have got to bear in mind that the Gathering is not an empire, not a federation, not a set of alliances. Or—no—it is certain of those things, in a certain wise, to certain of its members. But the rest see it quite differently. What common terms do these delegates have? Why, many of them aren't even delegates!

110

And he rehearsed the accounts of the past and present as if he were newly arrived and hearing them for the first time.

Civilization in South Beronnen did not perish utterly when last Anu came near. Folk had built storehouses, fortresses, yes, vaults where books and instruments could be preserved; and they had a few legions. Longevity helped too. A bright young Ishtarian might study under a master, be in the prime of life when the catastrophes began, and survive to teach in the next cycle. (Also there seemed to be the factor of creativity. If most men are at their most original between the ages of, say, twenty and thirty-five, the corresponding Ishtarian ages would be about fifty to one hundred fifty, with all the advantages of accumulating experience and insight.)

Civilization thus could rebuild and then expand vigorously, exploring, trading, colonizing. This meant guardians were needed. Ishtarians might have less innate violence, power hunger, and general irrationality than men; but they were equally able to see that robbery often yields more fun and profit than honest labor, or to fear becoming victims themselves. Humans have tended to handle resultant troubles by subjugating the troublemakers. But Beronnen had no government to establish a hegemony. The legions were the closest thing to governed organizations, and they were autonomous. They hired out to whoever would pay, on whatever terms could be mutually agreed on—though never to anyone who attacked Beronneners.

Less developed areas found it worthwhile to engage these crack troops, or detachments thereof. They got protection, plus valuable civilian services; a legion was by no means exclusively military. They also got trade with Beronnen and each other, and access to the learning and technology that centered around Sehala.

It was a good idea to meet at intervals, exchange information, negotiate accumulated disputes, plan joint undertakings. Sehala was the natural if not the invariable site for this. A society might send its leader(s) or might send diplomatic representatives . . . or some thing else. It might dispatch a single person or several. Formulas evolved for apportioning votes reasonably

111

fairly, irrespective of numbers. But the assembly was not a legislature. It recommended.

True, the recommendations were normally followed, by legions and nations alike. A dissenting minority would find it more expedient to obey majority will than to risk being left isolated. The soldiers regarded themselves as custodians of civilization, but—in contrast to counterparts throughout human history—not as being on that account its policy makers. (Longevity helped. An officer of Larreka's age had seen countless issues burning for a while, ashes not long afterward.)

Thus the Gathering was different things to its different members, not to mention outsiders. Their languages included names for it which was not mutually translatable. To some folk it was a kind of police; to others it was the bearer and preserver of everything important; to some, this gave it mystical significance; to others it was a foreign culture, not inherently superior, whose captaincy it was good, or at least prudent, to acknowledge; and on and on.

To the Valenneners—scattered, anarchic, backward—it was an alien, which sent traders and, reasonably enough, guarded these . . . but which replied to attacks with punitive expeditions whose targets were shrewdly if not always correctly picked . . . and which forbade with its garrisons and patrol ships the good old custom of raiding . . . and which, while it kept its strength, would never let them take new lands, distant from the Cruel Star. . . .

Owazzi finished. The consensus appeared to favor Jerassa. Of course, nobody could compel the Zera Victrix to come home, and perhaps those who had much to lose in Valennen would support it, did it choose to stay. In any case, it had independent income, from services which personnel of it performed in many separate places. But the bulk of this assembly felt that it should urge the legions to pull in closer to the heartland; and probably Larreka's colleagues would rather do this than join him in a doomed cause; so was it not best that Larreka reconsider? That was the general feeling, Owazzi said. A minority had been pointing out that the kind of military aid the humans would give had not been specified, and should be before any further thinking was done. Would the speaker for Primavera, if such he was, care to comment?

"I must," Sparling said harshly.

He wished he were on a Terrestrial-type stage, safe behind a lectern, not surrounded by these eyes and eyes and eyes. As was conventional, he faced the Law-speaker. He filled his lungs and said to her old face:

"I think most of you here will understand how grieved we are at the tidings I bear. Prepare your-selves." *Useless human phrase. Ishtarians speak straight out in public matters. They save oratory for art, where it belongs.* "Very lately we have gotten word that our hands may be tied for years to come, in helping you in any way.

"Any way. I do not know when work can continue on my dams, nor does Jane Fadavi know when she can get the air seeders to abort tornados, nor have we prospect of synthetic food and prefabricated shelters being sent for refugees in the near future, nor aircraft to evacuate them from stricken parts, nor—anything. In-cluding weapons.

"At best, we can do minor jobs, we can advise, we can try to keep Primavera going. I do say this: We will not abandon you. For hundreds of us, this is our home too, and you are our people.

"You have doubtless guessed the reason. You know that war goes among the stars, between our world Earth and another. Thus far, action has not been in-tense. Both sides were busy marshaling their forces. Now it is in earnest, and will consume resources we had counted on.

"But I have worse news yet. Part of Earth's effort in-volves establishing a base on this world. Be not afraid. You are remote from the fighting. The base is not nec-essary. We of Primavera will strive to persuade the overlords of Earth that it is not necessary."

Shall I tell them the war isn't? No, not here. They'll soon observe our bitterness.

"If we succeed in that, we will at least release our home production. For instance, the dams can then be finished in time. But unless the war proves brief, we cannot expect shipments from Earth as early as we had planned. And we may not be able to stop construction

113

of that base. We will almost surely be in no position to help you fight. Oh, I suppose we can keep our private guns and vehicles, and you can keep those you already own. But a few small arms, a few cars and flyers, will not check the barbarians.

"I do not know what will happen. Conceivably this will all end in short order and we can go on as we'd hoped. But I think we had better batten down against the worst."

Sparling stopped. *Lousy rhetoric for a human audience*, he thought. *How good for a mixed bag of Ishtarians? Not awfully, I'm afraid.*

Into a terrible hush, Owazzi took the word. "We must think a multitude of stiff thoughts over again. No doubt this assembly will stand for longer than expected, to consider ways, means, and contingencies with our human friends." The language allowed her to separate those, by a suffix, from human unfriends. To him: "I wonder, though, since Larreka accompanies you, I wonder what your ideas are about holding on in Valennen."

Taken by surprise, Sparling stammered, "I, I don't know, I'm not a soldier, not competent to say—"

Jerassa spoke from the floor: "The Lawspeaker is right; we must more than ever move carefully toward judgment. But does it not seem, colleagues, that this triples the reason for recalling our forces to Beronnen?"

Protests arose in a storm-wave. Nobody wanted the legions to withdraw from his or her country. Yet— voices were sufficiently soft for Sparling to make out what individuals said—few opposed the principle that civilization should pull its outposts closer in and, specifically, abandon all holdings north of the equator.

Owazzi ended the low hubbub by signaling Larreka to the dais.

When he had silence, the commandant said, flat-toned for an Ishtarian:

"No. I tried to explain earlier, and you still don't see. This is not a question of protecting a few commercial interests. It's a question of heading off a conqueror. I know that, I tell you, know it from military intelligence and from what's lately been happening and

114

from a cold shiver that a lifetime on the frontier has taught me how to feel.

"If we can't get human war-aid, we'll not just be wise to stick in Valennen, we'll have to. Else the enemy can strike however he feels like, throughout the Ehur and Fiery Seas. He can throw more against an island than we can put on it; and when the garrison's been reduced, he can go on to the next. A battle or two won by us won't mean a futtering thing, long-range, when he's got a whole mainland to withdraw to and we no troops there to welcome him.

"Soon we'll lose those waters. Soon after, he'll be harrying North Beronnen while his ships range west into the Argent and east into the Cyclonic Ocean, picking off whatever he pleases, raising allies, breeding fighters—And maybe afterward we can keep him from taking over this half of this continent, but we'll've had to haul in everything we've got left to defend it.

"Which'd be the end of the Gathering. Civilization might limp on, but only in South Beronnen. And only *for* South Beronnen. Doom and blast, can't you see the Gathering is what this cycle's all about, the best thing we've got to pass on to the next?

"Yes, you can stay safer for a while by letting Valennen go. My judgment as a soldier is, it'd be better to let several of your homes go, and send the strength to me there that I need to clean the place out. But vote as you please. The Zera stays."

X

"Gwine to run all night!
Gwine to run all day!
I'll bet my money on de bobtail nag—
Somebody bet on de bay."

As SHE ENDED the old song, Jill Conway kept fingers flying on her guitar and began to whistle. Trills, glides, notes, chords, now shivery shrill, now bell-deep, flew out beneath the stars, entered ears and danced along

115

nerves till the whole body seemed to tone with them. Those were rollicking ghosts they raised, nevertheless ghosts.

Meanwhile her gaze wandered aloft. On this warm night she had rolled back the porch roof of her cottage. She and Yuri Dejerine sat under the sky only. Primavera had no need for street illumination; a tall hedge around the yard screened off windows of neighbors, who weren't close anyway; here was nothing except a glowglobe on a table where stood the cognac he had brought to follow the dinner she cooked. Above shadowy sweet-smelling masses of trees, the stars marched in brilliant armies on either bank of the galactic river. Caelestia hastened tumbling and glittering between them. But her eyes sought past Ea, toward the Wings. In that constellation lay Earth, which had begotten the words and music she offered her guest—had begotten her entire race, though scarcely an atom from it could be in her. . . .

Wings, passed over her mind. *Is it part of a different idea for Yuri? We've naturally come to use the star-pictures of Beronnen; but across a thousand light-years, he can recognize a few of man's, however strangely changed, he told me. Which are they?*

Light-years. Light . . . It glimmered on grass, glinted where it caught insignia on the man's dress uniform or, she knew, the silver in her headband; maybe her unbound hair shone a little for him. She finished the music.

"*Nom d'un nom!*" Dejerine exclaimed. He struck hands together. "I have never heard anything like! Where is it from?"

"America, I believe." Jill lowered the guitar to the floor, leaned back in her chair with one long leg crossed over the other, and lifted her glass for a sip. This Earthside brandy was heady stuff. She warned herself to go slow. *Well not too slow. Moderation in all things, including moderation.*

She had made that remark to Ian Sparling, and he had said, "My dear, your idea of moderation would've strained Alexander the Great," then at once retreated into impersonalities. *Is Ian really in love with me? I*

116

wish I could be sure, to help me know what to do, whatever that would be. She continued, smiling a bit:

"Odd, that you should have to come this far to hear a song off your native planet. But maybe it's forgotten there. I daresay we preserve many quaint archaisms. Shall we charge admission?"

Dejerine shook his sleek head. "No, no, Jill," he said. They had gotten on first-name terms in the course of the meal, which he praised with a knowledgeability that proved he was sincere. She had been pleased, being rather proud of her skill. "I meant your incredible ... coda? It fitted so well, yet it cannot be of human origin. Can it?"

"Yes and no," she replied. "I spent a couple of seasons doing field work in the Thunderhead Mountains. The locals there communicate across distances by whistling, and they've developed a music based on it. I learned and adapted what I could. That wasn't much. Ishtarians are better than us at producing and hearing sounds. Their music, like their dance, is nearly always incredibly sophisticated by our lights."

"What you can do is remarkable."

"Yeah, I've made it a minor art of my own. You should hear some numbers." Jill grinned. "Downright obscene."

Dejerine chuckled and bent toward her. She hoped he hadn't misunderstood her jape as a suggestion. To change the subject, and because the sudden fancy amused her, she said, "Apropos peculiar cultural creations, that expression you used. *'Nom d'un nom,'* wasn't it? If you'll forgive my pronunciation. Am I right that it means 'name of a name'?"

He nodded, relaxed, picked his cigar out of the ashtray on the table, and puffed.

I reckon he got the hint, she thought. *Maybe not consciously. He's sensitive.*

"A French phrase," he said. "I have never grasped the logic of it."

"Oh, but I do. What is the name of a name? For instance, my name is Jill. But the name of my name—" She cocked her head and laid a fingertip to chin. "Yes, I believe my name is named Susan. And yours ... m-m

117

... Fred? Why, we may have founded a whole new science!"

They laughed together. Then a silence fell, wherein they heard a nightringer sing.

"What a lovely evening," she murmured at last. "Enjoy it. We won't get a hell of a lot more like this in our lifetimes."

"Lovely in every way," he said, "though chiefly because of you." She gave him a quick glance, but he stayed where he was and his tone came earnest rather than glib. Therefore her look stayed with him. "I am truly grateful for your invitation, your all-around kindness. It has been, it is hard work getting settled here. And then nearly everyone is chilly toward us, if not outright hostile."

"That seems wrong to me. You're wearing the same uniform as my brother. This war wasn't of your making, and you're doing your duty the most humane way you can."

"You know I support the war. Not for conquest or glory—*ad i chawrti,* no!—but as the lesser of two evils. If we keep the balance of power today, we should not have to fight on a far larger scale in ten or twenty years."

"You've told me before. I—Yuri, I like you as a person, but you're too bright not to realize I'm also trying to influence you, get your help for the help of Ishtar. You talk about sacrifices for the greater good. Well, what value have millions of thinking lives? A whole set of societies, arts, philosphies, all we could learn and make of ourselves, from a race which quite possibly balances out as ahead of us in evolution."

His free hand made a fist on the arm of his chair. "I sympathize with the fact that you have friends here who will suffer if your programs are curtailed," he said. "But as for the more abstract issues—Jill, excuse me, but I ask you to ask yourself: How much scientific advance is your brother's life worth?"

"That isn't the point!" she flared. "Your wretched base—"

She broke off and he stepped quickly into the gap. "The base is a detail, important here but still a detail. If it were cancelled, you would become able to do cer-

118

tain things. Nevertheless the war would go on engaging resources and shipping you need for most of your projects. Engaging them for the sake of humans who can hurt just as badly as Ishtarians."

"Well, I don't know." She stared past him, into darkness. "Are we obliged to bail out the Eleutherians? Would we need that 'balance of power' you say is our real reason, if we hadn't first encouraged and then underwritten their land grab?" She shook her head. "I don't know. I only know, here we're letting a chance—purely from a selfish, practical viewpoint we're throwing away a chance at knowledge that could make as big a difference to us as, oh, molecular biology."

From the corner of her eye she saw him frown; but she felt he was as relieved as she at this way to steer clear of a partisan fight. "M-m-m, I'm not sure," he said. "I'll take your word for it that the Ishtarians have done unique things, sociologically. Yet how relevant can their experiences ever be to us?"

"No telling till we've tried. But I'm talking about straight biology. Look, what do you imagine it was like to live in a world where people got cancer? Or any of those foul things we tossed out after we understood our cell chemistry? *Our* chemistry. Since, we've begun getting in-depth knowledge—barely begun—knowledge of extraterrestrial life. I'll bet it brings on a, an Einsteininian revolution in Terrestrial biology too. And one of the most enlightening cases is right here on Ishtar. Maybe solitary in the universe."

"You . . . your research needn't be affected by the war, Jill."

"I doubt if mine matters—natural history, and in the most Earth-similar parts of the planet. No, I mean T-life. And to study T-life, we have got to get safe, steady, large-scale access to Valennen. Now the Gathering is in danger of losing Valennen. My honorary uncle Larreka's been in charge there; he's come down to plead for help in keeping a foothold—" She turned her gaze full upon him. "How do you like that, Captain Dejerine? A possible rebuilding of all our ideas about how life can work—possible immortality for man, or

119

you name it—in the hands of one battered old legionary mudfoot!"

"I don't quite follow you," he said softly. "I will be happy to hear you explain."

Surprise jolted her. In their encounters hitherto, he had shown he'd done his homework. His questions were well informed and he needed answers less elaborate than she had given him at first. Why this sudden ignorance?

A put-on, to make me enthusiastic and jolly again? she wondered. *And if so, for what purpose, plain good-heartedness or——?—He must know women the way he knows orbits. Or, anyhow, better'n any other man I've ever met does. For sure better'n I know men. Not that that's saying a valwas of a lot.*

In the warm and fragrant star-dusk he sat at ease, glass in his experienced right hand, cigar in the left, cordial but with a hint of the mysterious; and, holy Darwin, was he handsome! Her heart knocked.

No, I am not falling in love, I am not, I insist I am not. Though scientific objectivity compels me to note that it wouldn't be hard to do. Have an affair, at least. Which might or might not lead to, well, permanency. . . No. A hairy-brained notion. What kind of Navy wife would I make, or Primaveran settler he? An affair—

Her few men flickered before her. Not the boyfriends earlier; they and she were merely part of a group who styled themselves the Cartesian Divers, were considered wild in their staid community but really only dashed around at high speeds, did breakneck things in the outback, drank and smooched less than they sang rowdy songs, and rowdy songs less than ballads which filled them dripful of what today she called Weltschmalz; looking back, she saw that the boy Divers had been a tad scared of her, and maybe she of them. . . . Probably they'd prepared her to cannonball herself at Kimura Senzo when she was seventeen, Earthside eighteen. And for the two years he was here on his research grant, it had been a wholly beautiful, terrible, heavenly, hellish, shameless, furtive, merry, sorrowful, tender, angry, rainbow-colored thing they stole by divine right; and it wouldn't have been what it was if he weren't the kind who, after she made him surrender, kept warning that in the end he would go home to his wife because he'd have deprived their little girl of her daddy too long as it was—and then did. . . . She got over it in a couple of years. The three romps since were exactly that, fun, friendship, appeasement of the body for a while, though not for very long because Primavera *was* staid and she didn't want several people she liked to find out and be antagonized.

Ian—Well, I've never been sure, and besides, poor Rhoda—

Jillian Eva Conway, she said in Larreka's voice, *get your tail down! This man is the enemy, remember? A nice fellow, probably, but the object of the game is for you to seduce his mind.*

An irresistible image intruded, of one brain sexily rippling its cortex at another. She giggled. "Pardon?" asked Dejerine.

"Nothing," she answered in haste. "A stray thought. Unlicensed."

He gave her a quizzical regard. "If you would rather not talk science, I don't mind discussing my personal magnificence. However, I really would like to know what you mean about the, the T-life."

"Oh. Yes." She relaxed (*sort of*) and took a sip of cognac. It slid ardently over tongue and palate. "Short for 'Tammuz-descended life.' As distinguished from what we call 'ortho-Ishtarian,' the life that originated here. You must know—I know you do, but I'll repeat to make sure we're using the same terms—Anu has a planet which is, or was, terrestroid, and about a billion years ago had evolved a sentient species. When their sun started ballooning, we think they tried to plant a colony on Ishtar."

Dejerine raised his brows. "You think? My sources took that for granted."

"It's a theory." Jill shrugged. "After a billion years, what physical evidence is left? I must lend you some stuff on what the archeologists have have done on Tammuz. Fascinating reading, if occasionally grim." She refreshed herself again. "In our style of thinking, it is reasonable to suppose the Tammuzians developed an interplanetary transport capability and tried to colonize

121

Ishtar. Not all of them, that'd doubtless have been impossible, and Lord knows what epics of endurance the mother world saw while its sun slowly roasted it to death. We presume they hoped to save a few, who'd give the race a fresh start."

"Let me see if I have the facts correctly," Dejerine said. "Because Ishtar had already developed an incompatible biochemistry, they sterilized a large island and seeded it with their kind of life. The effort proved too great, or perhaps the survival margin was too small. At any rate, the colonists died out, and the plants and animals they had introduced. Microscopic forms did come through, did establish an ecology and in time evolved new multicellular species. Do I have it right?"

"You have the most popular theory right," Jill replied. "It's certainly colored our notions here on Ishtar. Countless bad poetry, songs, science fiction plays for our amateur theater. . . . But it's a theory, I say. Maybe Tammuzian spores were borne here by meteoroids. Maybe the sophonts rocketed spores here on purpose, for some weird reason. Maybe simple exploring expeditions of theirs happened to leave bits of life which survived. After all, a Tammuzian bug wouldn't be edible to the local microfauna. Or maybe the sophonts did start their colony, and then discovered how to use Mach's Principle—we did long before we'd've been able to mount that kind of interplanetary effort—and their whole race went whooping off into the galaxy. Maybe they're still around, away out yonder, a billion years ahead of us." The lightness departed from her. She raised her face to the stars, where they glinted in their secret hordes, and whispered, "Now do you see? Even the archeologists aren't necessarily turning over dry bones."

She thought from his voice that the spaceman felt a tinge of the same frosty awe. "A big idea. Too big for us."

She regained a matter-of-fact tone: "Plenty of theories, yes. The data they try to account for are fewer. First, on this planet Ishtar with its otherwise pretty terrestroid biochemstry, there occurs T-life: also built out of proteins in water solution, et cetera, but too alien to have developed here, since it is in the minority.

122

Uses dextro amino acids, levo sugars, where we and the ortho-Ishtarians are the exact opposite—to name only a couple of the differences, and say nothing about those we haven't yet identified.

"Second, the planet Tammuz is dead, but fossil traces and such-like clues show it did once carry T-life.

"Third, on Ishtar T-life is fairly well confined to Valennen. The northern three quarters, at that. It does spill into the rest of the continent and nearby islands, but there it has to be sympatric—share the range with ortho-life, which dominates. This suggests northern Valennen was the original site, a big island that later collided with another to form the land mass we know. Before, it was isolated, giving T-life a sanctuary to evolve in. Hence the notion that long ago, would-be colonists sterilized and re-seeded it. But we haven't any solid proof. That's unknown territory."

She took a further drink, feeling the glow in her stomach—and, yes, in her heart, at his look of shared excitement.

"Unknown, after a hundred years of man on Ishtar?" he wondered. Before she could explain: "I see. Orbital surveys, cursory overflights, landings almost at random, samples, specimens, yes. But nothing more. You have had too much else to do."

Jill nodded. "Right. Nobody's lacked for projects in the ortho sections. Nor will they for decades to come.

"But we have been accumulating a little knowledge, in the interzone of South Valennen. We've started learning something about T-life. And, if the Gathering can be saved, we've got the support base for a really massive attack on the riddles further north."

In unwonted earnestness, she continued: "Don't you see, this makes Ishtar directly valuable to Earth? Sure, I know about planets that carry analogues of T-life. But they have nothing else! Nothing we can eat, for openers; no chance for a base to practice agriculture, in a not-too-different surrounding ecology; no strong civilization of highly intelligent beings eager to help. Everywhere else, everybody who wants to study our biochemical mirror image in action, has to do it at the end of a long, thin, expensive supply line. Here it's a matter of an aerial hop.

"And then there's that absolutely unique interzone."

"Interzone," Dejerine said. "I take it you mean where the ranges of ortho- and T-life overlap?"

"What else?" Jill answered. "In a way, it covers the whole planet. The theroids incorporate a few T-microbes into their symbioses, and that alone is worth learning more about. But only in the South Valennen area do you get interaction between metazoans, or higher plants, or oddball things that we don't yet know quite which what are."

Dejerine blinked, then laughed. "You win.'"

She grinned back. "Two distinct ecologies, neither able to exploit the other. At least not till the ortho-sophonts came along. The phoenix tree is valued for more than being hardwood. Once out of the interzone, that lumber doesn't rot nohow. There've been attempts to raise it nearer home, but none succeeded. Likewise for a few more T-species, plus ortho-species and miner-als—plenty reason for the Gathering to want to be present in Valennen.

"But otherwise, well, very limited interaction. Plants crowd rival plants out of soil and sunlight, and so re-strict the scope of animals. Possibly lia is the main bar-rier to T-life spreading further than it has. Animals . . . no mutual nourishment, so as a rule the two kinds sim-ply don't bother each other."

He startled her by obviously quoting: "What, never?"

"Hardly ever," she warbled back, maybe startling him in turn.

"Actually," she added, "what interaction does go on is co-operative, as far as we know—though we know itchingly little." She combed fingers through a strand of hair. "Um-m-m . . . let me give you an example. I'll change the names to those of Earth types, to help you keep 'em straight; and bear in mind, the real critters are small." In a high-pitched singsong:

"See the ferocious tiger. See the fat, juicy antelope. Is the tiger going to jump on the antelope? No, the tiger is not going to jump on the antelope. The tiger does not think the antelope is fit to eat. But see the tiger watch the antelope. The tiger knows the antelope has very fine eyes and a very fine nose. See the antelope peer. See the antelope sniff. See the antelope gallop off. See the tiger follow. The antelope locates a herd of deer. The tiger can eat deer. The tiger does eat a deer. The antelope is a fink. See the leopard. Leopards like antelope steak. See the tiger chase away the leopard. The tiger is a goon. Children, this is called co-operation."

Jill tossed off the rest of her brandy. Dejerine moved to pour her a refill. "After all that lecturing," she said, "I suppose I should fetch me a beer. . . . Aw, a shame, on top of this gorgeous stuff. Go ahead, thanks."

"You certainly make your subject come alive," he said, the faintest accent on the first word.

"Well, your turn. Tell me about places you've been."

"If you will give me more songs later."

"Let's find songs we both know. Meanwhile, please do reminisce." Jill looked again skyward. Caelestia had dropped out of view and the stars shone forth still keener. Wistfulness tugged at her. "So much wonder. Damn it, I haven't got *time* to die."

"Why have you never visited Earth?"

"Oh . . . I dunno. Seems as if everything interesting there—wait, yes, I realize they have natural extravagances left like the Grand Canyon, but Ishtar has them too—mainly, everything is man-made; and our data banks hold millions of pictures, recordings, whatnot."

"The best hologram isn't the real thing, Jill. It isn't the totality of, oh, the cathedral at Chartres . . . which besides beauty includes the fact that countless pilgrims for hundreds of years walked and knelt and slept on the selfsame stones under your feet. . . . And you can have fun on Earth, you know. A lively person like you—"

A chime sounded from the open door. Jill rose. "Phone," she said. " 'Scuse." Who'd call at this hour? "Maybe an officer of Yuri's, in need of him?"

The fluoropanel she switched on was harsh after the majestic dimness outside. The room leaped at her, comfortably shabby, slightly untidy, its plainness defiled by scarlet drapes on which she had painted gold swirls and by a fireburst feather-plant cloak from Great Iren. Other souvenirs included native tools and weapons hung on the walls among pictures, landscapes and portraits, she had done herself with camera or pencil. Printouts were shelved and piled around, both flimsies for recycling and permanents which she had liked sufficiently well to pay for.

The phone chimed anew. " 'Bong' right back at you," she grumbled, sat down before it, and tapped the accept plate.

Ian Sparling's head sprang into the screen. He was haggard, the lines trenched in his long face, eyes burning blue-green out of hollowness. The gray-shot black hair was totally unkempt and no beardex could have touched his skin for two or three days.

Jill's pulse stumbled and began to run. "Hi," she said mechanically. "You look like outworn applesauce. What's wrong?"

"I thought you should know." His voice came hoarse. "Being as close to Larreka as you are."

She caught the table edge and hung on.

"Oh, he's safe," Sparling told her. "But— Well, I'm calling from Sehala. We've been here arguing, pleading, trying to bargain, this past eight-day. No go. The assembly has voted to abandon Valennen. We couldn't convince them the danger there is as bad as Larreka claims." He hesitated. "Well, hell, I had to take his word for that myself. I don't know from experience. And . . . not only did the Tamburu commandant declare we—the Gathering could absorb the loss and survive elsewhere. The Kalain's boss did too. Sent a courier clear from the Dalag to say his ground and naval forces are in control but could use whatever help they might get which is now tied up in less vital areas. Larreka doesn't believe any legion will agree to join his Zera. The cause looks too lost."

Rage leaped in Jill. "Those idiots! Couldn't they investigate for themselves?"

"Not easy to do, especially when they've such growing demands on their attention right at home. I suppose I can try to talk a few key people into letting us fly them there for a look-around. If we can get a vehicle." Sparling sounded dubious. "What gets you involved is Larreka. He's taking this pretty hard. You could . . . encourage him, console him, whatever you gauge is best.

126

He thinks the world of you." His weary eyes dwelt on her image as if to add Larreka was not alone.

Tears stung. Jill must swallow before she could ask, "What's he plan to do?"

"Head straight back. He's already left. You can catch him at the Yakulen Ranch, though. He'll stop off there to collect travel gear and say good-by."

"I c-can fly him."

"If our dear naval governor will release an aircraft of the right size. Ask him. It'd sure help. Larreka's not simply got to take charge—he says the new vice commandant is overcautious—but he's got to persuade his troops to stand fast."

Jill nodded. A legion elected a chief by a rank-weighted three-fourths vote of its officers, and could depose him by the same. "Ian," she half begged, "is it necessary? Does he really have to stay on? Won't he be spending himself, his males, for nothing?"

"He says that's the chance he must take. He'll keep a capability of evacuating survivors, should worst come to worst. But he hopes to do more than harass the barbarians. He hopes he can draw them into fights that'll show their real strength, their real intentions, before it's too late; and this'll get him his reinforcements. Sounds forlorn to me, but—" Sparling sighed. "Well, now you know, and I'd better report to God."

"You called me first?" she blurted. "Thank you, thank you."

He smiled the wry smile she had always liked. "You deserved it," he said. "I'll be home in two or three days, after tying up some loose ends here. Come see us. Meanwhile, *daryesh tauli,* Jill." It meant both "fare you well" and "fare in love." He was silent for an instant. "Good night." The screen blanked.

She sat briefly in an equal blindness. Dear, awkward Ian. Did he suspect how she admired him, he who had roved over half the planet readying to do battle with the red giant? Or how fond of him she had grown, his patience and decency, the good company he was when a dark mood had not taken him? Sometimes she daydreamed about how things could have been, were she born twenty years earlier on Earth.

She blinked hard, wiped her eyes with the back of a

127

hand, blinked again. *Damn! Why am I woolgathering on a sheepless planet? I've got a job to do. Except I don't know how.*

Surging to her feet, she went back outside. Light from the doorway caught Dejerine sharp athwart a night where she could not at once see stars. He rose, concern upon his features. "Bad news, Jill?"

She nodded. Her fists were clenched at her sides. He came to take them in his hands and raise them. His gaze captured hers. "Can I help in any way?" he asked.

Hope sprang. "You bet you can!" Abruptly controlled, she related the situation in a few unemotional words.

The mobile face before her congealed. He let her go and stared past her. "A pity, I suppose," he said, toneless. "That is, naturally I regret your distress. As to the wisdom of the military decision, I am not qualified to judge. You realize my orders are clear. Apart from self-defense, my command is forbidden to intervene in native affairs."

"You can appeal. Explain—"

He had never before interrupted her. "It would be futile. Therefore it would be undutiful, wasting the time of my superiors."

"Well ... okay. Let's talk about that later. Right now, Larreka needs quick transportation. I hear you've classed flyers big enough to hold an Ishtarian as, uh, Federation resources."

"Yes," he said, half defiantly. "You have few. We couldn't bring many more. To construct the ground installations in a short time will take every available freight carrier."

"You can let me borrow one for a couple of days, can't you?" she inquired around a tightening in her throat. "Full-scale work hasn't started."

"I was afraid you would request that." He shook his head. "No. Believe me, I wish I could. But if nothing else, the risk from storms—how bad do equinoctial gales get during a periastron? Nobody was here last time to study the meteorology. It must be unpredictable."

Jill stamped her foot. "Damn you, I don't need protection against myself!" She gulped. "Sorry. My turn to be sorry. Somebody else can pilot if you insist."

128

His eyes shifted back to hers, and the least sardonicism touched his lips. *Huh? Does he think I think he's worried about losing delightful me?*

He turned grave, even gentle. "I cannot authorize it for anyone," he said. "The aircraft would be put at hazard for a purpose irrelevant to my mission. Worse, this would be a kind of intervention, however minor. Given such a precedent, where can I draw the line against further demands? No, there is no way I could justify myself to my superiors."

Rage and grief whirled upward. "So you're afraid of a reprimand!" Jill yelled. "A check mark in your file! A delay in your next promotion! Get out!"

Astounded, he stuttered, "*Mais* ... please, I don't ... I didn't mean—"

"Get out, you gonococcus! Or do I have to throw you out—like *this*?" She snatched the bottle and hurled it to the porch. It didn't break, but the contents ran forth as if from a wound.

His mouth compressed, his nostrils dilated. He gave her a bow. "My apologies, Miss Conway. Thank you for your hospitality. Good evening."

He walked off with metronomic strides and was lost in the dark.

Was I foolish? chopped to and fro. *Should I have—? But I couldn't! I couldn't!* She sat down by the spilled cognac and wept.

XI

As LARREKA AND his escort neared the headquarters of Yakulen Ranch, a storm drove ponderously out of the west. Wind sighed cold through the heat which had brooded earlier, like a sword through flesh, and sunscorched lia rippled and rustled across yellow-brown kilometers of range. Far off, a herder and his wo were bringing in a flock of owas; they seemed lost in that hugeness. Single trees tossed, brawled, threw splashes of russet at flying murky clouds. Between land and low heaven swept a hundred fleetwings; their cries creaked

129

faintly in the whine and boom around. Where light-spears, fire or brass color, struck, they changed the look of the world. Westward stood a purple-black cliff down which lightnings torrented. The noise of those streams rolled steadily louder.

The trooper from Foss Island said, "If I was home and saw that weather coming at me, I'd haul my boat as high ashore as she'd go and cable her fast." Larreka could barely hear him.

"Well, it's not a twister, but I'd sure appreciate a roof over me when it gets here," the commandant agreed. "On the double!" He flogged his tired body into a smart trot.

The familiar buildings made a clustered darkness to north. He saw that the sails were off the windmill and the flag was descending a pole whose horned bronze finial swayed in arcs above the hall. Letters from here, to him and Meroa in Valennen, had told how nobody took a chance any longer on a gale not turning into a hurricane.

The first raindrops lashed nearly level when he entered the courtyard. Long, low, half-timbered, peak-roofed in tile, the lesser structures of the ranch walled in its paved rectangle—barns, stables, kennels, mews, storehouses, granaries, workshops, bakery, brewery, cookhouse, laundry, surgery, school, ateliers, observatory, library—not everything a civilized community needed, but ample when it could trade with other ranches and the towns, Yakulen's publishing linked to Nelek's ropewalk and Sorku's iron smelter and thus outward over South Beronnen and the whole Gathering. Folk scurried about, battening down. Just before a hireling closed the door, Larreka glimpsed a small flyer parked in a shed. *Ng-ng, we've got a human visitor,* he thought. *I wonder who.*

Hail whitened the wind, danced across flagstones, rattled on walls, bit at skin. He shielded his eyes with an arm and slogged to the hall.

It rose enormous at the middle of the court, stone, brick, and phoenix, many-windowed, many-balconied, gargoyles time-worn but mosaics still bright after ten sixty-four-years. That was at the east end, the oldest. As the Yakulen family grew in wealth, numbers, retainers, and guests, they added new units, each enclosing its own patio. Changing styles (the latest incorporated heraklite and armor glass from Primavera) flowed together as do bluff, crag, and canyon.

Somebody must have been watching out of the warm windowglow, for Larreka and his males had scarcely loped onto the verandah when the Founders' Door swung wide for them. Beyond its copper-sheathed massiveness waited an entryful of servants who took their baggage and toweled them dry. Larreka hung onto his Haelen blade. It was a trademark; the soldiers said One-Ear slept with it. The rest, such as fire-crackle profanity in a score of languages, he needn't keep up here among his kindred. The heroic capacity for drink—well, he'd take as much tonight as he felt like, and no more; he was getting along in years, after all.

At the head of his six legionaires, he walked down a corridor to the main room. It was brick, carpeted in deep-blue Primavera neolon, wainscoted in woods of several hues and grains. Flames leaped and sang in four hearths, bracketed lanterns shone along the walls. Between them hung pictures, trophies, ancestral shields; high overhead, the rafters bore banners which had flown over battles or rescues. At the far end of the chamber, half hidden among unrestful shadows, was a shrine of She and He. (Few of the household attended it; most of the family were Triadists, while their help were drawn from a wide reach holding many different cults. But if nothing else, respect for tradition demanded it be kept.) The room was chiefly floor space, a long table, mattresses strewn about, some chairs for occasional humans. The warm air smelled of woodsmoke and bodies. Windows on two sides, closed against the storm which dashed itself on them, muffled its noise.

About sixteen persons were there, talking, reading, thinking, idling, doing minor chores. The chamber dwarfed them. Most of the hundreds who dwelt in the hall were at work, or in their private apartments. His wife came to meet him.

Meroa was a large female, which made her the size of her short husband. She had the Yakulen features, big gray eyes, curved muzzle, pointed chin. Age showed in dried and darkened complexion, the thinning down of hump and haunches that had once been rounded enough to make a male bay at the moons. But the embrace she gave him wasn't the dignified gesture of her relatives, it was the hug of a soldier's wench.

From across two and a half centuries, flashed through him the awe of miracle when she agreed to marry him. He'd been brash toward her, and they'd had fun together. However, she'd turned down two earlier proposals of his (following a proposition—which she'd had the sense not to be offended by, recognizing that a legionary was almost expected to make a pass at every attractive female). He'd never dared imagine she found more in him than the yarns he could spin about his fifty footloose years prior to enlistment.

Her yes turned out to be only the gold before the dawn. He had sworn, "I, I'm not a fortune hunter, believe me I'm not. I could almost wish you were poor."

She had widened those beautiful eyes, where she nestled against him so close that they felt the tendrils of each other's manes. "What do you mean? I'm not rich."

"Your kin—the Yakulens have one of the biggest ranches in the country—"

"*Chu-ha*! I see." She laughed, "Silly, you've forgotten you're not back in Haelen. A ranch isn't a wretched little stead that a single household owns. It belongs to the family—the land, the waters. But members work for themselves."

"*Yai*. I had forgotten. You make me forget everything except you." Larreka braced his will. "My term in the legion has another three years to run, you know, and next year we're due for an overseas post. Well, I'll be back, and ... and by the Thunderer"—he had not yet taken the Triadic faith, though he invoked the gods of his youth out of habit rather than belief— "I'll make us a fortune!"

She drew away from him. "What is this nonsense? Do you suppose I want you nailed down here? No, you're going to re-up, and I'll be there to watch."

That was when the Sun sprang over the world-rim.

Today she whispered a lusty suggestion in his ear,

132

adding. "We'll have to wait a while, confound it. Still, I'll have you here a tad longer than you figured."

"What?" He decided she'd explain when she was ready. They disengaged and he exchanged proper greetings with the others. Presently he was sprawled on a mattress beside Meroa, his pipe alight, a mug of hot spiced jackfruit cider to hand. A couple of family elders lay nearby. The rest of the folk gathered around his troopers in different parts of the room, since these would have things to relate from Sehala less depressing than Larreka's word. He had of course used his walkie-talkie, via radio relays to keep his wife informed; and she had passed the news on.

(They had already settled it between them: When he returned to Valennen, she would stay behind. It would not be the first time; they had erstwhile met reasons, like undue hazard or shortage of transport or a small child, why she could not accompany him. She had protested: "The youngsters are grown. And if the barbarians do overrun you, I want them to know they've been in a fight with me too."

(He answered starkly, "I can't be both places. Foul years are coming to South Beronnen also, and nobody else around the ranch has the kind of military knowledge you've picked up. For the family—the whole futtering future—we'd better get the spread properly organized. You're tapped, soldier.")

"Who's our human guest?" he asked.

"Jill Conway," Meroa said. "She grew restless and went out with Rafik. They'll doubtless draggle in pretty soon."

"Gr'm." Larreka told himself not to worry. His youngest son should be able to last out even as vicious a storm as howled and drummed outside. But Jill—

Well, they died, they died, the poor all-powerful starfarers. If you started caring for them, you had to make it a bond to a bloodline more than to a single person. And thus it had been between him and the Conways. Yet there had always been something special about Jill, maybe because she used to stump across the yard before she could talk, laughing for joy, whenever he called. Chaos! Why hadn't she bred and given him a new little girl to uncle?

133

Meroa chuckled and patted his hand. "Stop fretting," she said. "Your pet's an adult. She knows what to do in worse weathers than this." Businesslike: "It's due to her that you won't simply overnight here, you'll stay a few days."

Larreka sucked smoke and waited.

"She heard about the vote against you, and called me, since you'd left Sehala," his wife said. "She was either bleeding or snorting live steam on your account—I'm not sure which; I don't know humans that well—and she wanted to help. It seems that new boss or whatever he is in Primavera won't let her fly you north. Sometime you must explain to me why in destruction's name they listen to such a creature. Anyhow, I had an idea. You know those dried rations humans carry in the field, the food they must have that natural soil doesn't bear. I asked if she could make the same kind of thing for you. Meat, that is. You can forage along the way all right, but you need meat for the strength to move fast. If instead of hunting, you stir powder into a dish of water— You see?"

"I blazing well do!" Larreka slapped her rump almost as loudly as the thunder went. "Why didn't I think of that?"

"You doubtless did in the past, but never felt this urgency before," said an in-law. "And of late you've had a great deal else on you mind."

Larreka scarcely heard. His attention clung to Meroa. *By the Three,* he rejoiced, *I've got a soldier's wife, if ever a male did.* The sixty-fours of females he had mounted when she wasn't around were as if they had never been. (They'd always been incidental, maybe more of a habit than a need. Noncoms in the legions seldom married. Meroa used to purr when he happened to mention an encounter and tell her how much better she was.) He couldn't think of words, but, catching her eye, he snapped his tail in salute.

"Jill put the apparatus together—she wheedled a friend out of it—and brought it here," Meroa went on. "It'll take two or three days to make an ample supply, she says. You'll save more than that on the trail."

And I will have you meanwhile, said her look.

This was the thing that humans might come to know

134

about, but never to know: What it meant when someone who had been a part of you for two or three hundred years was gone. Larreka and Meroa would bid each other farewell, and though the blessed radio carry their words after he reached Port Rua, they could not be sure they would ever touch again.

Well, she was a soldier's wife; and he was a soldier's husband.

(It wasn't that simple. The legions had learned to do everything possible which made for lessened sorrow. They did not accept enlistments of close kin into the same one of them; rather, they kept the companies and regiments wildly diverse, a practice that Hanshaw had remarked would be unthinkable for his race. They discouraged marriage and, through their traditional standards of maleness, encouraged promiscuity; but the very camp followers were made to shift among them from time to time. They exchanged stations every octad, and two successive stations were always far apart. And even so, even so, there had to be rituals, customs, tokens, help, to keep a trooper going after his long-term sword brother was dead. . . . Larreka dismissed the passing thought. He and Meroa had the Triad and their work; the survivor would survive.

(He had decided in these latter years that the work would be more use to him than the Triad.)

"I'd better let Jill tell the rest herself," Meroa added. Her glance flickered around the group. "No insult. What you don't know, you can't be guilty of concealing from that Primavera boss; and Yakulen may have sore need of his good will."

They signified assent.

"What we can discuss openly," Meroa said to Larreka, "is Rafik. He wants to enlist—in the Yissek, because of your ideas about the Fiery Sea coming under attack soon, where they are." Dryly: "Also, I suspect, because of what he's heard about balmy tropical paradises and eager dusky maidens."

"No," Larreka replied. "Not if I can talk him out of it. Can't he see, his best service is right here? If we can hold Valennen, a few raids on the Fieries won't matter. If we can't, then we've lost the Fieries too, and Beronnen is next in line."

135

"Chu, do talk to him. Bear in mind, he probably doesn't care for the idea of his mother being his military chief."

"He'd care for those islands less. Already the Rover's made them the opposite of paradise. The Yissek's fighting typhoons and flood tides and famines oftener than it's fighting barbarians. The dusky maidens are too busy staying alive to be particularly eager any more."

"I tried to tell him that, but it only fanned his idealism. Service where service is needed, no matter the risk!"

"Then I'll tell him that a soldier who willingly takes risks is a soldier the legion is better off without—Speak of a rammer and he'll stave in your boat."

The noise from the entry was immensely relieving, foot-stamp, servants busy, Rafik's deep young tones and Jill's bugle clarity. He heard the girl say, "—we thought of taking shelter, but no tree would be safe with all that lightning blatting around, so he took me on his back and galumphed his hardest—"

His son staggered in, soaked despite a rubdown, hailed them, and collapsed onto a mattress. That must have been a real fiend's race he ran. Well, Meroa had birthed him on a vessel beating through Ripship Straits in the teeth of an easterly, and a tinge of that had remained with the lad. *I'm proud of you, of you and all the rest. I'm no Yakulen—only by marriage—I'm not in the way of seeing my family as octads of cousins sharing the same land. I'm an old Haelener, whose world has his wife and kids at its core.*

Jill followed. She had shed her clothes. Her skin glowed from toweling. The hair stayed as wet as Rafik's foliage, trailing firelight shimmers. Having been carried, she was not exhausted, and sped to hug Larreka. "Sugar Uncle! Hello!"

Watching her come, he thought how oddly lovely she was. Once in her adolescence, when they'd been for a swim, she had commented on that. "Tell me for honest, won't you? How horrible do I seem to you? Sure, you like me, but how do I look? Four-limbed, a torso tottering along, no whiskers, no hump, no tail, no plants, bald except for ridiculous little patches, breasts dangling on top and . . . and genitalia right out in front too, in sight of the world and everybody—"

"How do you think I look?" he had replied.

"You're beautiful. The way a cat is beautiful."

"Okay, you remind me of a saru in flight, or a sword-leaf in a high wind, or whatever. Now shut up and break out our lunch."

For a blink of time, while she dashed across the floor, he wished he could spend an hour being her human lover. To gaze into those curious half-white eyes, rub beak against beak and taste thick pink lips, send fingers down the long slim blue-veined throat, across the softnesses beneath to their sunrise-colored tips and on over a many-curved slope till they rested between her thighs. . . . Did humans ever have such wonderings about Ishtarians? Unlikely; humans were too frail. His was the merest flicker of sadness that he could never be closer than now to her. Damn! When would she grab herself a mate and start whelping?

She cast herself onto her knees and into his arms. Her nails dug through the leaves of his mane.

Larreka bellowed for more cider. Jill liked it too. "I brought you a kilo of tobacco," she said.

"You brought more than that, I hear," he answered. "Freeze-dried rations—You're grand."

She switched to English. He saw and felt the bleakness upon her. "You know about the ban on transport, don't you? Instead of battering my skull against that wall, I kept quiet and . . . went around collecting firearms and ammunition. You've got mighty little in Valennen. I couldn't be very bold, in case that Dejerine bastard got wind of it. But I bought, begged, borrowed, a couple of times I stole—about twenty rifles and pistols, plus a few thousand rounds for them."

"Jill, you're a laren!"

"The least I could do. Uncle. Let's be practical, though. First, you'll have to arrange for porters while you're here, to help lug that stuff to the north coast."

"Couldn't you just flit it to Port Rua in a small vehicle?"

"Uh-uh. Too obvious. Dejerine could wonder why Miss Conway took a junket. He could check back and confiscate what he found. Whereas if I go off overland on a field trip, and the weapons aren't really missed for weeks—You see?

"Another thing. Several thousand rounds aren't that flinkin' many. You know how ninety-nine percent are bound to miss in action, no matter how skilled the marksmen; and you have maybe ten skilled marksmen in Valennen, right? You'll want an instructor who can spend a minimum of ammo on training more. And it'll help if, come combat, that instructor is there in the line, firing shots that go where they're supposed to."

He understood before she had finished. "You don't mean you aim to come along with me?" he exclaimed.

She nodded. She had drawn knees close to chin and folded arms around them; the ends of her wet hair stroked her breasts and left gleaming streaks. "I mean exactly that, Uncle."

XII

DEJERINE HAD FOUND it astonishingly hard to acquire a site for his ground installations. He wanted a place not too far from Primavera, and discovered an area two hundred kilometers eastward which his planetological team reported was suitable. It was otherwise useless land, stony, dusty when rain didn't make it muddy, barren aside from scattered leathery shrubs, deserted by the natives. Repeated periastrons were doubtless responsible for that, droughts which killed off vegetation followed by cloudburst after cloudburst to wash away exposed topsoil. The planet had many such regions. Yet a substantial water table remained, the bedrock was solid, the surrounding hills could be quarried for building material.

He expected that the Tayessa family, to whose ranch this desert belonged, would be glad to sell it. No doubt they'd jack the price as high as they were able, but he had plenty of gold along, plus authority to draw pesos if Federation currency was demanded. He was dumfounded when, after conferring, the owners refused.

On the basis of what xenological knowledge he had,

he replied to their representative: "I am aware that no individual owns the land, but rather the Tayessas do, and you must consider the rights of generations unborn. However, surely titles change hands, for one reason or another. Have you the right to deny the unborn what my gold can buy?"

"What can it?" she answered through the interpreter Hanshaw had supplied. "The Red Sun is here. Who can eat gold, or shelter in it?"

"I can pay in money of my people."

"How can we spend that, if no shipments are coming from Earth?"

In the end, he negotiated a contract which bound the Navy to send specified goods within a specified period. His superiors were going to give him hell for it; but no Ishtarians were likely to offer a better deal. The alternatives were either to set up in the antipodes, where only goblins lived, and thus complicate his job without end, or to seize and hold a spot by force. (Ah-ah-ah! Imperialism!) In writing his report, to go home by the next courier boat, he indicated tactfully but unmistakably that if the Navy did not honor the contract, he would resign his commission—and speculated how to let Jill Conway know he had done this.

Immediately upon taking possession, he brought down his men and established camp. Then he phoned to Primavera and requested a visit by Ian Sparling. The engineer should have a large amount of good advice in him, if he could be conciliated.

Sparling's flyer landed the next day. Ever nearer to each other, both suns were aloft in a breathless sky. The cracked red clay wavered with heat; the hills around were gray and unreal. Prefab barracks clustered offside, ugly hemicylinders, while machinery cluttered the rest of fifty square kilometers, brawling like dinosaurs among sweating men. Dejerine, who had been making a general inspection, conducted him to an office small and bare but air-conditioned.

"Coffee or tea?" he asked as he settled down behind his desk. "And would you like a cigar?"

"Nothing, thanks." Sparling's voice might have blown off the south pole. He folded his lean length into a chair, took forth pipe and tobacco pouch, and got busy. "I don't expect to be here long."

"I was hoping you would."

"Why should I?"

"I mentioned a consultant's fee. And with your project suspended, you have nothing else to do, have you?" Dejerine considered the aquiline face. "I won't make noises about patriotism. Let us be frank, you are hostile to my mission. But the sooner I complete it, the sooner I can release your resources back to you. Won't you help to that end?" He paused. "Furthermore—please don't misunderstand, this is neither a threat nor a bribe—I would like to see regular supplies coming to you from Earth again. My recommendations will carry more weight if I have done a good job fast."

Sparling in turn studied him. "All right," he said at length. "I think probably you are a decent sort. As we foulup humans go."

Dejerine inhaled a cigar alight. However tiny, this thawing was an encouragement, especially since the engineer was a close friend of Jill. He should use the opportunity to learn a little more about these people. "Will you bear with a personal question?" he asked.

Sparling smiled sourly. "Go ahead. I may not answer."

"Why do you long-term dwellers here have such an inferiority complex with respect to the Ishtarians?"

The other man was startled. "Huh? Who says we do?"

"Perhaps I phrased it badly," Dejerine conceded. "But I have heard repeatedly how many superiorities to our species they have, both physical and mental. And yet . . . they fight wars too, don't they?"

"Not every war is as senseless as yours," Sparling snapped. He sat quiet for a few seconds. "No. Excuse me. I shouldn't have made that remark, no matter how true it is. But as for, m-m, combative behavior, it can be a survival mechanism. To the best of my information and belief, no Ishtarians fight for anything but strictly practical reasons." A new pause. "Not quite correct. Pride or revenge can be a motive, particularly in the young. However, always an individual motive. No Ishtarian ever tried to force a nationality or an

140

ideology on someone else. Under all circumstances, killing is looked on as a regrettable last-ditch necessity."

"Still, they do have ideologies, don't they? Such as various religions."

"Yeah. They aren't fanatical about them." Sparling seemed to grow more amicable as he talked. "I don't believe any Ishtarian can become what we'd call ardently religious. Certainly this planet has never seen a proselytizing faith."

"Not the—Triadic, do they call it?" Dejerine ventured a smile. "I have been reading, you see. How does that church gain converts?"

"By making more sense, to many people, than paganism does. At that, it isn't easy to get into. There's a lot of hard study required first, and examinations, and finally an expensive sacrifice. But you know, if I had a religious inclination, I'd think wistfully about joining."

"What? You can't be serious. Personifying the three suns—"

"A symbol. You can suppose they are literal gods, but you don't have to; you can take the personalities as allegorical if you prefer, tokens of the reality." Sparling looked thoughtfully at the smoke drifting from his pipe. "And the mythology does contain a great deal of truth about life, with poetry and ritual to help you feel it more directly. Bel, *the* Sun, the life-giver, who can also be terrible; Ea, the Ember Star, a diadem on the Dark which is winter and death—but the world needs them; Anu, the Rover, bringing both chaos and a chance for renewal. Yes, it strikes me as quite a bit more reasonable than a Christian God who's simultaneously one person and three, who's called merciful but left us to handle creations of his like cancer and stroke."

Dejerine, who considered himself a Christian, refrained from saying more than: "Have there been conversions among humans?"

"No," Sparling said. "Nor will be, I'm sure. If nothing else, since we can't dream right, we'd miss half the significance. We'd be like a Catholic forever unable to attend Mass or take communion. No, worse off; he could read his missal."

141

"Dreams?" Dejerine frowned. "Like the medicine dreams of primitive humans?"

"Not at all. You don't know? Well, it's so subtle and difficult an idea—for us—that I suppose it's not gotten into the average popular account of this planet. Ishtarians sleep like us, and apparently for the same basic reason: the brain needs time off the line, to assimilate data. But the Ishtarian's forebrain doesn't shut down as thoroughly as ours. He keeps more consciousness than we do. To a certain extent, he can direct his dreaming."

"I've had that experience myself, when barely asleep."

"Most humans have. With us, though, it's rudimentary and unusual. It's normal for the Ishtarian. He can choose what he'll dream about. It becomes a major part of his emotional life—maybe one reason why, in spite of using a few drugs, Ishtarians never become addicted. Of course, some have more talent for it than others. There are actually professional dreamers. They use that blend of consciousness and randomness to experience marvelous visions, and an entire art of communicating the effect afterward to an audience. Words, tone, gesture, expression, music, dance, an enormous body of ancient conventions, all go into it." Sparling sighed. "We'll never be able to share that, you and I. So, since I can't dream the Triad, it can't be anything more to me ever than a philosophical concept."

Dejerine drank smoke. "Yes," he said slowly, "I see how the Ishtarians could have a ... a rather overwhelming impact. But I don't feel they are necessarily inherently superior, except in a few departments."

"Nor do I, nor any sensible person," Sparling answered. "For instance, insofar as we can separate culture and heredity—which isn't very bloody damn far—they seem to have less sense for three-dimensional geometry than we do. Maybe because of having no arboreal ancestors? A lot of them are terrified of flying, though they know our vehicles are safe. Et cetera. No, you're wrong about an inferiority complex. We simply consider them our friends, from whom we can learn a huge amount if Earth's politicos will get off our backs."

"Will you believe that I too have been close to nonhumans?" Dejerine asked softly.

142

Sparling nodded.

It flashed in Dejerine: *He is becoming better disposed to me. Perhaps he will carry an olive branch to Jill?*

Am I in love with her? Or is it merely charm that met a longstanding celibacy, like steel meeting flint? I don't know. I never will know unless I can see her again. Often.

He said with care, "Would you mind mentioning that to Miss Conway, if opportunity should arise? I'm afraid she is angry at me because I couldn't help her native official. She gave me no chance to explain how sorry I was."

Abruptly Sparling froze over. "How can I do that?"

A hand took hold of Dejerine's heart and squeezed. "Is something wrong with her?"

"No way to tell," Sparling clipped. "She's gone north with Larreka. They've been on the trail for days."

"What? Why, that is crazy!"

"How'd you stop her? If she chooses to do research in Valennen before it's closed to us, who has the right to forbid her? At that, she sent notes to her parents and me by a messenger who was not to deliver them till she was well on her way. I flitted over the route but saw nothing. Didn't really expect to, that small a party in that big and rugged a landscape. I called, but naturally they'd switched off their transceivers when they passed beyond ordinary relay range."

"Why in cosmos would she do so mad a thing?"

"Because she's Jill, and wants to help. Yeah, 'intervention.' But she calls it research, and you'd have a sweet time proving different, Dejerine. She'll phone when she reaches Port Rua, and quite likely I'll find a research project for myself in those parts at that time. Now dog your hatch! Haven't you done enough harm?"

XIII

"And lang, lang may the maidens sit,
   Wi' the goud kaims in their hair,

A' waiting for their ain dear loves,
    For them they'll see na mair.

"O forty miles off Aberdour,
    'Tis fifty fathoms deep,
And there lies gude Sir Patrick Spens,
    Wi' the Scots lairds at his feet."

JILL FINISHED THE ancient words which she had put into the tongue of Sehala—for Ishtarians who didn't know English were often eager to hear the music of Earth—and kept her guitar ringing on while she whistled in the way of a wind over cold seas. It flitted through her awareness that she had always taken such performances for granted; but what would the unknown maker of the ballad think, could he be called from the dust and across a thousand light-years to this night?

In it, Larreka's party were camped on the northern slope of the Red Hills. Ahead of them reached the Badlands, the Dalag, and at last the coast where they would take a legionary ship. In that open tropical country, under two suns most of the day, they would travel after dark as much as might be. But here they had forest to shade them, and to make them half blind, thus slow, when stars and moons alone gave light. Therefore they rested.

A low fire tinged faces, manes, forequarters of her companions, where they reposed in a circle and every eye gleamed toward her. Further off among shadows glinted the spearheads of the watch; if nothing else, tree lions might be made sufficiently desperate by dwindling game to attach sophonts. Closer hunched the bales of supplies and a tent raised for her protection against any sudden, flayingly violent storm. She didn't expect one. The forest walled this glade in unstirring murk, stars smoldered above, the air hung warm and full of heavy pungencies. She planned to shed her few garments and sleep outside on top of her bag. Still, nobody could tell for sure what weather Anu might bring.

Her tones died away. For a time, legionaries and porters lay thoughtful, only switching their tails in the male sign for "Thank you."

144

Finally a young trooper asked, "What did the females do?"

"Eh?" Jill was brought from a reverie. *Ah, well, just speculating about what it all means, life and death, suns and worlds, the kind of question which has to get asked over and over but I don't suppose can ever be answered.* "The human females in the song? They mourned."

"Yes, but how?"

"Oh. I see. At first, when someone they love dies, most humans sob and, uh, shed water from their eyes. Afterward they carry on their lives as best they're able."

"Who helps them through?"

"We . . . we don't have institutions like yours to uphold the bereaved. Prayers and some ceremonies are all, and not everyone uses them. The need is less." Quickly, Jill added, "I don't think this is because we care for each other less than your kind does. How could you measure?" Her mind presented an image of a dolorimeter, neatly crackle-finished for maximum sales, calibrated against the International Standard Snake whose belly people feel as low as (thus making the unit of grief a length). It did not quite undermine her seriousness. "Besides, when this particular song was composed, people believed they would meet again in an afterlife."

"Like the Valennen barbarians," observed a soldier. "I reckon that's what keeps them going. They don't seem to have much else, except for eating their dead if they can."

Larreka sat up on his haunches, abruptly looming over Jill, who was on the ground leaned back against a leatherbark bole. "Don't despise 'em for that, son," he drawled. An Ishtarian voice carried so many nuances that the other might just as well have spoken words of open contempt. "Giving your body is your last service in a hungry land; and they think that eating it is a service to you, freeing the soul faster than ordinary decay would." Reflectively: "My guess is, the notion got started in the Dalag, same as a lot of different religious notions did. And there are a lot of them, never forget.

145

Who're we to say any system—including what humans have worked out—is better than the rest?"

"Well, sir, I've seen a few practices myself, and heard of more," the trooper replied. "Most make sense. But who could take some of them seriously? Like, ng-ng, in the back country on Little Iren they torture themselves after a death. I've actually seen an old female stick her hand into boiling water."

"Certain humans used to practice self-mutilation in sorrow," Jill told them. "Less extreme; but then, our bodies can't repair themselves as fast or fully as yours. Pain in the flesh—in your case, the effort to control it—covers pain in the spirit. Not that I'd try it myself, understand."

Larreka took forth pipe and tobacco pouch and began to stuff the bowl. "What's right is what works for you," he said, "and no two yous are alike. A good thing about the Gathering, maybe the best thing, is it gives you a chance to look around and find what way of life suits you the closest—or start a new way, if you can corral a few disciples."

Without being preachy, his tone was unwontedly earnest. Jill thought: *I read you, Uncle. You want to strengthen the faith in these males. They're young, they don't have your perspective on civilization, throughout their lives they've known only that it's likely to go under in the time that's now on us. In such a case, a legionary in his first or second eight-year enlistment might wonder if it's worth standing fast and dying for. Especially when it won't support us in the lonely place where we're bound. You'll take every chance you can get to tell them.*

She felt sure she was correct when he went slowly on: "Take me. If 'tweren't for the Gathering I might've become a bandit, or at best dragged out a pretty dreary existence. Instead, well, life's done me right, chopped me up a bit here and there but no more than was reasonable for all I've gotten out of it."

Ears pricked. Jill's would have too, were they able. Larreka had told her scores of stories from his career, but few from his beginnings.

"Would you like to hear?" he asked. "I'm in a kind of backward-looking mood tonight—"

146

You dear old fraud! Jill thought. *Or, if you really feel reminiscent, you've got a king-sized ulterior motive as well.*

"—and the happenings are too long ago and far away to be very personal." They murmured assent. "Okay," Larreka said, a word which had passed into the Sehalan dialect. He paused to kindle his pipe.

The fire sputtered sparks. A porter fueled it and the flames licked higher, red and yellow. Stars touched with faint light the smoke which rose straight toward them. Out in the darkness an animal hooted, the single forest sound.

"You know I'm a Haelener born," Larreka commenced between puffs. "Spent my first fifty-odd years there. The song Jill gave us raised these memories, because Haelen is like what she's told me about that Scotland on Earth, only more so, I imagine, being out-and-out polar. Even in summer, when the sun—the proper sun—never sets over most of the country, even then it's cloudy, misty, rainy, stormy, moors and bare mountains, treacherous gray seas beating on stony shores ... well, you've heard. No wonder Haeleners have a name for being skinflints, and many of them become soldiers or merchant sailors or whatever will get them out.

"But me, I wasn't restless. Clan Kerazzi, that I belonged to, counts for wealthy. You know they're organized in clans, the Haeleners. Mine holds first-rank fishing and sea-hunting waters, and inland a wide chunk of grounds for what game can be found, not that that's much by Beronnen standards. And my family was well off. My father owned the sloop he captained and a share in three more. We lived in a big snug house on the coast, at a spot where currents brought driftwood. Not needing to buy coal, we could trade our catches for other things. *Yai-ai,* a pretty good life.

"Haeleners marry young, like around twenty-four, barely out of adolescence. They have to, because they lose a lot of kids in that climate and need all the breeding years they can manage. Besides, since you marry into a different clan, everybody's anxious to make ties. Could be that's the reason for the law of a single spouse at a time and outside romps theoretically forbidden. Parents arrange the marriages, but do check with the youngsters; when your life may depend on your partner, you'd better have one who likes you."

Larreka smoked for a while in silence. When he continued, his vision was past them and into the night woods. "Saren and I were happy. We could've asked our families to raise us a house near my parents', and I could've gone on working for my father. But we wanted independence. So the Kerazzis deeded us a spread on Northwind Bay, bleak as a usurer and sterile as his wife but with, ng-ng-ng, possibilities. You see, the fishing wasn't bad thereabouts; and storms often drove in big critters, well worth the trouble and risk of hunting; and in the hills behind, a tin mine was getting started. The miners took the stuff off overland, but I figured in time they'd be digging out enough to make sea transport better—and any ships which put into that bay would need a pilot who knew it. Eventually this came true, and we opened a small tavern as well. Saren's cooking tasted mighty good to sailors in from a long haul, and I was a popular tapster, I don't mind boasting. Meanwhile we had four kids who lived, three males and a female, fine 'uns.

"Sure, I'd no reason not to sacrifice to the gods. Having yarned with a lot of outlanders, I knew our gods didn't rule the universe. In fact, I sort of doubted they were more than a story. However, we'd suffered less than most folk, and fair's fair. Besides, respectability's useful to have. Why not go through the rites?

"Until, after twenty-three years, we were bound for Daystead—"

Larreka broke off. Jill stroked his back. He threw her a smile . . . of thanks?

"Daystead, sir?" asked a soldier from the Fiery Sea.

"A rally place," Larreka said. "Or maybe you don't know about those? Well, think. Most of Haelen gets no sun in winter. Your skin-plants would die, that long in the dark. A few peninsulas stick north of the Circle and catch a little daylight. Everybody has to crowd into them in season. Law and custom turn on this. The clans pitch in to build and maintain housing, stock food—all the necessities, including ways to keep people

148

from hating each other after they've been packed in like that for a while.

"We, my family belonged at Daystead. We'd always gone to and fro by boat, there being a mountain range in between which is apt to have killingly foul weather. This year"—Larreka's tone flattened—"the weather was at sea. We got dismasted, swamped, and driven into the surf. None but me made shore alive. I'd kept a grip on my daughter's mane, but the vines tore loose. . . . Never mind. I raised a cairn over what drifted to the strand and limped on into Daystead, mainly to let our kinfolk know."

He puffed again for a spell, during which the flames died back, the darkness crept near, and then very slowly, almost timidly, a crooked Urania rose above treetops which it tinted silver, the sole cool thing in the night except for his memories of winter Haelen.

"I've gone on like this," he said at last, "not to make you feel sorry for me, but to show you the situation. One more thing you must know. Remember, different nations have different ways of taking a member over a loss. What the clans do is to provide him or her company, day and night, until the wound seems to've healed. Somebody's always beside the mourner, ready to lend a hand or talk or whatever. Usually several persons are. For most this is good. At least it's better than brooding alone, in a country which is often ghastly empty. Besides, the way of Haelen is to help your neighbor without stint—you save your grasping greed for outsiders—because you never know when you might need him. Yes, people meant well by me.

"But . . . for the past three octads, my household had dwelt aside. We had visitors, but they were hunters, miners, sailors, fishers, traders—friends but not intimates, if you follow me. I'd gotten used to being on my own, me and my wife and our children. We hated the crowding at Daystead, and kept to ourselves as much as might be without giving offense. Here, suddenly, I was allowed *no* privacy. And—well, Jill will understand. I hurt like fury, but there was no call to treat me as if I'd lost a family I'd had two or three sixty-fours. They did. It was the custom. Also, I suppose, it was something to do, to keep interested in, during those stretched-out blacknesses between glimmers of sun.

"And they expected me to honor the gods! 'After what the gods have done to me?' I answered. That shocked my clan worse than it would have otherwise, midwinter being a time when you live on such a thin edge. Me, I challenged the gods to come down and fight like honest males.

"No reason to say much more. I'm sure you can see how trouble got worse and worse, the bulk of it my fault."

They didn't assume he'd gone a bit crazy, and bear with him till he recovered, Jill thought, *because Ishtarians practically never do go crazy.*

"In the end, I walked out," Larreka said. "By then, the sun was far enough returned that I could live off the country, though that was mighty lean living, what shellers and seaweed I could scrounge on the beaches, what fist-sized animals I could knock down with a rock inland. Yet my bad temper was lucky for me after a fashion. You see, soon afterward a late blizzard hit Daystead, really vicious. It brought the deaths of several people and great hardship to the rest when fuel gave out.

"Now, mostly the Haeleners are not ignorant. Mostly they didn't think my ranting at the gods and our folkways had caused this. But a few did. I don't blame them for falling back into old superstitions. You northerners can't know what that season does to your soul, the cold and gloom, aye, the auroras that're called the Dead Fires. . . . As for the majority, well, I was not popular. I'd made it hard for them to get through winter.

"So I wasn't likely to be offered another wife. And a bachelor there can't hope to be more than an ill-paid hirling. Unless he turns robber, which in my bitterness I actually considered.

"Yet—there was the Gathering. There was the trade it makes possible. In the spring, the merchant ships started coming again for our hides, minerals, salted ichthy, preserved bipen eggs. By then I was in sorry shape, but somehow talked myself into a deckhand's stall.

"And for the next forty-eight-odd years I wandered half the world. I'd never imagined how big and wonderful it is. Eventually I joined the Zera, and later found me the female I still have. Everything came to me out of the Gathering.

"Lads, this isn't all that civilization is about, not by a long spearcast. But it's a sizeable part of the thing. Take a while to imagine what your lives would've been like without the Gathering. Ask yourselves if you don't owe an equal chance to your children."

Larreka folded his forelegs and settled back down. The group took the hint that he wished to speak no further, and made ready to retire. Jill scrambled to kneel beside him and throw an arm across his neck. The mane restled scratchily. His warmth, the blent smells of iron maleness and tobacco smoke, a sense of rubbery muscles beneath the moss-like pelt, flowed through her.

"Uncle, you never told me," she said in English.

"Never got around to it before." He left unspoken: *How much can I tell you of a life which has already been four times as long as the most you can hope for?*

"What say we get some sleep?" he went on immediately. "Anu'll soon be up, blast its bloated belly; and we've stiff country to cross. Never miss a chance to flop your bones, soldier."

"Yes, sir. Good night." She brushed lips across a leathery cheek. The cat-whiskers tickled her.

Stretched out on the bag, arm across eyes, she wondered what he would choose to dream of. And what would come to her?

Or who? If she could pick, whom would she most like to have join her in dream?

XIV

EVER AS MIDSUMMER drew nigh, the True Sun paced closer on the heels of the Red One. Meanwhile the Cruel Star grew and grew in heaven. At its nearest, said old stories, it would loom seeably larger than its rival.

Drought seared Valennen, but storms lashed the Fiery Sea.

Likewise did the Tassui. During the past octad, Overlings had been building fleets to harry islands from which the legions were departed, and the commerce between them. Arnanak had been too busy ashore for much buccaneering of his own. However, he used all the labor he could spare in Ulu's shipyard. Some vessels he lent out to raiders whom he egged against the east coast and the Ehur archipelago. They pulled the attention and strength of the enemy in that direction while he readied his inland campaign. Some keels he held in reserve until now—now when his time looked ripe to close the ring.

For the Zera sat only in Port Rua. Its sallies were fitful into those hinterlands which, a bare year ago, civilization had imagined it dominated. United behind Arnanak, the warriors of Valennen beat off every such foray, or faded from sight and let it waste itself on emptiness.

He was not content with that. As long as the Gathering had a sea-supplied base here, his flanks and rear would be too unsafe for the ventures further south that he planned on. Due haste was needful. Though scouts and spies reported no sign of a movement anywhere in the Gathering to send reinforcements, this could change. Before it did, he wanted Port Rua under siege ashore and blockade afloat . . . and not a single soldier getting home to fight on a later day.

Thus he put himself at the head of a flotilla. They sailed afar to Castle Island, overcame a weak defense, pillaged widely, and tore down stone buildings raised by agents of the Gathering. Else these might have become fortresses. Arnanak meant for the inhabitants erelong to have Tassu masters, where they were not simply replaced in their still fertile home. Beyond this, his purposes were to learn by direct experience how well his naval organization, modeled on the legionary, worked: to exercise a number of quite young males; and to get away for a span from dull demands on the Overling of Overlings.

On their way back northwestward, a typhoon scattered his ships. He didn't believe any would be lost.

152

His people had a tradition of outfacing wild weather. But it was the reason why he had only two hulls with him when he spied the vessel from Beronnen.

"Sail ohai-ah!"

The lookout's call brought Arnanak springing to the poop. Seas ran high, gray-green and foam-laced, blue-black in their troughs. Spindrift flew blindingly and stingingly off wave-crests. Overhead, low clouds raced gray, high clouds roiled. Double shafts of sunlight struck through, double colored, to shatter in glints and spill in bleams. A wind shrilled nearly cold. The waters brawled and rumbled, the deck swung underfoot.

He picked the strange craft out, a fleck afar. Behind it, the peak of a volcano on Black Island thrust above a dim horizon. Smoke blew tattered from the mountain's throat. He focused a telescope he had once bought from a trader. The shape grew clear, not a lean low Valennener but a high-sided two-masted square-rigger such as plied out of Beronnen.

"A Gathering transport, bound for Port Rua," he decided, and offered the telescope to Usayuk, the mate. "Surely alone. Steer to intercept and signal *Devourer* to come along."

"I'd say yonder's a legionary, not a merchantman," Usayuk replied carefully. "Belike they've guards aboard and ballistas ready cocked."

"The better reason for a close look. Fear not. We can maneuver around them like fangfish closing in on a sea judge."

Usayuk stiffened. "I never said I was afraid."

Arnanak gave him a stark smile. "Nor did I. Let me own, instead, that I am he who feels a little unease, at what their faring may portend."

For if the enemy has decided after all to pay the cost of holding fast north of the equator— No, now. What use a single shipload?—Well, a convoy may have been flung apart as we were. Or if it carries something those humans are giving the legion to fight with—

Arnanak thrust the thought away. Worry was boot-less, the more so when he knew not with any surety what the will or the powers of the aliens were. Therefore let him go boldly forward. The Three would dance out his fate: in the mighty rhythms of Sun and

153

Ember Star, and in that chaos the Rover brought, from which free will might snatch a chance to begin a new cycle of destinies.

Commands and responses roared the length of *Leaper*'s decks. It had been tacking. To catch the foreigner meant a nearly straight downwind run. The mainmast boom came over in a thunder of cloth. Arnanak considered ordering the topsail unfurled, but abided by the mate's judgment that jibs and mizzen simply be kept poled out wing and wing with the mainsail. *Devourer* did likewise. Both gaudy hulls bounded ahead.

Males busked themselves. Deckhands fastened onto ankles those hooks whereby they could swarm into the rigging at need. Some climbed aloft as archers. Others went below to stand by the oars. The rest of the crew unlashed timbers and dovetailed these together to make a platform and gangway forward of the mast. There several took stance, while followers waited beneath. Arnanak was among the former. Aside from helmet and shoulderpieces, he had left off armor—it would drown him should he go overboard—and carried just shield, spear, and cutting weapons.

The platform jutted slightly over the water. He stood at its edge, feet braced against roll, pitch, and yaw. The wind from aft thrummed in shrouds and tossed the leaves of his mane. It smelled of salt and wildness. To him came Igini his son, who asked in a growl, "When we board, may I take the lead?"

"No, that's for me," Arnanak said. "You may come right behind." An old thought passed through him, how foolish it really was that a leader must always be in the van. But he might not live to see his Tassui become a soberly calculating civilized race. "Anyhow, if they're strong they won't be worth the risk and loss of attacking, when our holds are already stuffed with booty."

"What? But then they'll go make war against our brothers ashore!"

"Say, rather, they'll enter the cage we're building. Frankly, I'd have steered wide of them, save that a glance across their decks should give a hint as to whether Sehala is serious about keeping Port Rua." Arnanak lifted his telescope again.

They were preparing for battle on the southland craft. He saw only a few legionaries among the sailors. They might have more below, ready to spring a surprise, but he doubted that; they could not have foretold this encounter. To be sure, as Fire Time neared, merchant crews also got trained for combat. Nevertheless, here was not likely any troopship. It must be a carrier of messages, incidental supplies, maybe a personage or two on a special mission.

Then should he close? They'd give a stern reply. Two lucky hits from those ballistas fore and aft could wreck his vessels. Or he himself might be killed, and the alliance he had forged soon rust away. . . . Well, he took that hazard whenever he trod into action. And he might win a treasure or learn a thing of unreckonable value. . . .

What was that form which came from a deckhouse? Two legs, no body-barrel whatsoever, wrapped in cloths though long yellow-brown strands fluttered from beneath a headband—

"We fight!" Arnanak bellowed.

While shouts rang and weapons rattled around him, he leaned over the platform edge and told Usayuk: "Hark, they bear a human among them. Can we capture it, who knows what it may tell us, what ransom we can get or bargains make? Bring us alongside and grapple fast. I'll lead our storm. But *all* we want is that human. The same eyeblink as we come back with it, cast loose and make off. Signal *Devourer* to take their starboard side, as we their port."

"Hu—man-n?" The mate showed unease. Like most Tassui, he had merely heard rumors about the strangers; but those whispered of wizardry.

"It may unleash a terror against us," Arnanak admitted. "*Vu-wa*, we can be no worse than slain, can we? And forsooth the Gathering will never of its free choice give us an opening unto those creatures." He raised his head and added in an iron tone: "Moreover, I am ally to the dauri."

Usayuk, and those others who heard, traced signs against ill luck. Yet they were heartened. Though nobody could be sure either what powers the dauri commanded, they lived much closer by than humans.

155

The Torchbearer cast a light out of the murk ahead, onto the Beronnener ship, as if to set it ablaze.

Arrows whined from topmasts to decks. A ballista stone made a fountain within a javelin throw of *Leaper*. On both barbarian craft, sails were struck and oars thrust forth. They had worked themselves ahead of the southerner in such wise that its sails—the sole motive power it had—brought it straight in between them.

Arnanak saw the human and a helper rush around, passing out metal tubes with stocks akin to a crossbow's. Soldiers and sailors took unskilled aim. He saw an archer of his crumple and fall from the shrouds, to smash on deck in a splash of purple. But how different was this from a dart-death? And there was no time for fear.

Inner oars withdrew again. Hulls grated together. Hurled at the ends of cables, grappling irons bit fast.

Swifter and more maneuverable, the northland ships did have less freeboard by a head-height. This alone had overawed many a would-be raider, in the bright days of the Gathering. But since then Arnanak had devised his knockdown platforms and caused them to be widely built.

That on which he stood thrust above the gunwale of his enemy. He pounced downward. His sword belled and sparked on hostile iron.

Beronneners swarmed against him. He laid around, struck aside a descending blade, caught ax-thunder on his shield, chopped into meat and bone. Few yells lifted. Breath loudened and hoarsened; in the chill wind, pelts steamed white. More Tassui boarded, and more. They cleared a space.

Above heads and helmets, Arnanak saw the human. It stood beside a legionary on the foredeck. In its hands was a sorcerer's weapon. But the maelstrom of infighting made firearms well-nigh useless. A shot was as likely to hit friend as foe, Arnanak deemed. *Anyhow—move!* He howled the war cry of Ulu and pushed ahead.

With him came his warriors. Their opponents had not awaited a breakthrough at a single place; that was not the way of boarders who sought to capture a ship.

Arnanak's gang hewed through their mass and sped across bare planks beyond.

Igini outdashed his father and pounded first up the gangway. The human raised its weapon and squeezed trigger. Igini's head exploded. He fell off the board and lay in purple-soaked shapelessness. Arnanak cast his ax. He could have thrown it to kill, but he meant to stun. The top of helve and blade caught the human in the midriff. It lurched and sat down. Its weapon clattered free. Arnanak reached the being and swept it into his grasp. The legionary had drawn sword and battled furiously. Sheer weight of arriving warriors drove him into the bows.

The southerners rallied and loped against this little band which had let itself be pinched off. Arnanak's males held the gangway. He himself went to the port rail. Gripped in his left arm, the human struggled vainly. His right waved at Usayuk. The mate ordered grapnels released. Driven by oars on the farther side, *Leaper* edged forward until its foredeck was below Arnanak. He sprang. Usayuk's rowers kept their vessel in place while the rest of the raiders followed.

They were not the whole group. Some, boxed amidships, must take whatever mercy the foe chose to give. Some lay dead, among them Igini, who had been young and glad. But a male could proudly lose a son or life in a cause like this—the capture of a human.

"Fall off!" Usayuk bawled. "Get away!"

Devourer came into view from around the stern of the transport. Its attack on the starboard side had had much to do with making Arnanak's exploit possible. Both Tassu craft set sail anew. Wind skirled for them. The Beronneners would have no hope of overhauling.

The human staggered to its feet and yelled words. The legionary who had tried to defend it appeared at the rail. He carried a chest which he must have hurried off to fetch from a cabin. Already a broad gap of water churned between him and his uncanny companion. He whirled the casket by a strap and let fly. His cast was heroic. The box boomed against the deckhouse.

"Overboard with that!" Usayuk cried: for it might be deadly.

The human could not have followed his Tassu, but

157

did see how sailors jumped to obey. "No!" it wailed in Sehalan. "Else I'll die—"

"Belay!" Arnanak called. "We'll keep yon chest." And in Sehalan to the human, harshly because of Igini: "I do want you alive for a while, at least."

XV

THEY SHIPPED ENSIGN Donald Conway to Mundomar in a large group of air corpsmen. The personnel carrier was old and overcrowded. You had to do everything by turns, by the numbers. To pigeonhole yourself in a bunk another fellow had been using, in the middle of a vast lattice of identical bunks, and lie there listening to your brothers in arms snore and smelling their farts somehow didn't relate very well to crusades for rescuing gallant pioneers threatened by monstrous aliens and securing mankind's future among the stars. Not that he had been naïve, exactly—old Uncle Larreka was blunt-spoken when he shared his memories—yet he had pictured himself as a kind of legionary. Was he, instead, a plug-in unit?

Well, he triumphed at the poker table, and refrained from admitting this was because he had learned the hard way, from his sister Jill. That made him wonder how she was doing, and Mother and Dad and Alice and her husband and their kids. He missed them more than anybody he had met on Earth.

Monotony became tension as the convoy neared its goal. In merely interplanetary space, it would certainly be detected by the Naqsans, whose fleet was likewise busy around that sun. If they decided on an assault—

Tension became terror. The Naqsans did attack. And the air corpsmen had nothing to do but crouch jammed together between blank bulwarks. If they took a direct hit, they would likely never know it. Conway learned how excellent was the American expression "sweating it out." To judge from the stink and clamminess, his skin exuded every poison his body could make.

After many hours—mostly devoted to maneuvers

and computations, then a swift burst of furies, then more hours when men must wait—the enemy evidently decided the price was too high, and withdrew. The convoy had suffered losses of its own. These included a ranger which had taken a near miss, peeling back half its hull. The crew was spacesuited, but a number of suits got ripped open, and all men took varying amounts of blast, heat, and hard radiation. The convoy rescued what casualties it could and divided them among the ships that remained.

Travelers on the personnel carrier gave up bunks and helped tend the wounded while the voyage proceeded through its last stages. Don Conway thus experienced men with pulverized bones, with faces cooked away and eyeballs melted, with vomiting and diarrhea and the sloughing off of hair, skin, flesh, intelligence. He had seen death before, in animals and a few sophonts; but the latter had been peaceful. Now he understood why, for a year after Aunt Ellen perished in the Dalag, Jill had had nightmares. He even guessed this was part of the reason for her closeness to Larreka.

But Aunt Ellen was the victim of a senseless accident. These men had died, were dying, would survive as cripples when cloning wasn't feasible, in a great cause. Right?

At first his unit was stationed near Barton, the capital of Eleutheria, largest human settlement on Mundomar. Action was slight everywhere on the planet. The front had stabilized, which Conway read as "stalemated." Desultory clashes occurred on land, in the air, at sea. "Wait a while," Eino Salminen warned. "The lull is mainly due to lack of supplies on either side. But Earth and Naqsa are pouring in matériel. Soon the fun begins."

"Why can't we blockade?" Conway inquired.

"They would try the same against us. We would get battles with heavy nuclear weapons at satellite altitudes, maybe in atmosphere. Bad enough to meet in deep space. Close-in fighting of that kind would probably ruin the planet we are supposed to be fighting about. Worse, it could provoke a full-scale war between the mother worlds."

Conway guessed he understood this wisdom. Neither Eleutherians nor Tsheyakkans missiled each other's towns. The latter, in their drive to regain Sigurdssonia, had occupied several communities of the former; but he learned to scoff (privately) at what atrocity stories he heard. If you checked, the proven horrors were incidental to combat—children got in the way of bullets, et cetera—and Tsheyakkan military governors, while strict, treated Eleutherians as humanely (!) as was the case where situations were reversed. Maybe more so, but censorship made it impossible to discover the truth of that.

He was glad to be out of the spaceship and able to stride about freely, in safety. However, he found little to do on leave. Barton had a few night clubs, live theaters, and whatnot. If you'd been on Earth, they seemed dull, crowded, overpriced. It was easier to stay on base and watch a 3V recording. A couple of philanthropic organizations made an effort to get the citizens and their new allies acquainted, by way of dances and invitations to homes. By and large, the results made Conway uncomfortable. These were good folks, no doubt; their courage and devotion were fantastic; but weren't they, well, rather dour?

A girl asked while she danced with him: "Why have no more of you come?"

Another girl declined his suggestion of an evening out: "I'm in war production, you know, working every day. No, please don't feel sorry for me. This is what I want to do—serve. It's different for you, of course. You've always been rich and safe."

His host at dinner got a tad drunk and said: "Yes, I've lost one boy already. Two more are down there. Earth supplies weapons, we supply warm bodies." He grew indignant when Conway remarked that this was equally true of Naqsa and the Tsheyakkans.

The countryside offered roads where a person might like. But Conway thought it unattractive. No matter how thoroughly terraformed, the district remained flat, hot, wet, almost always thickly overcast. Amidst regimented trees and fields, green though they were, he missed Ishtar's wild red and gold; he missed a sight of sun, moons, stars. Naturally the Eleutherians were

160

emotional about their homeland. But did *he* have to be?

The unit was ordered to the front. Action was rising afresh.

Yet "the front" was nearly a meaningless noise. Tsheyakkans held parts of southern Sigurdssonia. Occasionally they would withdraw before an Eleutherian advance—or vice versa—whether as the consequence of a battle or as a phase in a larger plan. Humans had leapfrogged to a similar spotty occupation of western Hat'hara and islands near that continent. Besides those lands, the ocean and skies between saw engagements.

Conway's squadron did on its first patrol. When his headset informed him that detectors registered hostile craft bound this way, he felt crazily that it couldn't be real, he was trapped in a fever dream, nobody could want to kill him whom so many people loved. Meanwhile his fingers did what was needful with drilled-in skill. And that was strange too, being a passenger in his body. Then the Tsheyakkans arrived and the dogfight erupted. He forgot to be afraid.

He noticed himself enjoying what he did, as if this were a poker game for stakes higher than he could afford to lose—

—where he suddenly drew a fourth queen. The enemy flyers were mean-looking elongated teardrops, against lead sky and mercury sea; but they were no better than his Shark, and their pilots didn't have even his hasty operant training. One plunged at him. He slipped aside from the rake of tracers, rolled about and got the bandit in his sights; automatons did the rest, fireworks and a long, long smoking spiral down into the drink. Accelerations made him giddy, quasi-drunk. He whooped his joy till the next opponent showed, whereupon he became strictly business.

He couldn't swear that he made a second kill. He did know that his outfit won hands down and went jubilant back to an otherwise dismal base in the jungle. At small cost to themselves, they'd practically wiped out the croaker escadrille.

Small cost. . . .Trouble was, it included Eino Salminen, who was Conway's best friend in the service and who'd gotten married very shortly before leaving

Earth. Twice Conway tried to write a letter to Finland. He never completed it. Each time, he'd start wondering if that pilot who burned under his guns had been married too. *Not that I feel like a murderer or anything. It was him or me, in a war. I only wonder about him.*

Rain roared on the barrack. Its unconditioned interior was a steam bath full of swamp stenches. Men who huddled near the 3V were stripped to their skivvies. Nobody dared go nude, Conway suspected—at least, he himself would have been afraid the others might thing he was projecting a proposition—or was that merely a quirk he'd acquired? An environment both womanless and weird did things to your mind. Ah, well, probably his bare ass wouldn't like direct contact with a chair anyway.

Barton was 'casting the latest news tape to arrive. Mostly it reported Christmas and Chanukkah festivities on Earth, this year especially elaborate because the Universal Love movement had grown so popular. But there were stories as well on a complete Neanderthal skeleton discovered in North Africa, and almost the whole of Apollo turning out to rescue a little boy trapped in a broken-down mono shuttle, and Lima's new fusion-power plant, and an acrimonious election campaign in Russia, and a spectacularly messy divorce in the Philippine royal family, and a riot in New York Welfare, and a Bangkok fashion czar decreeing triangular cloaks. . . .Toward the end, it was announced that a skirmish had occurred between Terrestrial and Naqsan space forces in the Vega sector. As for Mundomar, nothing special—

Major Samuel McDowell, Eleutherian liaison officer, stirred. "Did you notice the date on that tape?" he asked. "Happens to be the day my brother-in-law got killed."

"Huh?" somebody said. "Too bad. I'm sorry."

"He wasn't the only one," McDowell said. "Enemy came out of the jungle and shot up the whole village where his unit was. Lot of civilians bought it too. Filthy terrorists."

"You call your men in Hat'hara guerrillas," Conway couldn't help muttering.

162

McDowell gave him a whetted stare. "Where are your sympathies, Ensign?"

Against the inward-crowding heat, Conway felt his cheeks and ears flush. "I'm a combat flyer, Major," he snapped. *I don't owe servility to a ranking officer of a foreign country, do I?* He nearly added that they have a proverb on Earth about not looking gift horses in the teeth, but checked himself. If McDowell complained to Captain Jacobowitz, Ensign Conway might go on the carpet. Besides, the poor devil had suffered grief, and did see the war as a matter of survival. "No offense intended, sir."

McDowell eased a trifle. "Oh, I'm not a fanatic," he said. "If the croakers would be reasonable— But think. To Earth, what's going on here is a sideshow! Or less than that. Can't they see we're bleeding?"

In a quick and brilliant series of actions, human airmen cleared the skies. Tsheyakkans were no match for them.

After that it should have been easy to interdict supply lines and reduce cut-off invasion forces from above. Don Conway personally sent a surface watership to the bottom and probably a submarine freighter. But the next time around, a missile speared his flyer, as was happening unexpectedly often to his corps. He ejected, and bobbed about in the sea till a rescue bug hooked him out.

This earned him a week's R&R in Barton. A polite gentleman from Earth phoned him at his hotel room, requested an interview, and treated him to the kind of dinner he had not guessed existed on Mundomar. In time, after numerous cordialities, the gentleman got to the point.

"I gather you've been on the Shka coast. It's devilish hard to collect any real information about that area. The Eleutherian authorities sit on everything and— Well, see here, Ensign. You're not an Eleutherian, you're a . . . m-m-m, you're under the jurisdiction of the World Federation. Think of that as your nationality, where your loyalty belongs. And people, important people in the Federation would definitely like to know if their suspicions are right, about the oil in Shka."

"Oil?" Conway was astounded.

"Yes. I'm not a scientist, but it works like this. Mundomar had an unusual evolution, starting when the whole system was a condensing dust cloud and going on through a mess of complicated planetology and biochemistry. Its petroleum contains several pretty unique materials. Extremely valuable as starting points for organic syntheses, like medicines, you know? Sure, we can manufacture the stuff from scratch, but pumping it out of the ground here and shipping it home is a hell of a lot cheaper. (Say, do you care for another drink?) The question is, when peace comes and the planet's parceled out, will the rich sources be in friendly hands, or the hands of ungrateful sons of bitches who'll screw us on price, or even the hands—flippers—of croakers? If Earth knew for sure, confidentially, what territories have these deposits, well, we could better plan our military campaigns and make our political deals. I don't imagine you have the complete information; but every scrap helps. Helps the Federation, that is."

Conway almost said he had none, and if he did would still have seen no particular reason to contribute to the profits of producers or the kudos of commissioners. He halted his larynx in time, and spoke acccording to a swiftly devised plan. Item for item, he bought drinks with hints, and finally a night's worth of delightful girl with an outright work of his imagination.

He didn't think the Earthling would mind too much, being after all on expense account. Anyway, his furlough was soon over and he returned to combat.

For a while, that consisted of runs over wilderness. He blackened the areas he was told to blacken, and got no more reply than rifle bullets. The trouble was, the job had no end.

"They don't quit, the slimy bastards," said a captain of armored infantry. Conway had burned out a generator and landed for help at an advanced Eleutherian post. It was a village lately recaptured, ruins in the rain, full of a rotten-sweet odor. Humans rarely bothered to bury Naqsans, whose corpses couldn't infect them. The captain spat on one. "They can live off this country better than we can. And their mother world's getting war supplies through to them—"

His gaze went to a fence which confined a number of prisoners. They weren't mistreated; but nobody here spoke any language of theirs, and physicians who knew their ailments were in short supply. The big seal-shapes comforted each other as best they might. "We'll collect plenty more like those, though," the captain said. "A hard push is in the works. You'll be busy yourself, Ensign."

Conway flew high above the clouds, far into the stratosphere. Beneath him shone whiteness, around him deep blue and his companion warriors, above him the sun and a few brightest stars. But mostly he saw Ishtar.

And felt it, heard it, smelled it, tasted it. When he was little, how infinitely tall his father was, and how beautiful his mother. And Jill and Alice were pests he couldn't have done without. When Larreka came around, he'd smoldered with jealousy at the way the soldier favored Jill; but *he* took overnight boat trips on the Jayin with Dad, just the two of them waking up in an enormous misty morning. . . . He remembered woods and seas, his early discovery of the arts of Earth, an eo-sweetheart, O God, a triple daybreak seen from climbed heights in the Thunderhead Range. . . .

His earphones alerted him. What? Were any bandits left?

Their speed into his vision was terrifying. They were not the kind he had encountered before. Gaunt delta wings, these bore a wheel emblem whose recognition struck like a fist. Naqsa's. The League itself. Yonder pilots weren't half-trained colonists stuffed into unfamiliar machines. Naqsa had followed Earth's lead and sent air corps regulars.

"Hang onto your scalps, boys," said Conway's commander; and the two squadrons penetrated.

It was raining when he got his consciousness back. Jungle crowded the wreckage of his flyer. He had no memory of being hit or of a crash landing.

Mainly he knew pain. Blood was all over everything. His left leg was crimson pulp from which jutted bone

splinters. He thought dimly that he must have broken
ribs too, because each shallow breath hurt so. The universe had a scratch across it that he discovered was in
his right eye.

He fumbled at his radio. Nothing happened. The
canopy was burst open. Rain hammered and stammered over him. Where was his first aid kit? Where the
fuck was his God damned first aid kit?

He found it at last and tried to prepare a hypospray,
to dull the pain enough that he could think. His shaky
hands kept dropping the apparatus. Presently he quit,
since it hurt too much to bend over in his harness and
grope after the stuff.

Later he began feeling warm and numb. The crack
in creation faded, along with the rest of everything. *Go
away, death,* he thought somewhere afar. *You're not
welcome here.*

Why not? asked the gentle dark.

Because I . . . I'm busy, that's why.

All right. I'll wait till you've finished.

KILLED IN ACTION: Lt. Cmdr. Jan H. Barne-
veldt, Ens. Donald R. Conway, Ens. James L.
Kamekona. . . .

MOURN FOR: Keh't'hiw-a-Suq of Dzuaq, Whiccor
the Bold, Nowa Rachari's Son. . . .

XVI

THEORETICALLY, DEJERINE COULD have done all his
communicating with Primavera at his worksite. In
practice, he needed relief from that desert as much as
any of his men. Furthermore, an electronic image is no
real substitute for a live presence. It is immensely easier
to stay cold and impersonal toward the former. Hence
he flitted often to the town for consultations as well as
avowed recreation. The individuals who most strongly
resented his mission had the wit to see, in time, that he
had not instigated it, he too meant well by Ishtar and

might be persuaded to urge a change of policy upon the government.

After a couple of hours spent on technical problems in Sparling's office—the location and most efficient utilization of natural resources needed for the project—the engineer abruptly said around his pipe: "Tell you what. Anyef, the area's top dream artist, is giving a performance in Stubbs Park. Why don't you come to dinner at my house and then we'll see the show together?"

"You are very kind," Dejerine said, surprised.

"Aw, you've turned out to be not such a bad fellow. Besides, frankly, the more you see of native culture, the harder you may work to help save it."

"I have tried to appreciate playoffs from your data banks. It isn't easy."

"Uh-huh. It isn't simply foreign. Music, dance, and drama are more subtle, more complex than anything I believe our species has ever done. But while Anyef's conveying her latest experience, I can give you a running commentary."

"Won't that disturb the audience?"

"I've got a micro transceiver set in a bracelet, and I'll find you another you can hang on an ear. Whispering won't bother anybody: the wind'll be noisier. I think that's why she's performing this dream, whatever it is, this evening—she'll use the wind somehow as part of her language—" The phone chimed on Sparling's desk. "Excuse me." He punched acceptance.

Goddard Hanshaw's ruddy features apppeared in the screen, unwontedly grave. "Bad news, Ian," he said. "I thought you, being a particular friend of hers, ought to know right away."

The pipestem broke between Sparling's jaws. He caught the bowl automatically and put it in the ashtray with exaggerated care. The ashtray was an iridescent chelosaur shell—"Larreka called from Port Rua. Jill Conway's been captured by the barbarians"—which she had given him.

Dejerine sprang out of his seat. *"Qu'est-ce que vous dites?"* he yelled.

Sparling waved him down. "Details, please," he said.

"They borrrowed a ship from the Kalain Glorious on the Dalag coast, but the commandant refused to spare

167

more than a handful of soldiers for its protection; claimed he needs every sword he can get to hold North Beronnen safe," Hanshaw related. "He may be right. However, the upshot was that a couple of Valennnener galleys, doubtless out pirating, attacked the ship in the Fiery Sea. Their crews boarded, were either beaten off in short order or deliberately retreated after they'd grabbed Jill. On the basis of prisoner interrogations ‒Larreka didn't specify his methods‒he thinks probably the kidnapping was the whole objective, when their chief had seen a human was aboard. That does give hope. If they want her for a hostage or a bargaining counter, they shouldn't hurt her, on purpose anyhow. Their boats being too fast to pursue, Larreka proceeded on his way. The thing happpened, uh, three days ago. He's just arrived, made straight for the big transmitter."

Nausea rose in Sparling's gullet. "What do you mean, they won't hurt her?" he snapped. "'Unmixed Ishtarian food‒"

"Larreka's a smart old devil. The moment he saw her borne off, he ran to fetch her box of supplement, and managed to toss it onto the other deck."

Sparling sagged in his chair. *I wish God were more to me than the mayor's nickname, so I could thank him.*

Then: *But she'll be in that hell-country, alone among savages. They won't realize she can't endure many things they take for granted. Or any superstitious notion may enter their heads.*

Strength returned. "I'll go there." Sparling said. "Make sure I can have a fast long-range vehicle, will you? First, though, I'll check what else I can arrange. Shall I call you back?"

"Yes, please do. I . . . I've got to notify her family." Hanshaw's image blanked out.

Sparling swiveled around to face Dejerine. The officer's tanned countenance had become a piece of leather in which the eyeballs stood like white-ringed targets.

"You heard," Sparling said. "What do you propose we do?"

Dejerine worked his lips before he responded, "What have you in mind?"

"Don't worry, nothing rash. I'll try to negotiate her

168

release. But if they don't approach us about that soon, or if they demand impossible terms, we'll show them they'd bloody well better bring her back unharmed."

"You would threaten—?"

"What else? They savvy force. When we start sinking their ships, demolishing their homesteads, strafing every armed band we come on, they'll get the message." *And if Jill has died—*

"Aerial punishment." Dejerine nodded heavily. "My command is to supply the means."

"You've got 'em. We don't. We haven't a single military device. Never expected to need any." Anger lifted. "Well, how long are you going to sit there? You didn't need those battle flyers you brought along—till now—to justify your presence on Ishtar!"

Dejerine gathered resolution. "That would be insubordination on my part," he said. "Under no circumstances besides a direct attack on us may we, any man or any equipment, be used against natives. The policy has more reasons than idealism. If we got embroiled in local quarrels—"

Sparling's left hand squeezed that arm of his chair; his right fist doubled upon the other. He spoke slowly, congratulating himself on the levelness of his voice. "Don't you think you'll compromise your mission worse by provoking a complete boycott of it and all your personnel? That's what will happen if you abandon her, you know. I'll see to it personally."

Dejerine reached toward him as if across a gulf. "'Can you not realize?" he pleaded. "I willl dispatch a message at once, requesting permission. I am fond of her myself."

"How long will your courier boat take to reach Earth? How long will those lardbrain GHQ bureaucrats take to process your letter—and deny you?"

Dejerine's tone hardened. "If I disobeyed, I would be removed from this post. My successor would likely be much less *simpático,* considering what trouble you caused the Navy. I can carry on if you boycott us, but it will require using powers of confiscation and arrest, criminal penalties for refusing to give us essential cooperation." He stood; Sparling did too. "Sir, I will leave you. Please note, I have not ordered anyone to refrain from helping Miss Conway. Please do not be so conspicuous about whatever you do that you force me. And ... you would be wise to keep me informed of events ... and I will be more grateful than you can guess." He bowed. "Good day, sir."

Sparling stared at the door for a minute after it had closed.

Doubtless he's right, he thought drearily. *Well, I suppose I'd better go home and pack.*

When he stepped outside, it was into a hot blast, which hissed down the street and brawled in the treetops. Bel glared and Anu glowered where red-tinged streaks of cloud hastened through a sky that was otherwise merciless blue. The air smelled dusty. Few people were about. He didn't notice if they greeted him or not. As he strode, he was working on a set of plans, one for each contingency he could imagine.

Except Jill's death. If her laughter blew away forever on the wind, nothing would matter very much.

His wife was in their living room. With most undertakings suspended, Primavera's supply department required little staff. "Hello," she said. "What brings you this early?" He turned his face her way, and the happiness died out of her. "Something is terribly wrong," she whispered.

He nodded. The facts jerked forth.

"Oh, no. *Não permita Deus.*" Rhoda closed her eyes briefly, seemed to brace herself, then came to take both his hands. "What will you do?"

"Go there."

"Alone?"

"Might as well, since the Navy isn't interested in protecting mere taxpayers." An imp reminded Sparling that extrasolar workers didn't pay taxes. "Should things come to a fight, Larreka's troopers are preferable to us civilians. Or, if we do need human help, it can arrive in a matter of hours, even if we are only allowed small passenger vehicles these days. Meanwhile, till we have some solid information, why keep men tied down in Port Rua?"

"Must you go yourself? And immediately?"

"We'd better have *a* human on the spot." No longer able to meet her look, he regarded a picture of Becky

170

on the wall. "I'm idle here; the Navy will get no more advice from me. I have about as wide an experience of Ishtar and Ishtarians as any man. You know how I've perforce become a fairly good jackleg physician, in case she—she—Well, she'll've had a rough time at best."

Rhoda straightened her dumpy figure. "Also your top reason," she said quietly. "You are in love with her."

"Huh?" he exclaimed, shocked. "Why, that, that's ridiculous! We're friends, sure, but—"

She shook her head. "No, *querido*." She hadn't used the endearment of their early days for a long time. The tears would not altogether stay down. "I know you. I knew this from the start, and knew you were both innocent. You have always been kind to me, Ian. So I think, because you must go back into a dangerous place—you must—I should say you go with my blessing. Bring her home safe."

He hugged her to him, protesting, "You're wrong. I can't imagine how you got such a wild idea," since that felt like the only possible thing to do.

"Well, perhaps I was mistaken," she likewise lied against his breast. "We will talk no more of it. Let me help you pack. And I will call the Conways and ask if there is any way we, I can help."

Should I feel guilty that I chiefly feel embarrassed? he wondered. *Or that several of my contingency plans call for me to risk my life?*

A thought went through him like an electric shock. She sensed it in his body. "What is the matter?" she asked timidly.

"Nothing, Nothing." He spoke with his voice alone; his mind was elsewhere. "I just got a notion. It'll keep me here maybe two or three days yet."

XVII

PORT RUA WAS legionary barracks and their outbuildings, workshops, trading posts, warehouses, taverns, the homes of long-time dwellers, all crowded together on straight and narrow streets in order that a high, betowered stockade might enclose them. Outside sprawled tents, booths, and shacks where overflow people could shelter unless attacked. Further scattered were the steadings of farms and pastureland which had helped nourish the town. But most of these stood deserted amidst heat-sickened fields. Tassu raiders had plundered several. Legionary columns made sallies northward and westward as much to hunt and gather food as to harass their foes.

From that mountaintop where he waited at the head of warriors, Arnanak could barely see the settlement. Clearer in view were the long sweep of the Esali River through its brown-burnt valley till it emptied into Rua Bay, and the easterly glint of that great bight opening at last on the Sea of Ehur. His telescope found boats trying to fish—they didn't venture far, lest a native warcraft snap them up—and masts of ships tied at the wharf, supply line and escape for the Zera Victrix.

The sky seemed white-hot over the two suns. Though the air never stirred, and its dryness made pelts and manes crackle, somehow it seethed. Arnanak and his sixty-four males wore nothing save their shields and weapons, whose metal parts they did not touch, and still they felt consumed. What must it be like for the sixty-four from cold Haelen and gentle Beronnen, bound full-armored up the mountainside?

They came at a smart trot, though, which thumped the bricklike soil, snapped stalks of parched dead lia across, and kept their standard slowly flapping. They were in battle order too, squads knit into platoons (three heavy-mailed shock troopers with a porter for their gear; four pairs each of an archer and his arrowbearer, who held a big shield for them both; eight light troopers, swift scouts or close infighters as need might be) and one catapult trio (its bearer, its shooter, and its ammunition lugger). This left a single male in command, if the agreed-on number was not to be exceeded.

Actually, it had been, but Arnanak didn't fret. For the extra member was a human!

Clad in white, its head likewise decked against heaven, it moved mysterious to the sight. A murmur and growl went among the Tassui. "Hold steady," Arnanak told them. "This is a thing I was hoping for. Remember, such creatures are mortal. Do I not hold one of them captive?"

The new arrival was noticeable taller and broader than Jill Conway, doubtless a male. Arnanak wondered if a death tool lay beneath yonder flowing garments, to wipe his whole band out at a burst. He thought not. How then would the male ever learn where the female was kept? No, he must have arrived lately in a flying boat. Much earlier, the Zera's commandant had released a couple of Tassu prisoners with the message that he wanted to talk under truce. Arnanak set out from Ulu the day he got that word, sending a courier ahead to declare the place and terms whereon he would meet. He had barely arrived and pitched camp here. Thus he would not hitherto have heard of the newcomer.

The legionaries halted two spearcasts away. Their standard dipped thrice, their sign of peacefulness. Arnanak for his part thrust sword into ground. He and their leader stepped forward.

Startled, he saw this was none less than Larreka. All knew of old One-Ear. Arnanak had glimpsed him a few times, on visits to Port Rua before war began. So he was back from South-Over-Sea and gambling his life on the good faith of his enemies? *Why not?* the Tassu decided. *I am here in my own person, and I may well be more the keel of my people's strength than he of his.*

"Greeting, mighty one," said Larreka in the vernacular. He added no customary wishes for luck.

Arnanak returned a Sehalan salutation: "Honor and happiness be yours, Commandant, and fellowship between us."

Larreka stood quiet, his pale blue eyes probing the other's green. Hardly aware that he did, the latter took soldier's stance, torso and arms straight, feet squared, tail bowed outward. Larreka stepped near and offered his left hand. There passed between them the initiates' grip of the Triad, followed by certain phrases.

They let go. "Where did you serve?" Larreka asked.

"Tamburu Strider," Arnanak told him. "Combat engineer corps, mostly in the Iren Islands. But that was long ago."

173

"Yes, it would've been. . . . You're the Overling of Ulu, aren't you? Gods know I've heard enough about you." Larreka paused. "And we've met before. You don't seem to have recognized me then, in my helmet. But I'd know you in the Final Dark. You bore the human off my ship. I cast her ration box onto yours."

Arnanak's hearts clenched. Was this a fate—whether of Sun or Ember Star—or a whim of the Rover which might breed a fate—or might mean nothing?

Because Larreka stood unshaken, he rallied to his purpose. "Then well are we met anew, maybe. Let us swear a day's peace, and your folk can take ease with mine." He waved at the awnings they had raised. "We brought beer for hospitality."

"You and I and this human have work to do."

"Aye."

The fighters gave oath in their separate ways, broke formation, disarmed, and mingled, southerners more warily than northerners. In Sehalan, Arnanak acknowledged Larreka's introduction of Ian Sparling, and led them to his shelter. A regular tent, though two sides were furled for the sake of breath, it stood in a patch of wan blue blades. Already Starkland seeds, blown in on storm winds, were surviving Fire Time better than most of the plants which fed mortals.

Beneath the tent were shade, rugs to rest on, ale, waterskins, and goblets. The Ishtarians folded their legs. The human sat down jerkily, arms clasping knees, face haggard, insofar as that visage was readable. Arnanak told him: "She of your kind who names herself Jill Conway is well. She has suffered no harm, nor do I mean for her to."

"That . . . is good to hear," Ian Sparling grated.

"I seized her, when the chance came, as much to bring about a meeting like this as for any other reason. On my side we have ever stood ready to make peace. We got no word—"

"You sent us none," Larreka interrupted in a tone as dry as the land, "save that the legions must get out and stay out."

"This is our country," Arnanak said for the human to hear.

"Not every bit of it," Larreka retorted. "Our sites we

174

have held for octads, bought from owners willing to welcome civilized traders. Since, we've often had to punish banditry. But who in your ruck of barbarians has any claim to our towns?"

Arnanak addressed Ian Sparling: "Gladly would we Tassui have met your kind and dealt. You never opened a door."

"We sent occasional explorers here," the human said. Having talked a great deal with Jill Conway, Arnanak made out the strain in his voice. "But that was before there seemed to be any single purpose or leadership among the dwellers. Lately we've had troubles of our own—" He leaned forward. "Well, I've come about her release. If you truly wish the friendship of her friends, you'll fetch her to me at once."

"And afterward we will talk further?"

"What do you want of us?"

"Your help. I have heard how you will help the Gathering through the next sixty-four. Are my folk less worthy of life?"

"I . . . am not sure . . . what we could best do for you."

"Aye," said Arnanak bleakly, "no tales have reached me of almighty works or even of promised miracles in Beronnen."

Ian Sparling considered, before he won quick respect from the Tassu by saying: "I could swear every kind of reward, but why? You're too intelligent. Let's discuss instead, today, the female's ransom. Ask the impossible, and you will get nothing—no, worse than nothing: attack on your country, the ruin of your plans. Ask something reasonable, and I can likely arrange it for you."

Nevertheless Arnanak must pounce. "If you are able to lay South Valennen waste, why have you not struck ere now? We've given the Gathering ample woe, the Gathering you are supposed to rescue. Why have you held back your military aid? Is it because you have none to bring?"

"We . . . we did not come here seeking quarrels—" Ian Sparling collected himself. "Now is too early for threats. Name a ransom."

"What can you offer?"

175

"Our good will, first and foremost. Then tools, materials, advice, to help you outlast the bad years. For example, instead of this heavy tent cloth, stuff that's much lighter and stronger, rotproof and flameproof. That would let you range more freely in search of wild food."

"Ng-ng, I would rather have a supply of those weapons you've given the soldiery a few of." Arnanak stared at Larreka. "Also, you must withdraw help from the Gathering."

The commandant uttered a rough chuckle and jerked a demi-thumb at the goblet of ale before him. "This doesn't taste very good either," he said.

"I know you two spoke together beforehand." Arnanak had settled into a steely calm. "I did not truly believe the humans would or could abandon their long-held purpose for the sake of one of their number. Indeed, she whom I hold warned me of that. Honored be her pride."

"Then let's talk of what may be done in reality," Ian Sparling urged.

"Aye," Arnanak agreed. "Let us do that, Larreka. Will the Zera leave Valennen freely, with *our* good will, or must we destroy you? Dead bones are oracles here, but of no use to Beronnen. It is not too late to bargain about what Fiery Sea Islands you may keep," *until we're ready to cast you off them*, "though best for your cause would be that you returned the whole way home."

"Stop spilling time," the legionary snapped. "I thought we might dicker out a few meaningful things. If you leave our hunters and fishers alone, they'll keep their parties small and stop putting the torch to areas where they know you have homesteads. Like that."

"We might accord so far," Arnanak said. This was not unawaited either.

"Hold on!" exclaimed the human. "What about Jill?"

Arnanak signed. "You have offered nothing to match her hostage value in staying whatever hand your people may raise to uphold the Zera. Can you? If not, we will keep her till after our victory. Meanwhile we can talk

176

about her price from time to time—her price and much else.

"Do you not understand, Ian Sparling? My aim is that the Tassui shall live, not as a few starvelings but in power and fortune. Have you thought that we may become those whom it can best pay you to deal with?

"If naught else, here is the first real chance for us to swap knowledge of each other, which could well be worth more than a fleetload of goods. Therefore be not afraid for her. Think rather how we can arrange to have brought to her whatever she needs for health while she abides among my folk."

Ian Sparling stared long at him. The sounds of soldiers and warriors moving about, talking a little, came distantly. The air beneath the tent simmered. It smelled almost charred.

Larreka broke silence: "I knew the Valennener leader must be shrewd as well as strong. I didn't see till today that he's also wise. Too bad we must kill you, Arnanak. You should have stayed in your legion."

"I'm sorry that you do not surrender," the Overling returned in like courtesy.

Ian Sparling stirred. "Very well," he said. "I foresaw this outcome. Take me to her, then."

"What?" asked Arnanak, surprised.

"She's all alone among wild strangers. They may mean well, but they aren't her kind, nor do they know how to look after her should ... harm befall. Let me join her. Why not? You'll have two of us."

Arnanak studied not the face which was alien as a daur's, but Larreka's. The commandant looked stark. He and his guest had surely wrestled together with this thought.

Decision surged forward. What was life but the taking of risks? "I can make no promises," Arnanak warned. "It is hard travel for days to reach her. Nor have they an easy time there."

"The more reason for me to go," Ian Sparling said.

"I will first want to see everything you bring along, garb, food, everything, handle each piece myself and make you show me what it's for, till I am sure you plot no treachery."

"Of course."

177

XVIII

JILL HAD BARELY arrived at Ulu when Arnanak got a message that sent him off again. "They want to parley in Port Rua," he told her. "I make no doubt your presence among us has to do with that. Raise not your hopes too high. The odds are you must stay here for—maybe till fall or early winter."

She thought his advice was kindly intended. But then, the big black-skinned barbarian was not evil by any means. From the viewpoint of his people he was a hero, and might become a savior.

He and she had spoken together at great length and in growing intimacy, first aboard his galley and later on the overland trip from the fjord where he left it. He had done everything he could to help her across those high mountains. Often she had ridden on him or a warrior of his, as she used to ride on Larreka. And this was despite her having killed his son, with not so much as a bone brought home to call the soul back in dreams.

While he was gone, she found her captivity light except for being captivity. She got a room to herself, which none entered without her leave. She could walk abroad freely. Since her supply of amino acids and vitamins was sequestered between meals, she had no possibility of escape.

"Best you not fare beyond sight of the close," Innukrat said. "You could well get lost."

"I know woodcraft better than that," Jlill answered, "and I don't believe any animals in Valennen are dangerous to me."

Innukrat pondered, then decided: "First, go out twice or thrice in company and see if you can find your way back." When this had been done she made no further objection.

She was a wife of Arnanak's and, after he left, the sole native in the compound who knew Sehalan. That was due to her being a trader who, before the war on

178

civilization began, had ranged as far as its outposts in the Esali Valley. The sexual equality found in most Ishtarian societies—exceptions were as apt to be matriarchal as patriarchal—prevailed here too; but under hard and primitive conditions, there was necessarily more specialization of jobs than elsewhere. As a rule, males did the trading and raiding abroad, while among other skilled tasks, females took goods for barter across the home country. They feared no assault. While they stayed on the marked routes, their persons and burdens were sacred. Jill asked if that law was ever violated. "I have heard of it, very rarely." Innukrat said. "The neighborhoods tracked down the doers, slew them, and pickled them in brine."

Initially Jill, fascinated by her surroundings, enjoyed herself, until in abrupt guilt she would remember how those who cared for her must be worrying, and how she had become a high card in the hand of Larreka's enemy. The steading alone was worth days of exploration. Its basic layout resembled that of a southland ranch, but everything else was quite foreign. A hall formed one side of an adobe-paved courtyard, a great single-storied building of undressed stone, massive logs, sod roof, half of it a chamber where the housesold gathered for meals or sociability, the rest given over to service rooms and private cubicles. When she had grown used to their angular style, she deemed the carvings on roof pillars and wainscots as good as she had ever seen. The remainder of the court was defined by smaller, plainer structures: sheds, workshops, housing for subordinates and a few domestic animals. It always brawled with activity here, a hundred individuals going about their labor or their pleasures; Jill found the little ones as irresistible as they were at home. But without a common language, she was barred from doing much more than watch. The Valenneners soon came to take her for granted.

Ulu lay in the eastern foothills of the Worldwall range. Forest all around gave some shielding from the suns, though most trees were scrubby and this year their red or yellow leaves drooped, curled, withered. The occasional blue T-plants looked better, and in places a phoenix loomed magnificent. The household held frequent fire drills, and Jill recollected that the phoenix had its name, translated from a native equivalent, because its reproduction depended on the conflagrations which devastated these lands every millennium.

A trail into the woods soon ended at a cabin. Two armed guards waved her off. She asked Innukrat why and got an uneasy response: "Best not talk of that till the Overling comes back, if he then chooses." Jill decided probably it was a shrine or a magical site. And yet nobody minded her inspecting the family dolmens, though oracular dreams were supposed to come from them.

This was the single restriction on her freedom of movement. Every other path she could follow as long as hunger or weariness allowed. Ten kilometers southeast the forest came to a halt and she looked widely from mountain peaks sheer in the west, across umber hills and down over a remote veldt, ashimmer in the heat which billowed from the two suns.

Here and there she saw crofts. The social system appeared to rest on a kind of voluntary feudalism. An Overling dominated a region, led its fighters in battle or its workers in civil emergency, tried lawsuits upon request, officiated at the major religious rites. Lesser families could stay independent of him if they chose, but most found it preferable to become his "oathgivers," pledge him certain services and obedience in exchange for the protection of his household troops and a share in his food stores when times got hard. Either party could annul the contract for cause, and it was not binding on the next generation—after the latter had passed that sixty-fourth birthday before which the power of the parents was absolute.

Innukrat spoke of killings, especially among the young. Both sexes were raised haughty and quarrelsome. "They must be ready to fight, and know how, when raiders come or when we ourselves go raiding; for you see what a niggard land ours is." Nevertheless Overlings and oldsters kept bloodshed within bounds and eventually got unfriends reconciled. *Well,* Jill thought, *Ishtarians aren't human.*

Her loneliness began to press in on her. She craved

180

language lessons from Innukrat, and the female obliged as much as possible. That was no large amount, a wife's duties being countless. Jill offered to help, but soon discovered she was merely in the way. Beside lacking the strength to use these crude implements, she hadn't the skill.

She took to spending most of her daytimes outdoors. The open country theatened sunstroke; and besides, the woods held more nature to study. It was sparse compared to that in the southern hemisphere, but as she gained a little familiarity, she found herself just as captivated, and frequently stayed out late.

Thus it was that she had her encounter.

She was returning after both suns, now close companions, had set. Tropical twilight was brief. However, the moons sufficed through this scanty foliage. Often her trail went through what she would have called a meadow were it less parched. Entering one such, the path curved sharply around a canebrake, to bring her out in a single stride.

Low, gnarly trees made shadow masses around. Behind them on her right, the battlements of the Worldwall glimmered gray into a black-purple sky where stars burned fewer than usual. For Caelestia was rising near the full, and Urania at the half hung close by. No longer did either have two clear phases at once or avoid regular eclipse. Apart from a thin edging of silver, they shone pale red. Their glow upon dead lia and dry thornbushes made the air feel more hot than it was. Silence lay like a weight.

Jill stopped noticing, stopped moving. Her pulse alone jumped, a knock-knock-knock through head and throat, as she and the creature stood confronted. It had been crossing the meadow when she surprised it.

No—can't be—trick of moonlight—I'm hungry, heat-exhausted, my brain's gone into free fall—

The shape bounded from her.

"Wait!" she cried, and stumbled after. But already it had disappeared among the trees.

A moment's dread made her grip the dagger Arnanak had given her. *No, it fled, not I. . . . Regardless, I'd better get on back.*

While she strode, faster and faster, she tried to con-

181

jure the shape forth as it had stood in the red beams.
A T-beast, beyond a doubt. Whatever life had been like
on Tammuz a billion years ago, when it started anew
from microbes on Ishtar it did not follow the same
course as ortho-life, or Earth's. There were three sexes.
There was no elaborate symbiosis, nor hair or milk;
and instead of plant chemistry or perspiration, the
homeothermic animals, like many plants, controlled
temperature by changing color. There were vertebrates
of a sort, but none descended from an ancient worm,
rather from a thing like a starfish—no true head but a
branch, the fifth limb changed into a carrier of mouth
and sensory organs. There were a few bipeds—

But they were small. This had been a giant of its
kind. The petals atop its branch would have reached to
her chest. On the abdomen she thought she had made
out three eyes above the central bulge of the genital
sheath. Legs had been long and powerful for the size; it
was more a leaper than a strider. Yet the boneless-look-
ing arms were well developed also, ending in a hand of
five fingers arranged in a star.

Hands? Fingers?

Yes, if she wasn't crazy. She'd seen the right arm
lifted, digits spread, as if caught by astonishment at
sight of her. The left had been carrying what seemed to
be a knife.

*Illusion. Got to've been. I've made a remarkable dis-
covery, sure, a T-beast never suspected before. Probably come down from the north because of changing
conditions. Only a beast, though!*

Windows appeared yellow ahead of her. She burst
into the hall, pushed through its crowdedness, blurted
to Innukrat what had happened.

The female traced a sign. "You met a daur," she
said uneasily.

"A what?" Jill asked.

"I think best we wait for Arnanak about this too."

"But—" Memory stirred. Primavera did have xenological data on the Valenneners, mostly taken second-
hand from members of the Gathering, yet filling a few
books which she'd read. "Daur. Dauri." *Yes, I seem to
recall, they believe in a kind of elf or pooka or minor*

182

demon—"Are those, uh, are they beings that haunt the wilderness—magical powers—?"

"I told you, wait for Arnanak," said the chieftain's wife.

He returned some days later. Jill didn't know how many; she'd ceased keeping count.

She chanced to be home when he arrived. To save her human clothes, she'd begged a length of the coarse cloth the natives wove from plant fibers, and stitched together several knee-length shifts caught by a rope belt. She was no Ishtarian whose life depended on ample sunlight; hereabouts, Bel could burn off her skin. Head, arms, and legs were sufficiently tanned to be safe if she took due care. Next she wanted footgear. Her shoes stank from overuse.

The household produced most of what it consumed. Occasionally Valenneners needed boots. The female who was best at leatherwork proved quite willing to make Jill two or three pairs—maybe because that got her out of her ordinary chores, maybe because it was a challenge, maybe from simple kindliness, or a combination of these. She required the girl on hand, to be a living dummy and to explain with gestures and a few Tassu words how the things should fit.

Jill stood at the booth, holding up a parasol she had made against heat and glare. Shouts lifted, foot-thuds, a rattle of iron. Into the courtyard dashed Arnanak and his followers. Jill dropped the parasol. For a second she went dizzy. Then: "Ian!" she yelled, and sped heedless across adobe which tried to blister her soles. "Ian, darling!"

And into his arms— She burrowed against the human male strength, hardness, sweat, and warmth of him. She kissed him so teeth clashed together; after having drawn back just enough to look upon his beaky face through tears and wonder, she kissed him again with a trembling tenderness which turned into the way of lovers.

At last they stood apart, hands in hands, dazedly regarding each other. It made no difference that scores of Ishtarians milled around in the white and crimson dazzle.

183

"Oh, Ian," she stammered, "you came . . . to fetch me—?"

Joy drained from his countenance till the bones stood forth like reefs at low tide. "I'm sorry, my dear," he answered in a voice gone dull. "No release yet."

Her first emotion was bewilderment. "What? Then why're you here?"

"I couldn't leave you alone, could I?" He marshaled himself and spoke fast. "Don't be afraid. I'm here by agreement. Arnanak isn't ready to let us go—he and Larreka made a very limited bargain that didn't change anybody's objectives—but he's anxious to get on good terms with us humans eventually. Two hostages are better than one, he thinks. The idea is to exchange us in due course for concessions—which might amount to no more than establishing a kind of diplomatic relations with his kingdom—and for that, obviously we'd better be well treated meanwhile. We talked a lot on the road. He's really not a bad chap in his fashion. For now, well, I've brought along food, medicine, clothes, as much stuff as I could for you. Including, uh, what I think are your favorite books."

She searched the blue-green eyes and knew: *He is in love with me. How could I not have been sure?*

"You shouldn't have," she forced out.

"Like hell! I, I'll explain the situation—got a lot of news to pass on—but it amounts to me being the logical choice. How've you been? How are you?"

"All right—"

"You're looking good. Kind of thin; but, you know, that sun-bleached hair against that sun-tanned skin, you're damn near a platinum blonde." In haste: "Everybody was okay at home, at least they were when last we heard in Port Rua. They send their love. The whole community wants you back."

"*Chu*," Arnanak's Sehalan joined their English, "will you not come indoors? Go to your room, you two guests of mine. The males will bring your baggage. Later we will feast. But you must have much to talk about."

Most certainly they had much.

Sparling knew her better than to soften his tidings.

184

"No real compromise. Just a couple of minor arrangements to make the war less destructive on both sides, which can't affect the outcome either way. The Tassui won't stop till the last legionary is out of Valennen or dead in it. The Zera will hang on as long as it possibly can, in the hope of reinforcements. I can hardly blame the barbarians. According to Arnanak, if they stay penned in their homelands, Fire Time—he calls it Fire Time—will kill most of them. We, we humans, should've given more thought to that. We should've mounted programs for the relief of this country too. Not that that swine Dejerine would let us carry them out."

"Yuri is no villain," Jill said. This made Sparling look so grim and hurt that she must stroke his cheek and lean closer to him. They were sitting side by side on the boughs and straw mattress which made her bed, backs against a rough log wall, legs stretched across a clay floor. With a loose-woven blind over its single window, the room was dim and halfway cool. It had no door; a similar curtain in the entrance let through the sounds of readying for rejoicing which filled the hall.

"Neither is Arnanak," he said, milder the moment she chose him to be. "Still, they both have missions, and Lord help whoever gets in the way. Arnanak means for his people to grab off territory less hard hit by periastron and its aftermath than here—territory to live in, and live well. Of course, that involves breaking up the Gathering. It couldn't stay idle while that many of its members were overrun, displaced, subjugated, slaughtered. And when the Gathering's gone under, Beronnen will lie wide open. The end of civilization on Ishtar—again. Arnanak made no bones about that to me."

"Nor to me," Jill said. "Though he does think his descendants will inherit and rebuild it."

"In time. How long, considering Ishtarian life-spans? What horrors go on meanwhile, and how much gets lost forever?"

"I know, Ian, I know."

"For us, time's gotten damnably short, if we want to do anything to help Larreka. Arnanak told me he already has messengers out, calling ships and ground

185

forces to rendezvous. I don't give Port Rua another month before he cuts loose the storm."

Jill sat quiet a while. Somehow Sparling had not spoken like a man in despair. At last she ventured, "You sound as if we're not altogether helpless."

He nodded. His cowlick bobbed, ludicrous and dear in the gray-shot black hair. "We can try. Jill, I'd have come anyway to help you, but it happens I made me an excuse." He slid back the sleeve on the left arm against which she nestled. Braceleted on the wrist was a micro transceiver. "Arnanak checked my kit item by item before allowing anything along. But as I'd hoped, he didn't recognize this. He believed me when I explained it's a talisman."

She frowned. "What're you getting at? We must be three hundred kilometers from Port Rua, or worse. Under ideal conditions, a high-gain detector might pick this thing up at ten."

"Ah-ah-ah!" He wagged a finger. "You underestimate my low cunning."

In a burst of hope, she said, "No, if it's low, I've got to have overestimated it."

He rattled a laugh. "As you like. But listen. Larreka helped me work out the details. Part of the deal he made was, the natives will let small legionary bands hunt freely, in exchange for the soldiers not firing these woods and savannahs. Well, I brought along a few solar-energized portable relays—Mark Fives, you know, same as we've got around South Beronnen wherever a bigger, permanent unit isn't convenient to install. Certain of those foraging parties will plant 'em strategically when nobody's looking, well hidden in trees, on hilltops, et cetera."

"But, Ian, how can they come near enough—?"

"They can't, especially when they don't know our location. In fact, as Larreka must have mentioned to you, he's never learned just where Ulu is, where the enemy chief has his headquarters. Arnanak's been cagy about that; he's no slumpskull. Yet surely one of those relays will come within a hundred kilometers of here." Sparling drew breath. She noticed at the back of her excitement how much she liked seeing his pleasure. "Okay. I brought several plastic containers of protein

186

powder, different sizes to confuse the issue. He emptied and refilled each, as I'd expected. But he didn't think to check for false bottoms. In a particular can is snuggled a rather bigger and huskier transceiver, put together for this purpose. A signal from my micro will switch its main circuit. That'll be our primary relay— stepping down the frequency so we aren't limited to line-of-sight—and *it* can do more than a hundred kilometers!"

"O-o-o-oh." She stared before her while all her nerves tingled.

"Nothing can happen in a hurry," Sparling cautioned, "and the scheme depends on every link in the chain. First, I imagine it'll take a while before the rest of the system is in place. Then, second, we'll simply have audio contact with Port Rua. True, they can reach Primavera, but still— Third, with the rudimentary equipment I could bring along, I'll need a fair bit of time to survey this neighborhood to sufficient accuracy."

"Survey?"

"Sure. I think probably I can use the stars, and sights taken on local landmarks like mountain peaks, to pinpoint us on the map. Then we can hike to a rendezvous point where a flyer can land for us." He gave her a shy smile. "It was the best I would invent on short notice."

Notice—she thought. *I notice that funny little wrinkle at the corner of your lips.*

Damn, though! I don't want to be merely a captive damsel languishing for her knight.

It came to her what she might do for her share.

Arnanak was in alpine good humor. While he ate and drank and boasted prodigiously, standing at a trestle table in the hall, she jollied him along. Not that she pretended to have changed sides. He knew her too well. But she did make plain that her stay had given her a favorable opinion of his folk and she would gladly intercede for them. *No lie, either. We* should *be helping them, them and the Gathering both. My lie is a withheld truth, that our cruel, idiotic war makes this impossible.* She felt less guilty when he replied:

187

"We will talk more after I have crushed them in Valennen. If naught else, I must put on such show of might to hold the Tassui at my beck. I warned the legion again and again, if it did not leave it would be destroyed. Now my warriors are coming together. They will see Arnanak keep his word."

Sparling stayed short-spoken and noncommittal, on Jill's orders. The Overling must have gained some feel for human attitudes and expressions, and the man was better at outright concealing than at dissembling.

At the end of the feast, she turned grave and said, "I have to ask you about a thing. Could we three go outside?"

Arnanak was willing. Beyond the court, Jill tugged his elbow and pointed. "This way," she urged.

He stiffened. "That path goes to a forbidden place."

"I know. Come, a short ways."

He yielded. They stopped out of view of the buildings. The suns were beneath the Worldwall, though not yet the ocean it hid. Shadows lay thick among dwarfish trees and shriveled brush. Overhead the sky was an ever richening blue, a planet stood white, Ea red. A breeze carried a ghost of coolness and rattled came stalks.

Arnanak's eyes were green lanterns in the blackness under his mane. Fangs glinted when he said, bell-deep: "Speak what you will, but be quick: for I have my own errand here."

Jill gripped the comfort of Sparling's arm. Her pulse thuttered. "What are the dauri, and what have you to do with them?"

He dropped hand to sword hilt. "Why ask you this?"

"I think I met one." Jill described her encounter. "Innukrat would tell me naught, said I must wait for you. Yet surely there is common knowledge about them. I remember . . . hearing . . . somewhat."

His tension lowered. "Aye. They are beings, creatures, not mortal. They are believed to have powers, and many folk set out small sacrifices, like a bowl of food, when a daur has been glimpsed. But that is seldom."

"The food is no use to the daur. Is it?"

"What do you mean?"

188

"I think you know what I mean. Remember, my business is to learn about animals. The daur I saw was nothing magical. It was as mortal as you or I—a creature belonging to the same kind of life as the phoenix or the skipfoot, the kind of life which wholly possesses the Starklands. Yet it carried a knife. I saw the metal."

Did I really? "Arnanak, if the dauri were plentiful enough and far enough along to mine and forge metal, we humans would have discovered them. I think you gave it the blade . . . as part of a bargain."

A leap in the dark. But, Christ, I've got to have guessed right!

Sparling added, "I told you myself, we came to, to these countries mainly to explore them, find out what they're like. My fellows would be most grateful to anyone who gave them an important new piece of knowledge."

Arnanak had stood quietly. Now he sprang like a panther to his decision. "Well," he said. "The matter is not a dead secret, after all. I have told other Tassui somewhat of it. And I will keep you two till my hold on Valennen is beyond shaking." He turned. "Follow."

As they finished the short walk, Sparling stooped to whisper in Jill's ear: "Then you're right. An entire conscious race—and *you* figured out the truth."

"Sh," she answered. "Don't talk English here. He might decide we're conspiring."

They reached the cabin. The sentries lifted spears in salute and stood aside. Arnanak unbolted the door and led the humans in. He closed it again immediately, before his watchers stepped back to where they could see.

Within, a pair of clay lamps cast dim light and monstrous glooms; for the windows, too high for peering through, were full of dusk. A single room lay roughly furnished in miniature. Shelves held blue-leaved vegetation, odd-shaped butchered carcasses: food for T-life. A rear door, latch on the inside, gave egress at will to the three who lived here.

Sparling choked on a gasp. Jill squeezed his hand. Otherwise her attention burned at the starfish shapes. They scuttled back, letting out timid whistles and trills. The Ishtarian—the ortho-Ishtarian—reassured them

189

with Tassu words, and at last they came to stand before newcomers who must be hideous in their sight.

"Hear the tale of my quest," Arnanak said.

While he spoke, Jill stared and stared. Like most sophonts, the dauri seemed fairly unspecialized in body. She identified features, modified to be sure, she had seen illustrated in many works on T-biology. Inside those roughly spheroidal torsos must be skeletons arranged on a plan of intersecting hoops, with ball-and-socket joints for the five limbs. The top one, the branch, culminated in five fleshy petals which served both as chemosensor organs and as tongues to push food down into a pentagon of jaws. Under each petal was a tendril, an intricate set of fibers that received sound. At the ends of the arms, five symmetrical fingers could not grasp a shaft as firmly as man or Ishtarian, but no doubt were superior for an object like a hand ax. (Yes; Jill saw how their iron knives were hafted, and admired the ingenuity of Arnanak, who must have designed this.) The eyes at the roots of the arms were well developed, though strange to look into because the entire ball was self-darkening according to light intensity. Under the branch was a more primitive third orb, to co-ordinate visual fields which did not overlap. The remaining two eyes had changed into protuberances above the legs, whose varying shapes, colors and odors indicated that all three sexes were here represented. Otherwise, in this gloaming, the skin was dark purplish. In full tropical day it would be an almost metallic white—not too conspicuous, when many plants had the same protection.

Yes, remarkable but comprehensible, as T-life went ... except for the minds behind.

And when Arnanak finished, and from a chest took out the Thing he had carried from the Starklands—

Both humans cried aloud. A crystalline cube, some thirty centimeters on a side, held blackness full of many-colored gleam-points. When Arnanak gestured, the vision changed, and symbols glowed now beside this spark, now beside that.

"Look well," said the Overling of Ulu. "You will not see it again soon, if ever. It, and these dauri, go with

190

me a pair of days hence, to hearten my warriors for our onslaught."

A lamp had been lit in their room, and a bed heaped for Sparling, to rustle beneath feet when they entered. Oil burned with a piney fragrance, the air was merely warm, the window revealed the brightest stars.

"Oh, God, Ian, what a marvel!" Jill had not felt this caught up in splendor since—since—

His visage grew still more gaunt. "Yeah. But for what use? . . . Well, we'll pass the information on."

"We." She caught his hands afresh. "You were here, to share it. Can I ever make you know what that means?"

"I, I'm glad I was."

Borne on a tide, she said, "Ian, this is the first good chance I've had to thank you. I never will be able to, not really, but I aim to try my damnedest."

"Well, uh—" A side of his mouth bent upward, though he spoke almost uneasily: "Look, I should've insisted on separate rooms. If none're available, and doubtless none are, I— Okay, I'll go find my sleeping bag, wherever they've stowed it. Good night, Jill."

"What? Good night? Don't be ridiculous!"

He made as if to retreat. She threw her arms about his neck and kissed him. After a second, he answered.

"Stop being this bloody honorable, man," she murmured at last. "Oh, I'm fond of Rhoda myself and— You don't have to say it, you didn't expect a reward. But I want to!"

I do, I do. It's been a starvishly long time. And, I don't know, does revelation make a person horny? Anyhow, what harm, what besides kindness and caring, between two people who may never come back?

A wispy voice said through the drumbeats that there was a possibility her most recent sterishot had worn off. *Go to hell,* she told it. A thought flickered that the Sparlings had always wanted more children, but none were for adoption in Primavera.

"I think I'm in love with you, Ian," she said. "Already."

XIX

ABOUT THE TIME that Ulu celebrated midsummer, Bel solstice, by dance, chant, drumbeat, and sacrifice, the yellow sun overtook the red one in the sky. Thereafter Anu was the pursuer. Heat waxed; waterless winds roared; the veldt burned for days, and bitter smoke drifted into the hills; clouds surfed white against the Worldwall, but never broke past to birth their rain in this country.

Sparling ignored any discomfort. Jill claimed she did too. He believed her, and not just because she was the most disconcertingly honest person he knew. In near-zero humidity, temperature tolerance is a matter of relaxing and letting the body go about its business. Food was coarse but still in ample supply. Except for keeping control of dietary supplements, the natives were eager to please, whether by helpfulness or by letting their prisoner-guests alone. Most often it was the latter. For he and she were taking all they were able of each day and each night granted them.

He had never been as happy as now. That was a feeling laced with fret and, for him, a dram of guilt, less on Rhoda's account than because he couldn't bring himself to work full time on escape. But then, he reflected, joy never comes straight; only fear and pain do.

They seldom spoke about their private future. Such talk always ended soon, in a passage of love. Presently he, like she, ceased tallying the days; he let them happen in a place outside of time. But afterward he reckoned their number at forty-three, and wished they had been Terrestrial in length.

Being who they were, he and she found a great deal else to do together.

They sat where a shrunken brook muttered around stones it had formerly hidden. Sky showed pale behind boughs which did keep enough leaves that the forest floor was partly shaded, flecked with gold and ruby light-spots. A perching ptenoid, blue as a kingfisher and itself watching for ichthyoids which would likely never come by, hung on four-footed as if already heat and hunger sapped its life.

"Okay, we'll have another try," Sparling said, and turned the knob on his transceiver. Jill leaned close over his arm. The clean odor of her hair took him in a wave.

"Calling Port Rua," he intoned. "Please reply on this band."

"Military Intelligence Unit X-13 calling Port Rua," she added solemnly. "Secret and urgent. We need new disguises. An onion sandwich has made our false beards uninhabitable."

I wish I had her gift for having fun, Sparling thought. *Is that why she's so splendid in bed? Not that I have much basis for comparison. I didn't even know what a difference it makes.*

"Frankly, I'm getting worried," he said. "Larreka would have a technician on duty around the clock. Either our idea hasn't worked, or—"

Insect-small, but sharp in the silence around, an Ishtarian voice rose: "Port Rua responds. Are you the captive humans?"

Jill rocketed to her feet and did a whooping wardance.

"Yes," Sparling said, while his relief reached a lower peak than hers. "We're fine thus far. How're things with you?"

"Quiet. Too quiet, I feel."

"Uh-huh. Won't last. Can you get me the commandant?"

"Not soon. He is inspecting our signal system. We do not await him back until tomorrow. I can patch you in to Primavera."

"No, don't. That'd be an unnecessary drain on the batteries for our two sets here. You may know that I couldn't figure out how to smuggle in replacements that we'd have safe access to." *Nor what I could say to Rhoda.* "Do contact them and explain we're both being quite generously treated. I'll call again—let's say day after tomorrow, about noon. Meanwhile, good-by and good luck."

"May the Twain be kind to you, and the Rover do no harm."

Sparling switched off. "Well," he told the girl, "there's a long step taken."

"And *you* took it!" She cast herself upon him.

They walked under stars and moons. The light across mountains and along the treeless ridge was nearly lavender, purpling with distance as the land rolled eastward away from them until horizon hazed into sky. The air was gentle, sweet-scented. A creature akin to the cantor of Beronnen sang.

"You wouldn't think such a night was possible in Fire Time, would you?" he said. After regarding her: "It's like us, when everything is falling apart and burning, us catching gladness the way we have."

She tightened her fingers around his. "People must always have done the same," she answered. "Otherwise they'd be extinct."

He stared upward. "I wonder if that was Ishtar's ancient sky we saw."

"Oh, you mean in, m-m, Arnanak's Thing?"

"Yes. I wish he'd let us examine it closer. But I'd guess at its being a stellar simulacrum, variations determined by a solid-state minicomputer, energized by sunlight or a long-lived isotope, for space navigation or teaching or—" He sighed. *Here I am and here's my beloved and still I talk like a professor.* "Well, who can read a dead man's mind? Let alone a dead race."

"If they are dead," she replied, no less eager to speak of this than of themselves. "They might have gone elsewhere. Look, they could make an object that's resisted the sheer chemistry of a billion years. Somewhere in the north is a remnant of their colony—eroded, buried, or we'd've found it by now—nevertheless, recognizable as ruins. If they could do that, why shouldn't they have survived?"

"If, if, if!" he exclaimed in the prison of his finiteness.

"I often think that's the most wonderful word in the language," Jill said.

"Certainly we—you've come on a discovery like nothing since—"

194

"No, darling. We have."

"I'd give a lot to know how to pass the information on. How to make sure it doesn't—all right—doesn't die with us, should that happen."

"Why, we'll tell Larreka. What else? He can tell Primavera. In fact, look," Jill said, excitement lifting, "the truth should be broadcast everywhere. Arnanak's using myth and *mana* for his political purposes. Let the Tassui realize the dauri are mortal, that he's actually done no more than make a deal with certain members of a different species—they help him where they can, he'll see to it they get better lands after he's cleared civilization away— Ian, what a blow to morale!"

He shook his head. "No, dear. I've thought this over. If word gets around, he'll know his secret is breached; and who could have breached it but us? He told us in the cabin, he'd told others about that epic pilgrimage of his, but not about the practical politics which followed, because that'd spoil the awe."

"True," she said, reluctantly reminded.

"He doesn't have to know radio technology to decide we pulled a fast one somehow. And then—"

"I don't imagine he'd be vindictive."

"Maybe, maybe not. He might kill us as a precaution. I refuse to take such a risk with you, sweetheart."

"Ye-e-es, I see your point. I'm the only me I've got." She halted, making him do likewise. He saw her nose wrinkle at him in the tender light. "What matters more, though, you're the only you I've got."

He drew her to him. The turf here was descended from Tammuz, water-hoarding, soft to lie upon.

Later he raised himself on an elbow and looked at the miracle of her. Reaching up, she rumpled his hair. "I take back my remark," she purred.

"What?"

"About 'if' being the most wonderful word. Actually it gets second prize. The best is a four-letter Anglo-Saxoner, in your mouth and preceded by 'let's.' "

They could temporarily have foregone their extra ration. But when they announced their wish for an overnight trip, Innukrat doled out a supply. "Those are rugged heights westward," she told them. "You should feel as well as may be."

"You're a good person," Sparling said. His conscience jabbed him.

"If you truly mean that," she answered, "then after you have returned home and again wield power, remember—not me—my children."

The humans left the compound and trudged. He carried a pocket compass, allowed him since the Tassui knew of a crude version among the legionaries. Jill took notes to his dictation. Arnanak, conceding that they might as well put their stay to use by recording what they saw, had also admitted paper, pencils, clipboard. "Can you really pace that accurately?" she had asked.

"Fairly close," he said. "Oh, I'd prefer a laser transit and an integrating pedometer, but they'd've been hard to explain away."

And thus they were carrying out a survey whose results, referred to maps in Primavera, would locate Ulu within meters.

They were headed back next day, zigzagging down a furnace-hot talus slope, when the transceiver beeped. Sparling pressed accept. "What the devil goes on?" he snapped.

"Technician Adissa in Port Rua," said the tiny voice. "We have received a message for you from Primavera."

"Holy hopping Hanuman!" He felt as furious as the light around him. "What is this farce? You clotbrain, we might've been in the middle of our jailers!"

"*Kaa-aa*—" came a dismayed tone.

"Easy, darling," Jill counseled. "No harm done. He's probably a new recruitie, human-trained and anxious to serve." She leaned near the bracelet. "As we say in show biz, Adissa, don't call us, we'll call you."

"I beg forgiveness," the Ishtarian said humbly.

"Okay, you've got it; and we won't tell Larreka on you, either," Jill promised. "As long as talking is safe, what's your message?"

"First, what about the legion?" Sparling asked, mollified. He scrambled across the scree, which rattled and slipped, toward an overhang whereunder he saw a scrap of shade.

"Weapons continue sheathed," Adissa reported. "But fire has spoiled the nearby hunting grounds, and the commandant sends out no more parties. The ship that brought me carried supplies and a few soldiers. I am told it was the last that the legion—the units of our legion not already here—can afford; and nobody else will help."

The pair settled down below the cliff. Adissa switched on a recorded voice, Goddard Hanshaw's:

"Hi, there, you two. I thought you'd like an updating, though to tell the truth, very little about it is likable. We're personally well, I hasten to say. But things are pretty much at a standstill, or 'stand-off' might be more accurate.

"Fact is, you've become a symbol, a rallying point, *je ne sais que* the hell to call you.

"The usual situation. People live their lives meekly, but all the while their anger concentrates, and at last it's supersaturated and anything can make it crystallize out, rock hard. In the present case . . . well, I can't say exactly what. News from the battlefront, which is stalemated again, except not quiet: instead, a meat grinder. And on top of that, two popular, valuable members of our community are barbarians' pawns because of this same futile thing.

"Suddenly Primavera's gone on strike. Every longtime resident, and even most short-contract workers, refusing any kind of co-operation whatsoever. They won't as much as speak to a man in uniform or a 'collaborator.' Those who might prefer to behave differently, well, they don't feel it's worth becoming traitors in the eyes of their friends.

"Which is causing trouble aplenty, as you can guess. Captain Dejerine appeals to me damn near daily. By tacit consent, I'm the single Primaveran who can have to do with his command and stay kosher; it's recognized that somebody must. He made a few arrests, but as soon as he saw they were considered an honor, he released the prisoners and dismissed the charges. He's neither stupid nor wicked, you know. I feel sorry for him. He asked rather pathetically to be informed the moment any news of you came in. We haven't mentioned this communication line to him.

197

"Between us, I'm not sure the community is being wise. I have no notion what the resistance will lead to. Maybe we'll get cancellation of the Navy project; or maybe our last funds will be cut off; who can tell? I did feel you should know how matters stand, in case you do any dickering on your own hook. And I'll keep you posted. Meanwhile, don't worry about us. As the saying goes, the situation is desperate but not serious. *A vuestra salud*. Next, here's Rhoda."

"*Bom dia, querido*," said the woman's voice, and went on with a few endearments and wishes in Portuguese. Sparling clenched fists and jaws, and endured. "Jill," Rhoda finished in English, "your parents, your sister, her family send their love." Were those unshed tears in her voice? "I hope you will take mine too. Live well. Thank you for what you are, what you do. I pray for your safe return. Good-by."

Silence whirred. "That is the end," Adissa reported.

"Okay," Sparling said mechanically. "We'll sign off."

He sat for a while staring across the scorched mountains. Jill laid an arm around his waist. "You have a finer wife than *I* deserve," she said.

"No," he mumbled. "I mean, you're clean and brave and— Look, we can't yet do anything about anything, can we?" *Is that the question of a coward?* "In spite of my personal feelings," he slogged on, "I share God's doubts. A general strike against the Navy—the Peace Control—damnation, those men serve us all!"

"Don't agonize," she begged him. "Although—"

When her words trailed off, he turned his head and saw the clear profile against raw rock and cruel air, framed in tresses which were held by the circlet that a soldier of a legion had given her. "I wonder why Dad or Mother or Alice—even Bill—weren't on that tape," she said into emptiness. "Do I know them too well?"

She squared her shoulders. "Now I'm being a worry machine myself," she declared. "Hell with it. C'mon, hoofer, let's get back down to the hall. But kiss me first."

A while afterward, the time ended that had been theirs.

XX

FROM HIS EASTERNMOST watchtower, Larreka squinted across the docks of Port Rua and the legion's few ships, at the hostile fleet standing into the bay. Fifty-eight lean hulls he counted—fifty-eight mainsails tinged red by the newly risen Rover. The Sun, not much higher, dazzled his eyes with long rays that splintered and showered off amethyst wavelets. He could barely make his tally, and doubted that the garrison artillery could strike home a stone or a fire arrow against that glare. The barbarians had no such handicap; and the wind, already hot, was behind them too. It fluttered and snapped the banner above him.

"Kaa-aa," said Seroda, his adjutant. "Who'd have supposed they could muster that many?"

"Their chief's a wily beast," Larreka nodded. "He kept them in motion, in small groups, raiding amongst the islands and along the coasts. That way, we never got a real idea of the whole number of 'em. But he told their skippers to rendezvous at a particular time and place— I'd guess Plowshare Straits on Midsummer Day—and there they got their orders." He tugged his whiskers. *"Gr-r-rm,* that can't be his whole navy, not by a long cast. The bulk of it's doubtless out blockading, in case anybody should try sending us help."

"Then why are these here?"

"To cut us off. If we embarked on an unguarded bay, we'd have a fair chance of evading them at sea and geting home to fight on." Larreka's glance traveled across the town, low adobe buildings huddled together and painted in forlornly bright colors, to the river on which its western wall fronted, shallower now than erstwhile so that rocks gleamed like basking monsters, and over the brown and black land enclosing the rest of the world. Dust devils were awhirl out there, dancers who related some violent dream. "Yes," he said, "the campaign's begun. Their foot should arrive shortly."

In a moment he added, "Their top male is committing one foolishness, though. He's forgotten the good old military principle: Always leave your opponent a line of retreat."

"They must expect us to surrender eventually," Seroda added.

"A retreat of sorts, *yai?* But, you see, it isn't really. Those ships yonder say different. And in Valennen, especially these days, you can't support a lot of idle prisoners. Either they massacre us or they put us to work—as slaves, scattered around the country, in mines and quarries, chained to wagons or plows or mill wheels— Me, I'd prefer the massacre." Larreka ended on an oath, for he realized that he'd better assemble his troops while time remained and explain this to them. He hated making speeches.

After two sixty-fours in the legion, Seroda had no need to disclaim fear or lack of loyalty. He could say, "We might yet work out something. After all, it'd cost them plenty to take this post by force. They might still prefer to let us go."

"In that case," Larreka said, "it's our reason for staying."

Those barbarians whom the Zera Victrix killed in its last hours would not be available for an attack on Meroa and her children.

While the double afternoon blazed, the Tassu host reached Port Rua. They camped in their groundshaking thousands a kilometer from the walls, in an arc between river and bay shore. Their grotesque standards, pole-mounted animal or ancestor skulls, tails of slain foes, carven totems, made a forest wherein spearheads flashed as if it bore fruit. Their drums thuttered, their horns lowered, they shouted and sang and galloped to and fro in a smoke of dust.

The town walls were banked earth under a high stockade of phoenix, every log sharpened. Flanked by the towers at the corners, bartizans alternated with bastions. Each of the latter held a catapult throwing several darts at once, or a mangonel with incendiary ammunition. Below the landward slope was a dry ditch in whose bottom bristled pointed stakes. Soldiers lined the walkways back of the wall tops, mail and shields burnished, plumes and pennons flying like the banners enstaffed overhead. Spaced among archers were the few who had rifles.

Upon his return here, Larreka had shipped out most civilians, or they had left voluntarily. Those who remained were wives and servants, many native-born, practically members of the legion themselves. Their labor and nursing would be valuable. *We're not in such bad shape,* he reflected. *Yet.*

A horn resounded thrice, and two loped from a gaudy pavilion. The first was a stripling who dipped the flag he carried in a signal for truce. The second was huge and gold-bedight. *Arnanak in person!* Larreka thought upon his lofty post. *Should I go talk to him? Their ethics wink at treachery.*

No, wait, he is a brother in the Lodge.

And, over protests of his officers, Larreka ordered the north gate opened and its drawbridge lowered. Alone he went forth. He left off armor—why broil himself?—and wore simply his Haelen blade, a pouch, and a red cloak. The last was a confounded flapping nuisance, but Seroda had insisted the commandant couldn't look too shabby when he met their gorgeous rival.

Arnanak spoke to his attendant, who swung flag in salute. He himself stuck sword in soil. With Larreka he exchanged the handclasp and words of their mystery.

Then: "Hail and haleness to you, sir," he said. "Much would it gladden me if we could lay down the death-spears we bear."

"Good idea," Larreka said, "and easily done. Just go on home."

"Would you do the same?"

"I am at home."

"We couldn't set you wholly free anyhow," Arnanak sighed. "You had that chance earlier. Now I must make an end of the Zera."

"Go right ahead and try, sonny boy. But then what're we talking about, when we could be in the shade drinking beer?"

"I have an offer, because you are brave males. Surrender. We will cut off your right hands and keep you

201

fed till you recover, then release you in your ships. You will never soldier again, but you will return."

"Ng-ng." Larreka grinned into the earnest green eyes. "I could make a counter-offer, though I'd ask for a different part of your anatomies. But why bother?"

"I would like you to live," Arnanak urged. "Indeed, we'll leave whole any who join us."

"Do you think that kind would be worth having?" *Yes, they would be, on account of their skills.*

"Otherwise it is death for all, save those unlucky few we capture and put to work." Arnanak flung wide his great black hands. Light glinted and rippled off golden arm-rings. "You have no hope. If naught else, we can starve you."

"We're stocked up, including wells that give a better grade of water than you'll dip out of the estuary. This hinterland's picked clean where it isn't burnt off. Want to see who gets hungry first? I'll race you."

"Aye." Arnanak didn't seem annoyed at having his bluff called. "And you're in a good defensive position. Nevertheless, it *is* defensive, you're bottled, and we outnumber you eight times over. Do you look for help from Beronnen? Let them try it; our shipmasters will be gleeful at the plunder. Do you count on the humans? Why, they haven't even stirred to rescue those two of theirs that I hold."

"Don't underestimate them, friend. I've seen what they can do."

"Do you suppose I worked, fought, schemed throughout these years as I've done, without learning a great deal about them and taking it into my reckonings? My hostages only confirm what I knew. They're here for knowledge, they'll bargain with whoever can best slake that thirst, and they won't fight without provocation that I'll make sure they never get."

Arnanak paused. "You are right about our not laying siege, One-Ear," he continued. "We'll storm you. Unless you take my terms. Can you in honor refuse them on behalf of your folk?"

"Yes," Larreka said. "I do."

Arnanak smiled sadly. "I awaited naught else. But I had to try, no? Well, then ... Brother Among the Three, I wish you a bold journey into the Dark."

"And let Them be kindly to you," Larreka answered, the olden words; whereafter they two embraced as the Faith enjoined, and went their separate ways.

Toward evening the wind shifted around and strengthened, till dust hazed stars and made a thick, hollow-sounding darkness when neither moon was in sight. Under cover of this the barbarians moved their gear into position. It included the engines they took from those troopers who went north to regain Tarhanna. At the earliest dawnflush they started shooting, with these and with bows and slings. When the Sun rose, well-nigh red as the Rover, it saw a full battle.

Arrows whistled in sky-covering flights, stones went *whoo-oo-thump;* a steady barrage to keep down the heads of legionary sharpshooters. Thus halfway protected, Valenneners worked catapults and trebuchets to cast heavy missiles at the walls—every few minutes, a splintering crash, a shudder through the timbers. Howls, screeches, horn blasts and drum-thunder blew from the horde which roiled on the far side of the ditch. Both suns climbed, shadows shrank, heat grew. Grit, borne on gibing air, stung eyes and crunched between teeth.

Larreka moved about to supervise. A standard-bearer on the walkway above him held his personal flag on a long pole. Every commandant adopted an emblem on taking his vows. Among other values, it showed where he was, for those who might want to find him in a hurry. Of course, it attracted enemy fire too; however, Larreka figured he should be used to that. His device had puzzled many: a hand that pointed a shortsword skyward was clear, but not the English motto "Up Yours."

There were orders to give— "Get these love-tokens collected to send back"—and words to say—"Good work, soldier," expecially if the fellow had been hit—and surveillances to make and occasional things to do himself.

For a time, the archers who could shelter in towers and bartizans repelled attempts to throw planks over the ditch. Naked barbarians reeled back, ripped by shafts and quarrels, or tumbled down the slope to lie

203

impaled as the life ran purple out of them. But they got one trebuchet close and it kept hammering until a particular bartizan and its neighbor sagged into ruin. Nothing covered that sector save the bastion between; and a sleet of arrows had taken its crew.

Larreka watched through a peephole. The second strongpoint went out of action about midafternoon. Wildly cheering, the horde surged about before making way for a gang who carried long, heavy boards to bridge the gap.

"Okay," Larreka said. He had his arrangements— a fresh band to handle the mangonel, each member supported by two bearers of oblong shields that would somewhat protect him and themselves. They trotted forth and wound the weapon. Nobody appeared to notice them until Larreka fired a couple of rocks to get the range. Poorly organized, the natives couldn't recommence a proper barrage in a hurry. Meanwhile the planks had been emplaced and a vanguard of well-armored warriors started across. Larreka's third and fourth shots were incendiaries. Jars of blazing oil struck, burst, and scattered widely the pitch they also held. Casualties were heavy and the bridge caught fire.

"Best we go inside, sir," a legionary advised. The arrows were falling in earnest.

"Not quite yet," Larreka answered. *This is fun, sort of. Like old days.* "I think we can get that trebuchet too."

He needed three shots, and a pair of his males took mortal wounds. Nobody escaped whole-skinned. It was worth it, though. The engine that had been breaking down the defenses of Port Rua turned into a great red and yellow pyre. And the other injuries sustained were trivial—in Larreka's case, a furrow across the right haunch, easily willed shut.

He got skimpy time to admire his achievement. He had just led his group back behind the stockade, and was saying, "Well done," to a dying youth, when a runner brought news of six galleys rowing toward the estuary. Arnanak must have an amphibious assault in mind, doubtless conjoined with a fresh attempt on the shore sides.

Larreka considered, looked around the officers and,

beyond them, enlisted soldiers who ringed him in, and asked, "Who'd like to head a really wild mission?"

There was the briefest stillness, then a cohort leader whom he knew for a promising lad took a step forward. "I will," he said.

"Good." Larreka clapped his shoulder. "Get a few volunteers, enough to bend sail on a ship. Wind and tide are right; you can come in after those bastards. They could beach, but they'll use the fishery dock instead—I'm glad now we didn't demolish it earlier—that being a lot handier. Set the ship afire and crash it among them. Escape in a boat, or swim. We'll make a sortie, chop down the crews, and let you back in."

"Sacrifice a whole ship?" wondered Seroda the adjutant.

"We're not going anywhere," Larreka reminded him. "We'll torch the rest to keep 'em out of buccaneer hands. I've only delayed to see if we can find some use for them first, like this."

His main attention was on the young officer. Through heat and dust and wind, the noise outside the walls and the vigils and quiet dyings inside, their eyes met. They both knew what the odds were. In the face before him, Larreka recognized that the soldier had begun—at the back of his mind—to shape the dream he hoped would see him through his death. The commandant tightened his shouldergrip. "Fare in love, legionary," he said. That adieu went back to the last cycle of civilization.

A lull came in the combat. The Tassu ground forces grumbled back in a vast, disorderly mass, to take what rest and refreshment they could. Larreka figured the galleys would stand offshore till dark. Then the sailors would want moonlight while they established their beachhead and raised their scaling ramps. Probably they didn't imagine they could get over the stockade. But they must number in the sixty-fours; staving them off would occupy males who'd be sorely missed at the landward crunch.

I'd better slack off myself while I can, Larreka thought. Weariness was lead within his bones. Accompanied by Seroda, he plodded along thinly trafficked lanes to the headquarters building. The broadcast tower

205

on top reared skeletal against a sullen sky. The Sun was down and the Rover low: light the color of Terrestrial blood, shadows the color of Ishtarian. *At least the next round of fighting will be cooler.*

Irazen, vice commandant after Wolua's disaster, met him in the entrance, a stout, scarred veteran, lacking in flair or imagination but—since matters had gone this far—a good bet to hang in and make the enemy's victory expensive. "You're right in time," he said. "We have a call from the hostage humans. When they learned the situation, they—the female, anyhow—insisted on talking to you."

Jill would. Well, Ian would want to almost as much, but he'd be more patient about it. What a pleasant surprise. She rose before his inner vision, narrow headbanded face in its coif of dusky-yellow hair, eyes more blue than skies above tropical islands when he had wandered thither in his youth and smile more bright and ready than sunlight on their surf, tall slenderness where hid the ghost of a chubby little person who had stumped out laughing for joy to meet him. *Let the Three bring more such unto her, though he wouldn't see them. . . .*Larreka trotted briskly down a hall to the communications room.

"Here he is," the technician on duty said, and saluted his commandant. Larreka took stance before the blank screen.

"Uncle!" Jill's cry broke through. "How are you?"

"Still on deck," Larreka said, as they do in Haelen. "And you?"

"Oh, we, we're all right—went for a sunset walk, and we're sitting on a hilltop watching the dale underneath fill up with twilight—but, Uncle, you're being attacked!"

"They've gotten small joy of it so far," Larreka said.

"So far?" she pounced. "What's next?"

"More of the same. What else?"

Silence buzzed. Maybe Jill and Ian whispered to each other. Or maybe not. This room on this evening was of all the world the most eerily unreal place to be in. When she spoke at last, her tone was hard: "How long can you hold out?"

"Why, that depends—" Larreka said.

206

A legionary obscenity cut him off. "I quizzed your technie while we waited for you. No help is coming. Right? You haven't even had us, for what bit of good we might've done. Uncle, I know you, and God in heaven damn it, I claim soldier's privilege—you level with me."

"I thought we might simply gab for a spell," Larreka said into the cold countenances of instruments and controls.

"I'm beyond the age where a piece of candy will do me," Jill said. "Listen, I *know*. The rest of the Gathering has written you off. Supposing they did change their minds about what it's worth to hold Valennen, as you hoped they would if you held out—supposing that, they're too late. Arnanak's outsmarted them. My people are . . . paralyzed, or leashed by their own Navy. Your retreat is blocked and, since you won't surrender, you're to be annihilated. Arnanak was quite frank about that to both Ian and me. Your aim now is to make your annihilation so expensive that civilization gets a breathing space. Right?" Jill's voice broke across. "God damn it, I repeat, we can't let the thing be!"

"All die at last, dear," he told her in a surge of gentleness. "Look at it this way: I'm spared watching that happen to you."

The shaken answer came: "Ian and I have decided we'll get them off their asses in Primavera . . . somehow. . . . Ian, we will!" After she had shuddered, she spoke steadily. "Keep this circuit available to us. Stand by for a patch-in to Hanshaw's office at any hour. You savvy?"

"What do you have in mind?" Larreka asked. A fear sharpened his words.

"We don't know yet. Something."

"You must not risk yourselves. That's an order, soldier."

"Not to save Port Rua?"

Larreka stared into the abyss before he remembered how he had sent the chief of cohort off on a fire ship, and Jill had always liked to think of herself as attached to the Zera Victrix. "Well," he said slowly, "check with me beforehand, okay?"

"Okay, old dear," she whispered.

207

Sparling's dry, abashed tone: "Uh, considering drain on batteries, we'd better stick to immediate practicalities. Have you any estimate of how long you can hold out unaided?"

"Till sometime between tomorrow morning and the fall equinox. It involves a clutch of imponderables," Larreka said, while he thought what a grand mate for Jill this Ian would have been if twenty years didn't make such a grotesquely big difference to humans. "Eventually they'll cross our barriers and breach our walls. We can't shoot that many fast enough to prevent it. But if we inflict heavy casualties early in the game, Arnanak may elect to go slow, spending fewer males he'll be wanting later on. Once they are inside, we'll make them capture the town house by house." He pondered. "Ng-ng, split the difference and call thirty-two days a reasonable guess."

"No more than that?" Sparling asked low. "Well . . . we'll have to think and act fast. I may already have the germ of an idea. Luck be yours, Larreka."

Across the wilderness and those same two decades, little girl Jill said, "Smoo-oo-ooch." The connection broke instantly—lest he hear her crying, Larreka thought.

He turned to Irazen, who had waited. "Anything further to report to me?" he inquired.

"Nothing important, sir," his second replied.

"I want a nap. Action should resume shortly after first moonrise. Call me then."

Larreka sought his quarters. They had been Meroa's too, and still held things of hers and memories. As he doffed his armor, he stood before a photograph of the two of them and their latest child at the time, taken by a man in the early years of Primavera. Jacob Zopf had died a bachelor, his own race had no more memory of him than lay in their archives, but whenever she visited there, Meroa tended the Earth flowers she had planted on the grave of her friend. *Well, you're that sort,* Larreka thought to her.

He stretched flat on his left side because he had the double mattress to himself, closed his eyes, and wondered what to dream about. Fun and fantasy were probably wisest—let him, say, have wings and see what happened. It could be too saddening to wake with a mindful of ghosts. And yet, how much longer did he have for living back through the past and his might-have-beens? If he wanted a good death dream, he ought to start planning and experimenting now. Of course, he might not get killed in any way that let him depart from existence in the style and company he wanted. . . . "Ah, damn," he growled, concentrated on the wedding of Jill and Ian, and drowsed off into a feast which turned out riotously merry.

Seroda roused him by lamplight as per orders. The barbarians ashore were on the move again. Their galleys had raised anchor and were headed from midstream to the fishery dock. They had made no attempt against the larger ship that stood a ways off from them; doubtless they supposed its crew merely watched for an unlikely chance to slip past their fellows in the bay.

"Okay, I'll be along," Larreka said through what was half a yawn, half a chuckle at things which had happened at his dream party. Seroda gave him a bowl of soup and helped him back into his battle kit. He left HQ in a cheerful mood. Who knew, maybe his friends really would find a way to bail him out.

The assault on shore shouldn't bring any surprises that officers on the spot couldn't handle. The riverside was less predictable, more interesting. Larreka hied there. From a bartizan above the gate, he observed.

Caelestia had cleared the western hills and was rapidly swinging up among the stars. To him it looked like a red shield curiously emblazoned. Its light spilled through the hot air, across the barren land, sullen until it struck the water; then it suddenly turned silver-cool, a trembling bridge. The barbarian craft moved black across that glade. When they docked, the yells of their crews rent whatever peace had been in this night.

The trick would be to keep them busy till the fire ship arrived—same as they were supposed to keep the legion amused while their comrades hit the opposite end of town. Across moonlit roofs, Larreka heard the racket of that attack.

Bows droned, missiles whistled. Only those invaders stopped who were struck. The rest advanced in zigzag dashes, hard for sight to follow among shadows. Many

209

carried torches, which streamed and sparked from their haste.

Behind them, sails loomed phantomlike, limned by flames. The crash when ship smote dock went on through ground and bones. The blaze roared outward. Yet the Valenneners, however dismayed they might be, didn't break and run. They struggled over the earthworks to the bottom of the stockade; they poured oil out of leather bottles onto the timber, and their brands kindled it.

. .Did Arnanak deliberately fool me into thinking this was a diversion? Chaos, this is the main event! "Out, out!" Larreka bawled. "Sally—shove 'em back—before the whole wall burns!"

He pounded down the ramp and to the gate. Sword unsheathed, he led his troopers forth.

Metal sang upon metal. The barbarians rushed in, recklessly brave, hewing, hewing. Outnumbered, the legionaries stayed behind their shields and worked. They drove a wedge into the enemy that warded those of them who doused the fires. Then reserve forces reached the scene, and the soldiers could advance. Step by step, stab by stab, they drove the foe back down to the burning ships and the tides beyond.

"Good lads!" Larreka cheered. "Come on, finish 'em off, in the name of the Zera!"

A blow rocked him. Pain forked from his right eye. Darkness followed. He dropped the Haelen blade and fumbled at the shaft in his head. "Already?" he asked aloud. Amazement gave way to a whirling and thundering. His legs crumpled beneath him. A trooper crouched close. Larreka paid no heed. In the red light of moon and flames, he called on the strength he had left, before it ebbed wholly away, to help him dream what short small death dream he could.

XXI

MASSIVE-WALLED, THE room in the Tower of the Books was almost cool. Twinned sunlight slanted through windows curtained by strings of glass beads, to break in multitudinous hues on the stone floor. The same colors brightened the air, butterfly-like entomoids around Jerassa's mane. The scholar stood at a table whereon he had unrolled a parchment from the full shelves which lined this chamber. His English was precise to the verge of pedantry; but no Ishtarian could help turning language into music:

"Here are diagrams of various muscle-powered vessels in use when humans arrived. They may still be found in some areas. The problem is, you see, my kind may be individually stronger than yours, but we are considerably larger too. Fewer rowers, or crew-folk of any sort, can fit into a given hull. How best to apply available force?" He pointed. "This shows a supporting framework and system of sockets which enable forefeet as well as hands to work on an oar. And this shows a treadmill to drive paddle wheels or, in later models, a screw. But such devices are inefficient, and apt to break down when good steel is not present to withstand torque. The Valenneners and Fiery Sea islanders therefore combine fore-and-aft sails with ordinary oars, making a craft highly maneuverable though of limited displacement. We South Beronneners, as you may have noticed, favor large square-riggers. They have the drawback of sluggish response—for, in spite of arrangements like bosun's chairs and ankle hooks, the crews cannot get about aloft as readily as you.

"Since your emissaries have taught us improved metallurgy, designers have been experimenting with propellers turned by windmills. In due course, naturally, we hope to build engines, but as yet the industrial base for that is absent and now, given periastron, we will scarcely establish any for centuries."

He did not add, *We could, if Primavera were again free to help us survive.* There was no hint of reproach in the rich, sober voice. But Dejerine, standing beside him, winced.

"Those are exquisite just as drawings," the human managed to say, quite truthfully. "And the . . . the brains, the determination, to accomplish this much when Anu forever returns—"

All at once it must out. "Why have you received

211

me?" he asked. "Why do your people keep on being friendly to my men, when their own breed in town won't speak to them?"

Jerassa's eyes, which were golden, met his in calmness. "What would we accomplish by a freezeout of lonely youngsters, save to fence ourselves off from the many interesting things they can tell? Most of us are aware they had no choice about their purpose here. The Primaveran community hopes to exert influence on your ultimate leaders, through you, by withholding the skills—and the kinship—you need. We possess neither."

Dejerine swallowed. "You've certainly won our sympathy," he admitted. "For your plight; for the marvels we'd lose if your civilization dies." *And I too am brought to wonder about the war in space. Is it worth the cost and agony? Is it winnable ever? Is . . . it . . . even . . . any proper business of Earth's?* "But we have our duty."

"I belong to a legion," Jerassa reminded him.

The Ishtarian was about to resume his discussion of Sehala's prediscovery scientific and technological status, when Dejerine's com buzzed. He hauled the flat case from his tunic pocket, pressed accept, and barked into it: "Yes? What now?"

"Lieutenant Majewski here, sir," the Spanish came, tinny by contrast. "Police Intelligence. I'm sorry to disturb you on your day off, but this is urgent."

"Ah, yes, you're assigned to keeping track of our good local citizens. Proceed." Unease went along Dejerine's backbone.

"You'll recall, sir, they had accumulated a large stock of explosives for their projects. We left it in the storehouse under seal. After friction got bad, I decided to install a radio alarm, unbeknownst to them, and did under guise of re-checking the inventory. Shortly before dawn today, it rang. Unfortunately, we had nobody near town—well, the burglars would have made sure of that. By the time I could flit there with a squad from base, the job was done. Very professionally. The seal showed no visible sign of tampering. The interior looked so usual, too, that we had to count practically every object to find that ten cases of tordenite and fifty blasting cells were gone."

Dejerine whistled.

"Yes, high-powered technicians were at work," Majewski continued. "As for the reason why nobody was stationed in town—they'd have received the alarm signal as soon as my office did. But Mayor Hanshaw had asked them to help search for a flyer that had called to say a storm was forcing it down in the Stony Mountains. Well, sir, your orders are to grant any reasonable request. They all four went. A wild goose chase, I suspect but can't prove."

"This is crazy!" Dejerine protested. "*Hanshaw* wouldn't get involved with saboteurs. . . .Does he know you know about the burglary?"

"He asked why we were back in the storehouse. I thought I'd better consult you, and gave him a vague story about possibly unsafe conditions having been reported. He raised his eyebrows but made no comment."

"Good man, Majewski. I'll see this gets into your career file. *Pro tempore,* you and your group stay in quarters and answer no questions. I'm on my way."

Dejerine clicked off, mumbled an apology to Jerassa, and hastened out. Unseasonably, the day sweltered. Thunderheads towered black in the west. Light elsewhere seemed a still angrier red than before. He was glad to enter his vehicle and lift it.

On the short hop to Primavera, he called Hanshaw. It was a relief to find the mayor at home. No matter how unlikely, apocalyptic visions had jittered in the Earthman's brain. "Dejerine here. I must see you at once."

"Ye-es, Captain, I was sort of expecting you. Best we keep talk between the two of us, huh?"

Dejerine parked outside the house. Two passersby stared through him. He clattered into its shaded shelter. Stiff-faced, Olga Hanshaw brought him into the living room and closed that door as she departed. Her husband's big-bellied form occupied an armchair near a recorder. He didn't rise, but he lifted a hand and smiled slightly around a cigar. "Hello," he said. "Squat yourself."

Dejerine gave him a soft salute and tensed down into a seat opposite. In English: "I've just gotten terrible news."

"Well?"

"Sir, please allow me to be blunt. This is too serious for pussyfooting. Stolen high explosives, and reason to believe you may have connived at the theft."

"I wouldn't call it stealing. The stuff belongs to us."

"Then you admit guilt?"

"Wouldn't call it guilt either."

"That material was sequestered for Navy use. Sir, in spite of our disagreements, I never imagined you might get involved in treason."

"Aw, come on." Hanshaw let out a blue reek of smoke. "I do admit I'd hoped we could operate on the QT. You had the place gimmicked, hey? But relax. We're not giving aid and comfort to enemies of Earth. And you'll never miss that smidgin we, uh, reappropriated."

"Where is it?"

"Off in the boondocks, along with a few technies and their apparatus. I can't tell you where; didn't want to know, in case you interrogated me. You've no way of arresting them till they've completed their mission. And—Yuri, I foresee your grabbing any excuse you can, to let them off the hook."

"Tell me." Dejerine clamped fists together on knees.

"I think we should play back a conversation of mine a couple of days ago." Beneath Hanshaw's easy drawl dwelt bleakness. "I always record such things. You recall the situation in Valennen? Jill Conway and Ian Sparling prisoners in the outback, and Port Rua under near-as-damn continuous storm by what looks like every brave in the continent."

A twisting went through Dejerine. Jill—"Yes," he said.

"When Ian went there, he smuggled in a microcom, and brought relays for the soldiers to distribute which'd connect him to Port Rua. And therefore to us, if occasion demanded."

"You never told me!" Dejerine exclaimed. He felt sick with hurt.

"Well, you're a busy man," Hanshaw grunted.

Dejerine thought of streets where he walked like a ghost, and work in the desert slowed to a crawl, and the hours he spent composing reports euphemistic enough to stay the Federation's hand from Primavera for at least a while. "Didn't you think I'd be *interested?* Why, those two—they may have turned from me, but I am still their friend—"

Again Jill rode over the valley. the long hair aflow in her speed; again she jested and discoursed and showed him wonders which her eagerness about them turned into miracles; again she fed him in the amiable clutter of her home, and played and sang to him under the high stars of her planet. Again she came back when he lay sleepless, alone at night. Again he swore wearily at himself for being an adolescent inside, then claimed he wasn't really infatuated—attracted, as any normal man would be, but no more than a brief acquaintance would cause—besides, one should allow for a loneliness that other encounters, in bed and out, had never filled since Eleanor left.

Dejerine stiffened in a lift of anger. "If you are quite through punishing me," he said, "you can turn on that recording."

"*Touché,*" Hanshaw conceded. His expression turned warmer. "Understand, because of limited battery they hadn't contacted us directly before. Through Port Rua we heard they were in good health and spirits, well treated, on a sort of estate in the western uplands. I did pass on word about the strike, since that might conceivably affect their plans or actions. Then day before yesterday I got a call straight from them."

His finger poised near the on switch. "In case you'd like to visualize," he said, "we know that general area from air and orbit pictures, plus Ishtarian accounts. The hills and the mountains behind them are rather beautiful in an austere fashion. The woods are mostly low and gnarly, not much underbrush, red and yellow leaves partly shading off a cloudless sky. But in places you get T-vegetation, blue foliage; a couple kinds like the phoenix are impressive. It's hot there, kiln-hot and dry. With less wildlife than hereabouts and little running water, it's pretty silent. Jill and Ian hiked well

215

beyond sight and earshot of their keepers, two of them alone in that singed and dying forest."

"Thank you," Dejerine nodded. "I do visualize" *her withy-slim among crooked dwarf trees, sunlight flaring off her silver fillet and sheening copper along her hair, brilliant eyes and gallant smile . . . beside her a man who has long been her single companion. . . . Assez! Arrêtons, imbécile!*

Her tone shocked him, not the clear huskiness he knew but rough and uneven. "Hello, that you, God? Jill Conway and Ian Sparling here, calling from Valennen."

"Huh?" gusted Hanshaw's reply. "Yes, yes, it's me. Is anything wrong, girl?"

JILL: Everything is.

SPARLING: We're in no present danger personally.

HANSHAW: Where are you? What's happened?

SPARLING: Oh, the same place under the same conditions. We figured the chances were you'd be home at this hour. But are you private?

HANSHAW: No, I'm public. However, if you mean am I alone and can I keep it that way, the answer is yes.

JILL (not chuckling at his feeble joke): How about monitors? We won't want this conversation overheard.

HANSHAW: Safe, if you refer to the Navy. It doesn't listen in on transplanet sendings, probably not local ones either, so much talk being in Sehalan. I have Joe Seligman bring his kit around irregularly and check my house for taps or bugs, but he never finds any. Captain Dejerine's a gentleman at heart. And he must know I'm not conspiring.

JILL: You will be.

HANSHAW: What?

JILL: If I know you. After you've heard.

HANSHAW: Okay, let's get to the point. What's happened?

JILL: Larreka . . . is . . . dead. Killed. He—

HANSHAW: Oh, no-o. When? How?

SPARLING: (and a few fought-against sobs in the background): You'd have heard when the legion made its next report to the Mother Base. But we, being anxious because of the combat there, checked with Port Rua this morning. He fell last night, leading a sally.

216

The maneuver worked, but he took an arrow between his helmet bars and— Well, the garrison's hanging on; but I doubt they can last as long as they would have with him in charge.

HANSHAW: Poor Meroa. . . .

JILL: Let her get the news f-f-from the Zera's post in Sehala when it learns . . . as a soldier's wife deserves.

HANSHAW: Sure.

JILL: This tears it. We'd already sworn we'd find a way to get help to him. Now—he is not going to have died for nothing!

HANSHAW: What can be done?

SPARLING: We've given that a lot of thought. But suppose you describe matters where you are.

HANSHAW: Not promising, I'm afraid. The Navy sits tight on everything useful. I scarcely think a few civilian passenger flyers buzzing the barbarians will stampede them, do you? They'll've seen occasional overflights before, and heard about us. Firearms haven't fazed them, have they?

SPARLING: You can't persuade Dejerine to release real weapons, or look the other way while you do? After all, it involves rescuing us. I've got our location pinpointed on the map, and a grid to identify landmarks. A pilot couldn't miss who came to get us. You said our captivity, Jill's in particular, was a cause of the general strike. Well, won't Dejerine hope, maybe with reason, if we're freed, the strike will end?

HANSHAW: I, uh, I don't believe it would. Emotions here are mighty powerful under the quiet surface. Sure, we'll send a flyer after you. But as for Dejerine letting us use equipment or even risk Primavera men to save a part of civilization that wouldn't be in those dire straits if it weren't for his mission, his war— Children, I can foresee that kind of affair leading to secession, like Eleutheria's and New Europe's except that Primavera would join the Gathering. And next I can see Earth either losing us or having to send occupation troops it can ill afford, and Dejerine ruined for his "mismanagement." And I can foresee him forseeing exactly the same.

No, speaking as our resident politician, I can tell you that things are superficially tranquil because we don't

217

have such an involvement, such a commitment to the Zera Victrix. We're distressed at the pass it's in, maybe more distressed than we know; but it was the Gathering, not us, that chose to abandon it when it declined to come home. Let us join it in battle— Well, I said feelings are frighteningly strong, however tight-held. It'll be very hard for you, Jill, not to stay a flaming symbol when you return—twice bereaved now by this accursed war, since everybody knows how close you were to Larreka— Yeah, I beg you to resist the temptation. The last thing we need is a blowup.

JILL: Twice bereaved?

HANSHAW: What'd I say? Slip of the tongue. Let's not waste breath, let's discuss the wherefores of recovering you. Why didn't you get in touch immediately after you completed your survey, Ian?

JILL: Wait a minute.

HANSHAW: Uh—

JILL: Wait a bloody minute. You said, when you called before, my capture helped bring on the strike. But I'd been captured many days earlier. You were glossing something over, God. What happened next?

SPARLING: Jill, you wait. We'll get briefed when we get back.

JILL: God, what are you hiding?

HANSHAW: Ian's right, girl. Wait.

Silence.

JILL (a dead voice): It was Don, wasn't it? News about my brother.

Silence.

HANSHAW: Yes. He was killed in action.

Silence.

SPARLING: Jill, darling, laren—

JILL: Odd. I feel just numb.

SPARLING: You've been hurt to the heart already.

JILL: How's the family bearing up?

HANSHAW: Strongly. All you Conways are that sort. But me and my big flapping mouth— Jill, I'm, I'm sorry—

JILL: No, you did right. I'd want to know. . . . Ian, can I sit down on this log and hold your hand, and you discuss the rest?

SPARLING: Of course. I love you.

218

Silence

SPARLING: Hello, God? Excuse, please. A shock to me too.

HANSHAW: Everybody liked Don, and nobody liked the war. His death triggered the resistance.

SPARLING: (with slight difficulty): This doubles the reason for relieving Port Rua. A memorial— But see here. We've another reason yet. One that changes everything. Our way, we think, our way to force help out of somebody. In these parts and northward is intelligent T-life.

HANSHAW: Huh?

SPARLING: Yes. The weirdest little beings. Judas! I'd guess the study of their psychology alone could bring on a revolution in that field.

HANSHAW: Are you sure they're sophonts?

SPARLING: We've met a few. Seen them handle artifacts. Exchanged signs, if not words. Arnanak, the barbarian king, had contacted them, traveled way into their country and— He's using them to reinforce his power; the Valenneners think they're supernatural. In reality, he's made a deal. They'll share in the booty of better lands when he's finished his conquests. But here's the peak of it all. They're few and primitive, these dauri, as he calls them . . . but they know where an ancient Tammuzian ruin is. What it was like originally, what it's like after a billion years, I have no idea. However, Arnanak brought home an object, a portable star display is my guess, that time hasn't touched. Mull that over a while!

HANSHAW: Whe-ew-w-w. . . .

SPARLING: Obviously we humans can offer the dauri a lot more than he can, and learn about them and— (Oh, Jill, Jill)—but only if we can function effectively here on Ishtar. Which requires we have the Gathering to help us—which requires we save it—and with the dauri living in Valennen, Port Rua is the place to start.

Silence.

HANSHAW: M-m-m, yes, I agree. At a bare minimum, if we knack the barbarian organization, keep the outpost, yes, then the Gathering should be able to mount guard on the north; and there won't be that awful pressure on the south. . . .Yes. But how, Ian?

219

SPARLING: Would it be possible for the flyer, no, the flyers that fetch us to carry homemade bombs? Apparently the enemy makes massed charges, trying to reach the walls and break through by sheer weight of numbers. Bombs dropped into the brown of them—I hate the idea, but consider the alternative.

HANSHAW: Are you sure it'd work?

SPARLING: No. But we haven't thought of anything better to try.

HANSHAW: Uh-huh. Well, let me see. Our explosives are locked away these days, but—m-m-m— Well, I'll have to ponder as you suggest, and consult a few reliable men, and— You can wait some days, can't you?

SPARLING: Yes, we assumed we'd have to.

HANSHAW: We'll keep in touch. How about I call you daily at—shall we say noon?

SPARLING: That sounds reasonable.

HANSHAW: Starting tomorrow, then.

SPARLING: Now we'd better sign off.

HANSHAW: Until tomorrow. Jill, I'm so unspeakably sorry.

JILL: That's all right, God. Let's ... go on ... and salvage what they both lived for.

Click.

Half a minute passed before Hanshaw added slowly to Dejerine: "What all Primavera lives for. You try to suppress aid in the teeth of this news, and you probably will touch off a revolt."

Dejerine nodded. He felt stunned and drained.

"The single thing you need do," Hanshaw said, "is *not* react vigorously to the storehouse incident. Explain in your report that you're holding off action while you investigate. GHQ will agree that's a sound policy, I'm sure. We figure we can send off our expedition in maybe five days. Afterward we'll face the music."

The resolution did not burst upon Dejerine. It appeared to his awareness like something which had been there for a time, in embryo for a much longer time, and its strength lent a great calm.

"No," he said. "Delay is not necessary."

"What do you mean?"

"I will go, in a naval aircraft. Far more effective, not to mention safer for—for her, in case of sudden bad

220

weather. Tomorrow at noon when you call, I will be here to make arrangements."

"But 'effective'? You say you can't get into this fight."

"I can carry out a rescue, with part of my aim the improvement of the Navy's public relations. There is no need for Miss Conway or Mr. Sparling to be present when your bombers strike, is there?"

Hanshaw regarded Dejerine closely before he asked, "You'll go yourself, solo?"

"Yes. To preserve discretion."

"I see." The mayor rolled to his feet and thrust out his hand. "Okay, Yuri! How about a beer?"

XXII

THE MORNING BEFORE rendezvous, Sparling and Jill announced that they intended another overnight trip. Innukrat regarded them closely. "For what?" she asked.

"You know my work is to learn about animals," Jill answered. "I would observe those that fare by darkness."

"Aye. And yet—" Arnanak's wife sighed. "Your manner has changed of late. I wish I knew your kind well enough to guess how or why. But I see it, and hear it in your speech." Her nostril dilated. "I smell it."

Jill stood taken aback. Sparling jumped into the breach: "You are right. The battle for Port Rua must be well along, maybe ended. They are our friends yonder. Do you not fear for those you care about, and long for any word even though it be evil?"

"Are we that alike?" Innukrat said very quietly. "Then go you shall if you wish. I have my work here to keep me from thinking too much." She gave them a generous ration both of native food and supplement.

When they were afoot, Jill confessed: "I thought I was a fanatic (j.g.). Instead, I feel treacherous."

"Don't," Sparling said. "Nobody alive can be more

221

loyal than you. But loyalty to the whole of creation isn't possible."

As I have found out, Rhoda, jabbed within him. *Tomorrow I must face you, who've never stopped loving me.*

And I may do that with manacles on my wrists. Is this why I hope my crazy scheme will work? He touched the hunting knife which he, like the girl, wore. *Why the idea hit me in the first place, after what Dejerine told us? Could it be that the amateur bombing plot won't likely get me in enough trouble to make love unimportant?*

He glanced at her profile, envied her straightforwardness, then: *Stop groveling! What a waste of our last time alone.*

They spoke seldom through the next hour, for the climb was hard to their goal. When the subject arose of where that was to be, they had simultaneously named the same place; and their eyes met and they laughed. It had the required characteristics, distance from Ulu, easy identifiability, safe landing for a vehicle. Other locations were handier. But here they could spend an easy evening.

Timberline in Valennen was drawn not by cold but by aridity; and evolution in the Starklands had given T-life greater endurance of this than ortho-life. At the campsite, red and yellow forest had, kilometers behind, yielded to blue growth of different shape, fringed, leathery to the touch. Bushes grew well apart. Still wider spaced were trees. But where the mountain thrust forth an enormous outcrop, which the Ulu folk named Arnanak's Rump in his presence, a concavity on the south side cast shade. From under the foot trickled a spring. Nearby rose the dark bronze trunk of a phoenix, whose roof gave further shelter. The ground was padded with cerulean turf. Here and there sparkled bright orange not-quite-flowers. Westward the plateau became entirely open, and outlook ran unhindered to the gray awesomeness of the Worldwall.

The humans fell prone on opposite sides of the water, drank and drank. Sparling noticed blessed coolness and a tang of iron, but mainly Jill's cheek against his and a strand of blond hair in the rivulet.

222

Slaked, they settled down in shadow dappled crimson and gold. There was a curious absence of odor from the soil—human noses didn't respond—but no matter; his body and hers breathed forth a fragrance of flesh that had been at work outdoors.

"Hoo-ha," Jill said. "Let's just sit a while and sweat."

Sparling's gaze lingered on her as he chose words. "I'm happier than I can explain, seeing you aren't downcast."

She tossed her head. "I refuse to be. Don, Larreka—I'll mourn afterward. Neither would want me doing it here . . . nor you, Ian."

"I wish I had, well, your ability—no, your courage to be glad."

Her smile was lopsided. "You think that comes easy? It's a fight, and I don't win every round." She reached to ruffle his hair. "Let's help each other stay cheerful, *amante*. Captain's dinner tonight, followed by revelry. Tomorrow we make port."

"What then?"

"Who knows?" She grew altogether serious. Tears jeweled the thick lashes. "I ask one thing of you, Ian. One solemn promise."

"Yes?" *You can have any I dare give.*

"Your word of honor. Whatever I do, don't try to stop me."

"What? What are you thinking of?" *Suicide? Impossible!*

Her eyes dropped; fingers wrestled in her lap. "I can't rightly tell. Everything's tangled beyond redemption. But, oh, suppose I decided to—go propagandize on Earth, on behalf of Ishtar. I can claim accumulated leave, my right to a passage. You can't, and I doubt you can buy a ticket either while the war lasts. You could hold me back, though, by begging me to stay and be your mistress."

"Do you imagine I'd be that selfish? Making you act against your conscience? In fact—when we return, I have . . . my obligations, and you shouldn't spend more of your life on an old man who can't ever give you anything real—" *Assuming I'm there at all.*

She laid a hand across his mouth. He kissed her

223

palm. "Hush," she said. "We'll work that out later on, when we know what's best, least unkind." Rapidly: "See why I want your word, effective immediately, you'll let me find my own way, whatever it may turn out to be? I have to explore these questions freely."

He nodded. She released him to reply, "Yes. Maybe I should've expected this demand from you. Freedom," and wonder why she winced. But in a moment she pursued:

"Then I have your promise?" And he responded: "Yes, you do."

She cast both arms around him. "Thank you, thank you!" She struggled not to weep. "I never loved you more than now."

He comforted her as best he was able. In a surprisingly short time she could lift eyes full of mischief and breathe, "I'll start collecting right away. Guess what you mustn't prevent me from doing." And very soon after: "Ah, yes, I figured you'd co-operate."

Later, when Anu hung immense above the peaks, they built a fire and cooked supper. Then came stars and moons. They would sleep a little, and rouse to each other again.

The rescue vehicle arrived at mid-morning.

"There he comes!" Jill called. Sparling's look followed her upflung hand. A blinding-bright spark hurtled out of the south, became a winged barracuda shape, overshot, looped back, and circled far overhead, trailing thunder. They embraced a final hasty time and ran from rock and tree, into the heat and glare beneath naked heaven where they could be seen.

The aircraft slanted down. Jill whistled. "That's a *big* Boojum," she said.

A *Huitzilopochtli*, Sparling recognized. *Six machine guns, three cannon, an energy projector, and a couple of one-kiloton blast-focused missiles.* His head had felt a bit hollow and sandy, but the feeling vanished in a thrum of excitement.

The microcom on his wrist beeped. He admitted Dejerine's voice: "Hello on the ground. All clear?"

"All clear," Jill responded. "Come join the party."

The vessel did. Sparling's heart banged. Was the offi-

224

cer indeed aboard alone, as he had mentioned he would be? Sensors, computers, effectors, and whatnot, that was nevertheless a lot of machine to single-hand. *Part of me wishes he's got companions or—or anything. . . .* It halted. They jogged toward it.

A lock opened and extruded a gangway. Dejerine appeared at the top, a slim figure in a trim field uniform. He waved. Jill waved back. Metal thudded beneath hastening boots.

Dejerine shook their hands. His clasp was enthusiastic. But did he seem tired, nervous, even suspicious? *Well, after what he's been through— He bears no side arm. No side arm.*

"Welcome," he greeted. "I can't tell how happy I am to see you again." His attention was directed at Jill. *Where else? She told me he acted fond of her. Who couldn't?*

"Did you truly come by yourself?" she asked.

"Yes," Dejerine said.

Sparling knew both glee and grief.

"We may as well start right home," Dejerine said. "It's a glorious flight. This planet has more beauty than my mind can take in."

Then why won't you let us save it, you—no, not you son of a bitch—you military robot? . . . Hold on there, Sparling. You're too damn near hysteria.

They entered. The lock closed behind them. Conditioned air shocked with mildness and moisture. The main body of the craft extended ranks of instruments and equipment on either side of a passageway.

Dejerine wiped a forefinger across his sweaty mustache. "I can't imagine how you two stood that furnace this long," he said.

Jill sang *sotto voce,* "Shadrach, Meshach, Abednego—"

"I brought food, drink, medicine, fresh clothes," Dejerine continued. "When we're up, I'll put us on automatic; but can I do anything for you before we take off?"

Now! And there was no more time for doubt or regret.

Sparling drew his knife, gripped underhanded. "Yes," His voice resonated through his skull. "You can make ready to deliver the legion. Don't move! This is a hijack."

Jill gasped, Dejerine's olive complexion paled a trifle, though he stood oddly steady and his features merely went expressionless apart from the luminous dark eyes.

"My private idea," Sparling said. "Never a hint to Jill. But when I knew the circumstances—when I thought how our weak, clumsy effort from Primavera might not work, and at best could only give temporary help—while this monster can cow any warriors who escape it for the rest of their lives— Do you see? I'm prepared to surrender to you afterward, and stand trial and serve sentence. But please believe, Captain, I'm just as prepared to secure you and try being my own pilot if you don't obey my orders."

"Ian—" Her voice broke like glass.

Dejerine sprang. The distance was short, he was young and supple, trained in personal combat. Yet Sparling swayed aside and delivered a kick and a left-handed chop which laid him asprawl.

"Don't try that again, son," the engineer advised. "You're good, but I spent years in sections where I'd better know infighting . . . against Ishtarians. This knife is more emphasis than threat."

Dejerine climbed to his feet, gingerly touched the places where he had been struck, wet his lips, and spoke slowly: "If I refuse—and I'm sworn to the service of the Federation—you're practically sure to crash. They don't let anyone rated less than Master Pilot near the controls of a thing like this. What then about Jill?"

"I'll send her back to Ulu with a story that accounts for my absence," Sparling said.

She stepped forward. "Like hell you will, mister," she stated.

"Like hell I won't," Sparling answered; and to Dejerine: "I repeat, she's been in no conspiracy, she was unaware of my plan, her behavior has been correct throughout."

Jill clenched fists and stamped a foot. "You idiot!" she yelled. "Why do you suppose I snaked that promise out of you, not to block me, whatever I did? I intended the same piracy myself!"

He couldn't gape at her, for he must watch Dejerine

226

and she must keep beyond the latter's reach. He could only glimpse her in a corner of his sight, flushed, breath quick, fire-blue eyes and teeth agleam. *You would*, he knew. Aloud. "You're raving."

"That she is," Dejerine said in a hurry. "A touch of sun. I didn't follow her, she was so incoherent. Sparling, I will assume you're an honest man, however misguided. If I do your will, under duress, and you surrender to me later—we'll return here and fetch Jill. We'll have left her behind, you see, in safety."

The girl drew blade. "No." Her tone became one of the grimmest either man had ever heard. "I'm dealing myself in whether you want me or not. I hold you to your oath, Ian. Break it, and you'll have to fight me. Is that your wish?

"Listen. If you're alone with him, Yuri has a chance of taking you. He can pull a stunt—he's a spaceman and he's younger; he can take more gee force. He can black you out with a dive or a swerve and grab that shiv of yours, and there goes the game. But two of us—two of us'll be too many, too risky. Right, Yuri? Against two, you'll have no choice. Your duty'll be to stay at the helm—if only because you doubt a pair of klutzes like us can return the Federation's big expensive death machine undamaged."

I can't dismiss her now, whatever I do. She's torched her last line of retreat. The knowledge was like a blow to Sparling's throat.

Dejerine—Dejerine looked as badly shocked. His shoulders slumped, he gnawed his lip, in a muteness which went on. Finally, his stare never leaving the girl, he said rasp-voiced:

"Yes. Your analysis is correct. I will fly for you."

Turning, he led the way toward the command cabin. His back had straightened but his gait was stiff. And Sparling thought: *He guessed I might do what I did. Not Jill, that was a foul surprise, but me. He came here open to me.*

A glance at her showed pity on her face. *She sees this too.*

XXIII

Arnanak drew sword. Light flamed off the blade. "Forward!" he shouted.

A mighty sound arose as two dozen strong warriors strained against pushbars. Slowly, creaking, groaning, the bridge rocked into motion. Dust and cinders smoked from its wheels, sought eyes, ears, noses, mouths, plants. Sun and Marauder blazed ruthless in a glaring sky above a sere land. To the right, the river shone like brass. The earthworks and walls ahead loomed unreal through haze and heat-shimmer.

Yet the bridge toiled onward. Arnanak paced it at a distance. Its crew needed what heartening he could give. He and his big legionary shield would take their chances when he came within bowshot.

Pride swelled in him afresh whenever he glanced at the crude, ugly contraption. This was his thought, his doing. The engineers of the Gathering had never made anything like it; their foes had never built towns as well fortified as Port Rua. The beds of three wagons in a row carried massive timbers which jutted far enough ahead to cross the ditch. A load of stones at the rear balanced them. Behind, a bulkhead and roof warded those who shoved the huge weight along. Hardly a thing could stop it save the heaviest boulder a trebuchet might throw; and he had spent lives and his remaining captured hurlers to wreck every northside bastion.

Arrows whistled from the stockade. Many bore fire, and several struck home. But it was hard to kindle balks this big, which had furthermore gotten well wetted while being rafted down from Tarhanna and afterward by bucket brigades. Arnanak dodged to and fro. Regardless of weather, the surge of muscles felt good as he played tag with the shafts.

He still failed to see Larreka's banner. It had been gone for days, ever since the Zera inflicted that disaster at the riverside which made Arnanak order suspension of attacks other than bombardment and completion of his unfinished, untried device, no matter how much the warriors griped. Had the commandant fallen? If so, sleep well, Brother Among the Three. Yet Larreka was canny, and—

And they were at the gap!

A thunderstorm of joy broke from the massed Tassui when the bridge crashed snout against embankment. Arnanak whirled and sped back. The weary crew took out the pegs which held their shelter in place and retreated behind it. Trumpets on the walls bade archers stop uselessly shooting.

Arnanak signaled. The next engine moved, the last of those taken from Wolua's luckless band, a ram hung on chains under a testudo shifted by full sixty-four males. Though the copper that fireproofed its roof was tarnished, he could not look straight at it beneath the suns.

"Stand ready to charge," Arnanak told his guards. That word rolled on outward through the horde where it milled unrestful. Weapons blinked in roiling dust. Arnanak trotted clear of it for a view across the territory.

Flags wigwagged at him from afar. He laughed. "Aye, I awaited this." The east gate had swung wide and the drawbridge come down. Again he drew brand and broke into a run. His household troops torrented after.

Gallop, gallop, gallop! Light leaped fierce off armor yonder. A detachment had left the fortress to try to catch the ram crew, slay them, and bring back their tool, before it reached the walls.

Those soldiers were not few. They expected having to cut their way to safety. When they saw the Tassui bear down on them, they changed from close order to assault array and countercharged. Loss of them would sorely weaken the garrison.

"Spread out," Arnanak called. "Zigzag. Come at them fanwise." However much he had drilled his crack fighters, a reminder was best. Their old wild ways lay very shallowly buried.

He spoke none too soon. Portable catapults began sending whole bundles of darts, farther than a bow could reach. Through and through the sighing death he sped. He glimpsed males who struck the ground and

229

rolled. Some got back up, limped rearward or continued ahead; some lay still, abristle, and their blood purpled a soil baked too hard to drink it. But the smitten were few, and the time was short before the Tassui were upon the southerners.

Arnanak aimed himself and eight guards at a trio of heavy troopers in armor like his. Together they shocked upon the legionaries.

Shield bosses thrust, shield edges chopped, sword or hatchet hewed from above or around rims. Arnanak and a soldier strained, pushed, sought to find or force a gap in defense. Blows clanged on the helmet cages, thudded on backplates and greaves. Companions of his rallied around. With scant mail of their own, they could not stand before one that fully protected. But while their Overling held him engaged, they hacked and stabbed through any joint, any crack, any bareness. Erelong a pike head ripped the wight's underbelly. He shrieked when his guts spilled out, crumpled in the heap of them, and composed himself to die. His mates, worse outnumbered, were already slain.

Arnanak spied a light trooper nearby and attacked. That fellow could have outrun him, weighted as he was, but stood fast with his squad. Arnanak hooked his shield aside and slammed sword-edge into spine.

Elsewhere too, the skilled males of Ulu had served their end. They had broken the legionary formation, on which untrained barbarians oftenest broke themselves. Arnanak sped from the strife and winded horn. In a bellow and rattle and drum roll of footfalls, the horde came at the scattered soldiers and swamped them.

As dust settled, Arnanak saw that the testudo was across his bridge, up the slope, against the wall. He heard the ram boom. "Ohai-ah!" he roared in glory, and led his housecarls that way. They must not let a sortie cut off their sappers. They'd be under heavy fire till the stockade broke; and after that there'd be only a narrow gap, desperately defended; but the Tassui would get through. This day they would be in Port Rua.

Sixty-four years hence, we will be in Sehala.

A whine pierced the sky. Arnanak looked thither. A

metal shape glided down as if out of the Demon Sun. His hearts quivered. *Humans! What do they seek?*

From the vessel, something gaunt streaked at the massed warriors.

In flame the hue of lightning, heaven burst open.

Hurled on high, Arnanak flew. The noise was too great to hear, it filled him, had him, was him, and every bone of him tolled. He struck ground which heaved like the sea. The feel of his burns overtook him. His soul splintered in a scream.

Yet a part held fast. It was a stone called Arnanak, and though fire seethed over it in tide after tide, at its core lived the will to be a lodestone. Across a white-hot blindness where monster winds ran, it dragged home the tattered and destroyed soul of Arnanak. After a million cycles of the Cruel Star, he was.

He drew aside from agony and raised his eyes. He lay on an earth gone ashen quiet—for he could not hear the mangled whom he saw struggle amidst the heaped dead, he could not hear a sound. From the field a cloud lifted, taller than belief and on the top spread widely out, the phantom of an enormous phoenix. The town stood unharmed, ram abandoned beneath ramparts. *I must have been near the edge of the blast,* dripped through him.

I will go find my sons. But his hindquarters would not stir. When he saw how spearheads and knife points of bone stuck out of the seared flesh, he knew why. He hitched himself onto hands, rowed with forefeet, dragged the dead half of him along.

"Tornak," he tried to call, "Uverni, Aklo, Tatara, Igini,"—no, Igini died on the gentle sea, didn't he?—"Korviak, Mitusu, Navano"—his sons who had been here in pride and honor, but he could not remember the rest of their names—"Kusarat, Usayuk, Innukrat, Alinark"—friends, wives, everybody dear all whirling together while darkness ate at the edges of awareness—but he couldn't hear if he had any voice left.

"Humans, why?" maybe he called. "I would have been your friend too. I would have brought you my dauri and the Thing." Peering aloft, he was unsure if the slaughter ship hovered, as dim as his sight had grown. Nor was he sure if the corpse beside which he

231

must stop, because he could go no further, belonged to anyone he knew. He thought in the maelstrom that it might be Tornak's but it was too cooked for him to tell. Was he near the middle of the weaponstrike?

If he could reach that far in his weakness, then ... then not everybody was slain. Belike most had lived to flee, most would return home and some outlive Fire Time. If the humans did not vengefully follow— Why should they? The humans had no need. They were almighty.

Arnanak sighed and lay down to rest. The Night came on. Too swiftly for a death dream? No. It must not. He would not let it. He was no animal that merely died, he was the Overling of Ulu.

He rose and drew blade. "Give me my honor," he told the faceless. Light flew off the steel. It struck at the black wings which stormed around and around, rang against beaks and talons. They wailed, those winds.

Arnanak walked forward. He was on a whistling gray heath where cold blew till his sword sang with it. Claw grew there and raked at him, but he was well buskined. Packbags balanced across his back, armor secured above them, shield slung from shoulders so his hump took the weight, head high and eyes held steady, *right* front-left rear, *left* front-right rear,

Hark to the drum, the drum, the drum.
"Outward!" the bugles cry.
Finish your beer,
Gather your gear,
Bid every wench good-by.
"Farewell to them! Farewell to them!" the drum and
    the trumpet shout.
To hell with them, to hell with them. I'd rather go
    home than out.
Grumbling we come, we come, we come.
Settle yourself to hike.
How is the beer
On the frontier?
What are the wenches like?

and thus the Tamburu strides.

The Zera had joined them, for a bridge must be

forced. "What a winterful country I picked to be born in!" Larreka said, an obscenity bouncing after. "Best thing about Haelen is the ship that carries you away from it."

"You won't like mine any better," Arnanak warned.

"No. I didn't. We had to get through the world somehow."

"Are you sorry?"

"Of course not."

"Nor I."

The bridge was blade-edge thin. It trembled and glimmered above that canyon where the ocean plunges roaring into hell. They who stood on it radiated dread. "We'll have to take them by a rush," Arnanak decided. Larreka agreed. When they were armored, he took steel in his left hand. In that wise they two went shield by shield, warding each other.

Arnanak threw his spear. It burned in among the enemy. He and Larreka followed. Hew! They cast their foes down to the mist and querning of the waterfall, and passed over.

On the far side was a vast and tilted land, mountains athwart heaven, valleys scorched raw, silent under the suns. Its fieriness smote the bones. "Now do you understand why this has to be set free?" Arnanak asked. "But come. I know the way."

They were all there in the hall at Ulu to bid riotous welcome, sons, comrades, loves, strength after strength embracing him. He led Larreka to the place of pride. Here the air lay cool, a little dusky though lamplight gleamed off weapons hung on the walls. That whole night, merriment rang aloud. They feasted, drank, boasted, made love, swapped stories, wrestled, played games, clamored forth songs, never grew weary, and remembered—remembered—remembered.

At dawn the males took arms again, said their last farewells, and streamed outside. Ohai-ah, what a valiant sight! Spears leaped among banners, plumes tossed, blades and axheads clanged on shields, as with a single deep shout the host hailed its two captains.

"It is the time," Arnanak called, and, "Yai" Larreka said. Joyous, every Tassu and legionary who had ever fallen in battle followed them, upward on the windy ways to where the huge red chaos of the Rover awaited their onslaught.

XXIV

JILL WEPT. SPARLING held her close, on the bench they had in the rear of the command cabin. His face was a helmet's visor, save that an edge of his mouth twitched downward, over and over, and his eyes smoldered coal-dry.

Slow tears coursed along Dejerine's cheeks, bitter across his lips. From time to time a shudder possessed him. Somehow his hands walked steadily over the console and his brain measured what the scanner screens revealed.

The blast crater gleamed black, soil turned to glass. It was not unduly wide. The missile had been a precision instrument, shaped to cast its force in a cone and give off minimal hard radiation. This couldn't be perfect. A ring of unvaporized casualties lay around. For penance he magnified the view at random spots. Part of that meat moved, which was worst of all.

Abruptly he could take no more. He brought the energy gun into play. Bolts raved, forms charred, for a minute or two until the ground lay in a smoking peace. Maybe a few could have been saved, given proper medical care. But where was that?

Father, forgive me, he would have begged if he had been able, *for I knew not what I did.* He had never before seen combat. But it was as if he dared not pray. Instead, there belled through him:

For now thou numberest my steps; dost thou not watch over my sin?

My transgression is sealed up in a bag, and thou sewest up mine iniquity.

And surely the mountain falling cometh to nought, and the rock is removed out of his place.

The waters wear the stones: thou washest away the

234

things which grow out of the dust of the earth; and thou destroyest the hope of man.

Thou prevailest for ever against him, and he passeth: thou changest his countenance, and sendest him away.

His sons come to honour, and he knoweth it not; and they are brought low, but he perceiveth it not of them.

But his flesh upon him shall have pain, and his soul within him shall mourn.

Jill ceased crying. Small and shaky, her voice none-theless marched: "I, I'm okay. Thanks, darling. The sight was horrible, I'd no idea how horrible. But I'm only shocked, not killed, not crippled."

"Take it easy," Sparling said.

"No. Can't do that yet, laren." The soldier's girl rose. Dejerine heard her boots on the deck. Her arm crossed his shoulder. "Here," she said. In her hand were the knives she and Sparling had held, flanking him in the copilots' seats while he did their bidding. "Take them."

"I don't want them," Dejerine protested.

"For appearances' sake when we get back." Jill tossed them at his feet. The blades rang together.

He looked up out of his helplessness into her blue gaze. "What should I do?"

She came around her chair and sat down, no longer bothering with safety harness. "First, let's take a scout around," she said. More life resounded in every new-spoken word.

Dejerine felt Ishtar's gravity in his fingertips. The aircraft obeyed just the same. Lazily spiraling, it searched across kilometers. The screens showed bar-barians in blind, panic flight, on land and water alike. Meanwhile Sparling took the third seat, drew pipe and tobacco pouch from his tunic, loaded and lit and puffed. The odor was like a dream of Earth. Calm had descended on him.

At last, impersonal of accent, he inquired, "How many do you suppose we accounted for?"

Dejerine swallowed twice before he wrenched forth: "Two or three thousand."

"Out of, hm-m, didn't we estimate fifty thousand minimum?"

Laughter cackled from Dejerine. "Six per cent. They got off easily. We took a mere thousand lives apiece."

"They're rather more extravagant on Mundomar. And the garrison here numbers well above three thousand—each of whom would've been killed, or suffered out a few years as a slave before the most brutal kind of overwork did him in."

Sparling leaned closer. His tone gentled: "Do believe, I'm not happy about what we've done. I don't feel righteous. But neither do I feel guilty. And we're in your eternal debt. Yours, Yuri. You suggested a single big shot. I thought we'd have to hunt them with machine guns."

"What's the difference, in Christ's name?"

"None morally, I reckon. However, this took fewer of them, and most died too fast to know it. Besides"—Sparling paused—"they're a warrior breed. Bullets or clumsy chemical bombs might've checked them, but I don't think would have stopped them for long. They'd have found tactics, made inventions, stolen weapons from us, copied them ... come back to battle endlessly, till our final choices would have been to kill off their whole race or give in—throw civilization on Ishtar, if not ourselves, to them and their mercies. This today—I don't think they'll ever return against this."

"And," Jill said low, "a trivial point, no doubt, but now our people needn't make that raid out of Primavera. They can restore the stuff they, hm, borrowed. You'll close the case then, won't you, Yuri?"

Dejerine jerked a nod. "What shall we do next?" he asked them.

"Why, you're the boss," Jill replied, as if astonished at the emptiness in him. Her voice quickened, even brightened. "Well, let's radio the legion, reassure them, consult— In fact, could we possibly land? Spend the night? Check out the barbarian camp? Who knows, we might find that object from Tammuz. Or a few dauri. They'd sure need help and comforting, poor dears."

Things in the largest tent indicated that strange little starfish figures had indeed huddled there. But they were gone, fled in a terror and bewilderment beyond the horde's own. From what Jill told him, Dejerine

236

imagined them scuttling through this country that for them held only hunger, and was surprised at how deeply he wished they would make it alive across the Desolations.

The star-cube they had left behind. In awe he bore it to his flyer.

When he entered a gate of Port Rua, the soldiers saluted him who had delivered them. They did not cheer. Sparling explained they were too weary, they had lost too many, for rejoicing. That must wait. In what remained of the day they simply sent out burial details to cover the grisliness beyond their walls.

A wind sprang up, hoarse-throated, forge-hot, skin-withering. Dust drove before it till the air was a gray that stung and gritted; Bel glared as red as Anu.

"We will abide," Acting Commandant Irazen said, "if we get help."

He addressed the humans in the office that had been Larreka's. It was a white-plastered, rough-raftered room, mostly bare aside from a few mattresses, patterned in rainbows, on the clay floor, and a few books and battered souvenirs along the walls. The shortsword banner hung from a crosspiece on a footed staff opposite Irazen's. Windows were shuttered against the storm. Dull yellow lantern flames breathed pungency into a warmth less furious than outside.

Dejerine looked from the leonine being who also served a civilization, to Jill and Sparling hand in hand, and back. The girl interpreted. How slim and fair she stood. The light glowed on hair and gleamed in eyes. "What can I tell him?" she asked when silence had grown.

"Tell him—*Dieu m'assiste*—what can I?" Dejerine spread his palms in appeal. "He doubtless imagines Earth has had a change of heart. Have *you* the heart to tell him the truth?"

"No, oh, no," she whispered. "I'm not that brave." She turned to Irazen and spoke a few halting sentences. The Ishtarian rumbled a reply which eased her distress an atom.

"I explained this was a special case, that you stretched your authority and Earth can't give any further military aid," she said. "He's not too disappointed.

237

After all, he doesn't expect the Valennener confederation can outlive this blow. He'll just have individual warbands to cope with, sometimes to play off against each other. He ... he says that as long as there is a Zera Victrix, our names will be on its rolls."

"Probably the blockade will dissolve when the news has crossed the sea," Dejerine responded. Impulse snatched him. "But if not, I'll break it!"

Jill drew breath. Sparling let go an amazed, delighted oath. The girl told the soldier, who advanced to grip Dejerine by the shoulders till they hurt.

What a foolish promise to make, the human officer thought. *Why do I know I'll fulfill it? Why am I not dismayed at myself?* He saw Jill's vividness and knew why.

Or did he? She wasn't his. She and Sparling were bound across space to a judgment that might well bind them together for what was left of their years after the punishment. He, Yuri Pierre Dejerine, had nothing to gain but trouble. Then why this rising gladness?

Well, I doubt if I'll be called on to stir. The buccaneers will go straight home to their—what do they call it?—their Fire Time. Or if they don't, I can make a pretext to flit off alone, and carry out my mission in secret.

Blood guiltiness crowded back. *Yes, I can sink ships full of sentient creatures who are helpless before me.*

Jill winked. "We won't tell on you," she vowed. "Will we, Ian?"

"Absolutely never," the man agreed. The guilt grew incandescent in Dejerine's guts.

Irazen spoke again. Jill and Sparling lost a degree of their joy. "What now?" Dejerine demanded through a spasm in his pulse.

"He says—" The girl tightened her hold on the man. "He says he isn't Larreka. He'll stay while he's able, but the legion can no longer feed itself here, and if the Gathering doesn't supply them, he'll pull out."

She tried to smile. "Don't look glum, Yuri," she added. "Valennen won't be the menace it was, and the Zera will be alive down south."

"But it would be better if you ... if they could stay, would it not?" Dejerine asked.

"Oh, yes," Sparling said. "You're Navy; you ought to see that in a glance at the map. This is the anchor point for protection of the Fiery Sea, for keeping civilization going in those islands and North Beronnen, and keeping their resources available elsewhere—resources which'd be much wanted under the best conditions, and damn near vital if we of Primavera can't help as we'd hoped to."

Jill nodded. The tresses rippled along her throat. Within Dejerine, a nova burst.

—"What's wrong? Yuri, are you all right?" He realized that a minute or more had gone. She was holding him by the waist. On her face and Sparling's was honest, anxious concern. Irazen, sensing it, held forth hands as if to offer what help an alien could.

"Oui. . . . Ça va bien, merci. Une idée—" Dejerine shook himself. "Pardon. I must think."

He sat down, knees lifted, gripped his temples, stared at the rainbow beneath him, and—did not think—let understanding come, in great soft waves of peace.

Finally he rose. He knew why those two fared blithely toward prison. The same power rang through his words.

Not that he waxed eloquent. Rather, he stammered and groped for ways to tell his vision. He wished he had, or could at least comprehend, the dream art of the Ishtarians.

"My friends, I, I don't know what you can say to him here. Perhaps best you be, eh, noncommittal. Say that a limited amount of supplies will positively come. Say we trust the Gathering will decide to hold what it has and that . . . that civilization will retreat no further.

"Entre nous— Between us, I can let you know—for the present, work on the base is halted. Everything you had in Primavera goes back to you. And the Navy will serve you as best we can."

"Oh, Yuri," Jill sang. The blue eyes seemed, for a moment, blinded.

"Judas priest," Sparling said in voice that should have pardoned the Betrayer.

Dejerine hurried on. *I must make this irrevocable.* "Why? Well, I live in my head the same as you. I was

239

less and less sure I was doing right. Therefore I came north to fetch you with a vague idea that Ian might seize my aircraft and force me to, to do what we did. If he could succeed in that, ah, not my fault, was it? On him be the consequences. And you—everyone should feel kinder toward me, even though I was forced.

"But I did not expect you would bear those consequences too, Jill.

"I did not foresee how it would feel to burn people who could not fight back. Never mind how good or bad the causes, they could not fight back. You who will go to Earth are free of that.

"Yet it is never enough to kill. We must help and build. I am commander. My men will cheerfully obey the changed orders I give them until I am replaced. Primavera will stay in the Federation—also after they send for us three, because we will be those who go speak for Ishtar—

"Do you see?"

"I do," said Sparling. Jill sped to Dejerine and kissed him.

240

AFTERWORD

THE NIGHT WAS old when we finished our tale.

Espina had well-nigh told it with us, so sharp and knowing were his questions. He had not flagged though we grew weary who were two generations his juniors. But when at last he said, *"Yo comprendo . . . bastante,"* he closed his eyes for a while; and stillness brimmed the big room. Only the grandfather clock talked on, and that slow dk, dk, dk seemed only the falling away of time.

He had left the lights dim throughout. Hour after hour we had watched the stars wheel by. Now they were a faded crown for him, as the east turned silver. In hope and dread we waited.

The eagle visage swung back to us, the wrinkled lids drew away from brilliance. "My apologies," said the president of the Federation Tribunal. "I should not have kept you in suspense. But I had to contemplate this."

"Certainly, sir," I mumbled.

"No doubt you wondered if I wanted you for a game of cat and mouse—"

"Oh, no, sir!"

Espina grinned. "I gave you no hint of my real wish, my ultimate intention. I could not have done that if I wanted as complete a revelation as I have obtained. You thought perhaps by stating your case you could persuade me to give you a lenient sentence. But perhaps I was merely indulging curiosity or—in cold anger or idle cruelty—adding a more subtle chastisement than the law allows. Well, whatever it was, it is almost ended."

He bleakened. "Almost," he said. "Before I explain, there is one last necessary pain to inflict. You must realize in depth how grave the charges are against you.

"You, Ian Sparling and Jill Conway, committed piracy, and upon a naval vessel in time of war. You compelled the violation not alone of a directive, which would have been abundantly criminal, but of a prime policy of the entire Federation. Thereafter you, Yuri Dejerine, a naval officer, continued such violations. Falsifying your orders, you suspended the operations entrusted to you and employed the men, equipment, and materials in your care for civilian purposes irrelevant to your assignment. To those ends, the three of you continually conspired, which is a felony *per se*.

"Yes, yes, you have heard this before. Now I have heard, in detail rather than emotional catchphrases, your justification: that you had to assist a remote, non-human, technologically backward civilization, of interest to nobody except scientists; and that your action kept a few thousand residents, many of whom would not have stayed, from a secession which, could it succeed, would have been insignificant to Earth. In short, you deemed your tiny purposes and judgments superior to those of every authority and several billion private persons, and arrogated to yourselves the right to act accordingly.

"Why should your rehabilitation not require the rest of your lives?"

Before that sternness I surrendered my dreams, and surely my comrades did likewise.

No, not altogether, not for more than some clockbeats. Then Jill sat straight. Her voice lashed back: "Sir, whatever we've done, this law you claim to stand for gives us rights. Including, God damn it, the right to be heard. In public! Why the hell else do you think we went meekly along when the warrant arrived? We could've taken rations into the wilderness and stayed unfindable till your domesticated men left. But we wanted Earth to know!"

Ian and I took fire from her. "Yes," he said. "Captain Dejerine may be under Navy discipline, but Miss Conway and I are not. Your closed-chamber hearings, your holding us incommunicado, are illegal under the Charter of the World Federation. Your Tribunal can pass sentence, but it may not keep us from issuing our statement."

"Nor may the Navy," I joined in. "That's a reason why I was proud to wear its uniform—why I could be again."

242

Espina met our stares. The clock struck off an hour.

He smiled. "Excellent," he said. I had not imagined he could speak this gently. "I thank you for your spirit as well as your patience. Be at ease. Your torment is over."

He pressed the call button on his chaise. Steeliness returned. "This part is over," he corrected himself. "What follows will be in many ways worse.

"You see, what you have told me confirms and fills out what my studies had seemed to prove. God knows I am not a very merciful man; but I try to be a just one.

"When court reconvenes, proceedings will be open. Current rumors about the case will assure worldwide coverage. We will go through the motions, the indictment, your plea of guilty, the sentence, which my colleagues do indeed plan to make extreme.

"Then I, invoking my powers, will grant you an unconditional pardon."

I do not remember the next minutes well, except that we three embraced and wept through laughter.

When quietness was back among us, we found the servant had brought brandy. That was a noble cognac, a benediction. But after our toast, sitting crippled under the last stars, Espina started yet another cigarette, coughed, blew smoke, and told us in the same hard tone as before:

"Essentially, you aimed at a *cause célèbre* which would rouse sympathy for Ishtar, sufficient for the resumption of aid. Tonight you catalyzed my tentative resolution. With my help—I have managed things as I did in order to create the maximum sensation—you will assuredly wake a storm. Prepare yourselves. You do not know how all-consuming it is to be a symbol.

"My purpose goes beyond yours, though. In the long run, yours is the larger and more meaningful. But in the short run, it is incidental to mine. I want to end the war."

He puffed and sipped violently while we sat in an interior peace of exhaustion.

"The war." His mummy countenance grimaced. "This senseless, bootless, justiceless, finishless war. Our sole proper business there was to lend our good offices

243

toward settling the dispute. Instead, out of romanticism we turned friends into enemies. Out of sentimentalism we turned ourselves into butchers. Out of guilt-sense we turned reparation into a monstrously greater guilt.

"The time is overpast to make an end. It can be done. Between them, Earth and Naqsa can impose an arrangement that is not too unfair to either side, and certainly free of the unfairness that young men die while old men live. We have an undercurrent of wish for it throughout the Federation, as our cost and commitment rise without limit and without result. But as yet this is an undercurrent. The politicians, the media, practically no one and nothing public will take any initiative. They simply do not discuss the politically awkward subject of a negotiated peace.

"I will use you to whipsaw them into it."

The face grinned anew, the hand waved his cigarette. "Oh, I have my selfish reasons, too," he admitted. His chuckle went dry as phoenix boughs rubbed together by the Fire Time wind. "What a marvelous last battle! They will cry for my impeachment, a sanity hearing, revision of the Charter to strip my office of powers, every revenge that hysteria can mouth. And I will fight back in my fashion. . . .Win or lose, have no fears for yourselves. You will be protected by the double jeopardy rule.

"But—you must also be in the fight."

Contempt crackled forth: "Don't fear, either, that you need become fashionable radicals. Leave oratory, demonstrations, riots, denunciatory essays in chic magazines, solidarity with every grubby Cause that wants to hitch a ride, sermons which don't mention God because he isn't relevant—leave such things to the monkeys. Better, disown them, reject them. You shall simply be witnesses to the truth. You will not find that easy. The intellectual establishment that opposes you contains many skilled picadors as well as contortionists. Hardest of all will be to remain calm, reasonable, yes, truthful."

His lips twisted. "What truth can you state? What effects of this unnecessary war have you personally experienced?

"The preventable deaths of millions of beings who

244

may well stand above us in the eyes of eternity, made probable. Peril to a high civilization which we *know* has unguessably much to teach us, and someday not far off ought to take its place among the stars. You have verily seen destruction and grief which need not have happened, including—as far as can be discovered—the loss of two leaders who might well have worked together for incalculable good, had we provided them a chance.

"And Earth—on Ishtar, Earth has lost the trust of first-class minds, a trust not readily regained. Earth has lost the services of an outstanding officer; for though you be pardoned, Captain Dejerine, it is impossible for the Navy not to cashier you." Once more an unexpected softness flitted across him in a smile. "I daresay they will make a place for you yonder, and a hearty welcome."

The milder mood continued: "Providentially, you likewise bring positive news, of an entire intelligent species and relics of a powerful bygone race—from either of which we may quite conceivably learn what will open whole universes. But to do that, in living lifetimes, requires vastly enlarged assistance to the Gathering; furthermore, it requires help for the Valennen folk, that they in turn may help us. And this requires peace!

"I think, in a year or so, Earth will realize where its true interests lie."

His head drooped. Daniel Espina was mortal too. Soon we said farewell, and the attendant woke the pilot who would take us back to our hidden quarters.

We waited outside for him. The air was quiet, thin, relentlessly cold, exultantly clear. The sun had now cleared the peaks, down whose granite its beams hunted shadows, and heaven reached sapphire.

"A year," Ian breathed. Each work smoked white. "Or two at most. Then we go home."

And if we're fortunate, start over on our work, I thought.

"That many months—" Jill answered him. They had long stopped keeping secrets from me, or I from them. We are three. But this hour was theirs alone. "You'll send for Rhoda."

"How can she come?" he wondered against his own knowledge.

"The judge can fix that. You wouldn't be who you are, my darling, if you didn't ask him to." She squared her shoulders. "Meanwhile—" Presently: "Afterward— Well, we'll see." She did not trouble to speak of matters like the fact that loving and being loved bring duties. Her glance told me I was among her "we."

The pilot came. Jill led us to the flyer. Following her, I dared hope.

Exciting Space Adventure from DEL REY